I0600294

THIS FINE LINE
Copyright © 2025 by Zalyn Zofer

ISBN 979-8-9993516-9-2

Edited, Formatted, and Published by Represent Publishing

Cover Design by Brittany Evans @BEDESIGNS.CA

THIS
Fine Line

THIS
Fine Line

ZALYN ZOFER

Represent
Publishing

For Diane, who encouraged my literacy from the earliest days of my life and who allowed me space to let my head drift through the clouds while keeping my feet on the ground.

Author's Note

I wrote this book while teaching and tutoring in Chicago in 2010-2011. I was 25 and 26 years old. At the time, the novel served as catharsis, almost a journal for me to explore my own feelings about dating, marriage, friendships, family, and the general aimlessness that I was feeling. The story and the people in it are fiction, but it explores much of what I was going through mentally and emotionally. Many of the arguments or discussions are real discussions I had with friends, or just with myself trying to sort things out and get a hold of my life while also enjoying the first time in my life where I let loose a little. Like Lyren (whose name I completely made up. It's supposed to rhyme with siren), I went from being a straight-A student with all my ducks in a row to a flailing party girl completely unsure what I wanted to do next.

Finishing the first draft of the book in June 2012 was a major accomplishment for my rootless existence just to be able to say I completed a project. I shopped it to some agents, got a few bites, but it went nowhere. Eventually, I refocused my energy on a new career path, went to graduate school, and got back on solid footing.

Over a decade later, I decided to revisit this project and give it a shot at existing in the world. I did it. It doesn't have to be flawless or even decent. It's good enough that I did a thing, and I'm proud of that.

When I decided to self-publish this, I originally thought I should update it to be more current (it's amazing how much society changes in ten to fifteen years), but the truth is, this project exists best as a time capsule. I cannot write about current 26-year-olds. I don't know them. I don't understand their world. I will say one of the hardest things about doing current revisions was keeping the book set in a time before terms like "situation-ship" and "ghosting" were used.

What I do have is a story about a girl struggling to find a real career and sense of purpose in a crashed economy, surrounded by friends getting married while she flits between meaningless rela-tionships and doesn't know how to attract stability. A girl living in a world where Facebook is still a prime mode of communica-tion and connection, hailing cabs is how you get around, and girls publicly talk about their bodies and each other's sexual behaviors in a way that is less acceptable today. I chose not to edit some of the snide commentary and beliefs out, not because I stand by them at 40, but because I think it's OK to look back at a time and examine how we felt and what we once accepted. I'm glad that as a society we're calling each other to be better. But this was the reality of the world in which I was 26.

In revisiting this novel, I find Lyren to be an unlikeable (and often intentionally unreliable) narrator and main character. She's selfish, contradictory in her opinions, hypocritical in her expecta-tions of others, and sometimes just a downright whiny brat. But I guess that's what makes her real, and hopefully relatable.

Because reading her, remembering how and why I wrote her, and knowing what I know now, I also have some empathy for anyone trying to navigate the world when things just don't pan out the way you maybe were promised as a kid. It's OK, young Zalyn— err, Lyren. It gets better.

Chapter One

DECEMBER 2010

I'm gasping for breath as he pushes me against the couch, pressing into my body. No matter how hard I'm kissing him, it's not enough. I want to devour him. I want to let him devour me. He's consuming me with every move of his hand, every pull of his tongue.

Is this really happening? Am I really doing this? It doesn't matter. I don't want to be thinking right now. I'm so drunk that thinking is a pointless effort, anyway. We'd started drinking . . . what? Six hours ago? Seven? We were looking at travel pictures while he told me stories of his adventures. God, I should have known this was coming. Maybe I did. Whatever, I can figure it out in the morning.

My jeans and shirt come off in some kind of blur, and I wrap my legs around him while he stumbles over to his bedroom, paying no mind to the lights or TV. He's mentioned to me before that he prefers to hook up with girls on the couch because it's easier to get rid of them. *Victory point for me, I guess.*

I'm almost confused about why this isn't awkward, but I'm going with it. It's been a long time.

God, please don't think I'm fat, I think as he removes my underwear, the final piece of clothing between us. I'm thankful, first, that I didn't eat dinner, and second, that I shaved tonight and wore lace panties.

"Jesus, you're hot," he whispers, kissing my neck, and it makes me almost giddy. "I've been thinking about this ever since I met you."

It's easy to follow his lead. I find that despite the reasons sober me fought this over the past few months, letting myself go right now requires no internal coaching.

I pull him harder into me, showing him that I am every bit as into this as he's showing me he is. "I need you now, Alec."

I'm in and out of focus. Part of it's the sex; most is definitely the vodka.

A few messy but passionate moments and a one-sided crescendo on his end later, he looks me in the eyes, before crashing on top of me. We stay that way for a second, trying to recapture our breath and whatever remains of our consciousness. He rolls over, and I look at him and sort of laugh.

"Lyren . . . please . . . just," he hesitates. "Let's just not let this get weird, OK? I don't want to fuck this up . . . serious-ly . . . " He honestly looks worried, and I'm touched. "You were the friend I wasn't supposed to sleep with."

"Fail," I respond. He looks at me with concern. "Oh Alec, we're fine. I promise. I won't get crazy if you don't."

He smiles, and I playfully smack his butt as he shakes his head, getting up to turn off the lights.

"We better be fine. You're the coolest girl I know out here." He smiles again and gets back into the bed. Then he puts his arm around me, cuddling up and kissing my forehead.

"I'm the coolest girl you know, period."

"Keep telling yourself that."

Wow, this really just happened. We really went there . . . I'm still too drunk to think, and I don't want to ruin the moment. The world is spinning as I curl up inside his arm and crash.

ONE MONTH PRIOR

"Lyren, you've got to stop spending so much time with Alec if you ever want to meet someone," my mom said over coffee at Julius Meinl with my big sister, Emma, and me.

It is a favorite spot near my North Side Chicago apartment where we often find ourselves when my mom comes up from the suburbs to hang out with us. Emma lives over in Wicker Park with her fiancé.

"No nice guy is going to approach you if he thinks you're out with a boy, and obviously anyone thinks you're dating when they see a guy and a girl hanging out."

So let them think. *"Maybe I'm just out to have fun with friends rather than meet my soul mate, Mom."*

"But you never know who is around and who you could be meeting. I'm not saying it's the only reason you should go out, but you're limiting your chances."

"Look, when I'm out with Alec, usually we're with a group of friends, for one thing. And if there is a guy I find interesting, I don't not talk to him because of Alec, and if Alec sees a girl he wants to hit on, I don't care or stop him."

That isn't entirely true. Alec's favorite nickname for me is "cock block" and I rarely find anyone I want to leave my friends to talk to. He assumes I scare his potential women away, but I like to think he just prefers my company, even if it only ends with a make out.

"Well, you aren't getting any younger. You're 26, so you need to really think about who you are spending time with. I know you are having fun casually dating people, but you're at an age where it really is time to start thinking long term."

"I'll meet someone if and when I feel like it. It's hard when the only people willing to go out anymore are my guy friends. All of my girlfriends are getting married or at least are in serious relationships. Alec is always down to hang out and have fun. Besides, I know what I like and what I don't, and most guys just happen to bore the shit out of me."

Every time I go out with a guy, they are seemingly great on paper, but they let me walk all over them or do something totally repugnant within a few dates. Like that time an Italian guy and I were talking about food we liked, and seductively, he asked how I felt about Italian sausage. On a first date. Shoot me.

It isn't that I never go on dates. I'm not entirely celibate. I reconnected with Evan, a college friend, at a party about a year ago, and we jumped into an intense-though-not-quite-Facebook-official relationship for a few months. I hate admitting how much I'm not over that despite it ending without so much as a conversation or closure months ago. But I flirt. I sometimes make out with random guys in bars. I had a brief fling with a beautiful bartender named Scott. Honestly, probably the worst sex I ever had after a really fun flirtation over a few weeks. We fumbled awkwardly through what might have been half the Kama Sutra trying to find a vibe before I finally just made up an excuse and left, never to return to Schoolyard. Sad too. I liked that bar.

"Well, Mom is right though," Emma added. *"No guy will approach you if they think you are with Alec. Especially since you guys are always flirting with each other."*

"I think you like Alec."

My mom knows Alec and I make out from time to time. I

tell her everything, even things I know she is going to hate. She doesn't care if I casually make out with someone or anything, but she is really hesitant about Alec.

We've been flirting since we met at my friend Olivia's family party a few months ago. He is her older brother, who just moved back to Chicago from LA. He needed friends in Chicago. I needed friends who weren't settling down. Instant hit.

"Oh, Mother. We've been over this. I don't want to be dating Alec. He's cute, and he's a ton of fun. But he's not my type at all and you know that."

"I don't know. You like guys you can't get, and you'll never tie his ass down." My mom smirked with all of her maternal wisdom before taking another sip of her latte.

"I like guys who aren't all over me . . . "

"Because they don't like you," Emma cut me off.

I gave her a dirty look and continued. "I like guys who aren't all over me before they even know me, and who are smart and interesting and, most importantly, who are passionate. Alec is only passionate about partying and traveling. He's fun. He's not someone I'm ever going to fall for. We never even have serious conversations."

"I just don't want you to get hurt. I like Alec. I think he's a really nice friend, and I'm glad you're having fun and enjoying your twenties. That's what you're supposed to do. Just know that boy has a reputation, and you're not going to be the one to change that."

"Nor do I want to."

"Well, just don't come crying to me over this one. You know what you're getting yourself into." Sympathy was never my mom's strongest suit. She prided herself on telling it like it was.

"I won't come crying to you because Alec will never make me cry. We're just friends. And one day, I will meet a good guy.

And you know what? If I don't, I'll be just fine. Let's talk about something else."

"Oh, I wanted to ask you guys about something, anyway. I saw this floral arrangement in The Knot, and it used limes and oranges instead of flowers. I saved the clipping." *Emma brought the conversation back to her upcoming wedding, the other conversation mainstay, and for once, I was relieved about it.*

I wake up rather comfortably, save for a massive headache, in Alec's very white room. *Such a bachelor pad.* He's still sleeping soundly on the other side of his bed. The hangover has me feeling like death. Although, rubbing up against him in bed sort of turns me on and I'm hoping he makes a move when he wakes up. God knows when that is going to be. Of course, I had thought about it before. Sleeping with Alec. Alec is gorgeous and fun and flirtatious, and it's so easy to be around him. But unlike Scott, the build up did not disappoint. We had real chemistry. At least it seemed like we did. I was pretty browned out, so maybe we were just on the same wavelength of wasted.

I could just get up and go to make it clear that I'm not gonna be clingy about this, but the bed is so cozy, and I don't feel like walk-of-shaming it home yet.

Last night I promised Alec that nothing was going to change between us. We will stay good friends, the exact same way we were. We are adults. Sex doesn't change anything. We can be intimate without getting crazy and attached or fighting.

Right?

I can't say I've been successful in any sort of "friends with benefits" setting before. In fact, every guy I've slept with has been someone I legitimately wanted to be dating, even if it didn't exactly work out that way.

Whatever, this is different. This is Alec, and I don't secretly want to be with Alec. Everything's cool. Actually, the idea of having a sex buddy is rather appealing. All the good stuff without the drama of expectations and emotions.

We both phase in and out of sleep for a while until he finally gets up to go to the bathroom.

"Hey, what's your name again?" he jokes when he comes back into the room, adjusting his boxers. I throw a pillow at him as he shields himself. "Go make me some breakfast," he says.

"Yeah. Not gonna happen."

"Yeah, I don't have any groceries, anyway."

"Doesn't matter if you did."

"I hear you're a good cook."

"Who told you that?"

"Olivia."

"You talk about me to Olivia?" I solicit.

"She talks about you to me. I personally couldn't care less that we've been hanging out for months and I have yet to be treated to a Lyren Valence delicacy," he pretends to act offended.

"Pretty sure for that to happen we'd have to do something besides going out to drink."

"So let's go to your place and you can make me breakfast there."

"Still not happening." I know he's kidding around, but the thought of waking up with someone and cooking breakfast sounds so relationship-y that I start to question his intentions. *Could Alec actually* like *like me?* No way. He's kidding around. *Don't be a stage five clinger, Lyren!*

"I hurt!" he whines, crashing back onto the bed.

"Me too!"

"What did you do to me, woman?"

"Pretty sure that's the vodka, but if you want, I can blame you for my headache too."

He starts playing with my hair for a second in a way that

makes me melt. I massage his back in return, still sort of hoping for a little morning action but not planning on being the one to initiate it for fear of looking attached. But then he seems to catch himself, maybe in the same fear, and pulls back.

"Bears are on at noon. Gotta have something to watch in place of my Sox. What time is it?" he asks. I look at my phone.

"11:30. The Sox suck."

"You suck," he retorts. "Quite well actually."

I smack him.

"Ow woman! Who do you think you are?" He starts tickling me and smirks. "I told you I would get you eventually . . . "

He's right. He did tell me he'd get me eventually. And every time I denied it, I knew I was lying.

TWO MONTHS PRIOR

"Alec, the only reason we haven't had sex is that I don't want to have sex with you," I stated, over and over again, to his claims that if I wasn't friends with Olivia, we'd already be having sex. This time was in a bar after our other friends had left.

"Oh, but you do."

"You wish."

"I do wish. You're very attractive," he said, lifting his eyebrows suggestively.

"Yeah, well, you sort of look like a toad, and I'm not into toads."

What I am actually not into is inflating guys' egos, and Alec knows damn well that he is really good-looking. Everyone says so. I believe some of my straight guy friends think about him at night.

"Why must you hurt me so?"

"I have to keep you in your place. That's why you love me."

"I love you because you have a fantastic ass, and I can't hang out with it without hanging out with you, unfortunately."

"You've never seen my ass."

"Yet," he added, grabbing my butt as I feigned horror. "So where are all of your loyal following of men this evening?"

"I turned them all down already," I kidded, holding my nose in the air and flipping my hair.

"When are you going to start bringing your hot girl friends around to meet me? I have a rule against doing my sister's friends, but not my sister's friends' friends."

"They all have boyfriends. Why do you think I'm around you so much? Where are your guy friends? I'm running out of prey."

"In LA! You come out there with me, and my friends will show you a real good time . . . " He grinned.

"Maybe one day. Your friends seem weird."

"They are tons of fun."

"Not my type."

"What is your type, anyway?"

"I actually don't know that I have one. If you lined up all the guys I've been interested in, they would have nothing in common physically. The only qualities they all seem to have are intelligence, a sense of humor, and confidence."

"I don't have a type either. I don't discriminate. I love all shapes and forms."

"False! You love super plastic types who wear tons of makeup and have massive boobs. I see you on social media, you know. All of your groupies."

Alec attracts women like ants to a fallen sidewalk potato chip. He is tall and dark with the perfect amount of facial stubble, fit but not bulky. He has a casual but sharp style and an effortless charm that sends even the iciest skeptics off balance.

"You forget that I've been in the LA party scene for the past

several years. Those just happen to be the girls who were around. Doesn't mean that's all I like. I mean, don't get me wrong, I like me some big titties."

"See, you wouldn't want to sleep with me, anyway. I don't have big titties. Nor do I want to buy them."

"You don't have to. First of all, I've never seen them, but I'm sure they are great. They look a good size to me."

"I just don't like them." I'd always had a bit of insecurity about them, though why I admitted it to Alec, I wasn't sure.

"You're stupid. And, even if they aren't great, I do happen to know that you have a fantastic ass and gorgeous legs, and those? They can't be bought even if you DID want to buy your appearance. So be thankful. You've naturally got what all those girls you are so judgmental about are trying to have. Be nice to them."

"I just wish guys appreciated nature over plastic, that's all. It bothers me that girls feel a need to change themselves to meet a male standard and they can't see past it to what's really there."

"Sorry . . . that's never going to change. We're physical beings. Doesn't matter how it got there. We're still going to appreciate it."

"Gross." I cringed.

"And for the record, I don't want to sleep with you. Then you'll become a typical girl and get attached to my penis, and I'll have to stop being friends with you. I've never had a female friend I haven't fucked. So stop trying to get me into bed with you."

"Oh god," I laughed. "I need another drink."

———

Eventually, Alec gets out of bed without making a move, and by now, I've lost the desire. I want to go home and lay on my couch. And definitely discuss this with a girlfriend.

"Want to stay and watch the game?" He's putting his clothes back on, a good indication that I should do the same.

"Nah. I gotta get home." I try not to stare at him while I'm getting dressed to avoid an awkward moment.

"Alright, later, Lyren." He walks me to the door and hugs me goodbye, then sits down on the couch to turn on the game. Nothing has changed. This is perfect.

"And by the way," he says as I'm stepping out, "you're crazy. Your boobs are gorgeous."

I smile and say, "Thanks," then shut the door behind me.

I walk down the street in my clothes from the night before and grab a cab. It's December, and it's snowing. I can't help but smile to myself, considering how obvious it is that I didn't stay at my own place. It's out of character for me these days. And something about this feels different than when it was with Evan. *Fucking Evan.*

I don't feel like thinking about Evan right now, though. Alec and I slept together last night. And it was good. I'm touched that he remembered my insecurities about my breasts. That conversation was months ago.

I pay the cab driver and turn the heat up when I walk into my place. I want to call a girlfriend, but Olivia probably doesn't want to hear details about me banging her brother, and she's become my go-to with boy talk at this point. Emma will judge me. Sarah, my best friend from junior high, is out of town with her fiancé. To my luck, Gail, my best friend from college, is online, and she messages me first.

GAIL
Hey Girl

LYREN
Hola. What are you up to?

GAIL
Reading . . . what else is new? I'm bored.

I'm excited to have boy talk of my own, as most of my conversations with Gail revolve around her relationship at this point. But when I think about all the misery I made my friends listen to over Evan, I realize I have no room to talk.

LYREN
Sounds exciting.

GAIL
Yeah, not exactly. I cooked dinner for Brad last night, and then he went out to the bar with some friends, and I just stayed home. Pretty typical.

What are you up to?

LYREN
I just got home. Went drinking with Alec last night.

GAIL
Nice. How is that going?

LYREN
Interestingly. We copulated.

GAIL
Shocking.

LYREN

Hey! It's news!

GAIL

Oh Lyren, I'm sorry. It's not news. Everyone saw that coming. I could cut the sexual tension between you two with a pair of scissors. OK, tell me all about it.

Gail lives in Wisconsin, so I rarely see her in person. She's only met Alec once when she came to visit with Brad a couple months ago, but she had no problem pulling me aside to tell me how cute he was or how good we looked together.

LYREN

I didn't plan to sleep with him.

GAIL

Oh, I know you didn't PLAN to, but you obviously were going to at some point or another. And besides, kudos. He's really hot. He's like the second hottest guy you've ever slept with.

LYREN

Hmm, so you think Scott was hotter?

GAIL

Scott was the prettiest boy I've ever seen.

I know girls don't technically get feathers in their caps over guys they've slept with, but bartender Scott is the feather in my cap. He had the prettiest eyes, and was 6'2" and super quiet and awkward, which made me like him that much more. Sleeping with him would have been one of my life's greatest accomplishments if it hadn't turned out we had no chemistry and, oh yeah, also found out he had a serious girlfriend immediately afterward. Prick.

LYREN

Well, obviously, we were wasted. But we went out just the two of us after drinking at his place for a while. I mean, that's not weird. We drink together a lot. I was going to go home at like midnight, but we were across the street from his place and he was like, "Just come over for a little bit. I don't want the night to end yet. We can watch a movie or something." And I know that's the universal sign for "you're going to bang", but we've watched movies before.

GAIL

Yeah yeah yeah, get to the good part.

LYREN

I don't know. There was just something different about last night. The whole night I just couldn't stop thinking about how hot he looked. He'd been showing me pictures of his travel adventures at the bar, and it was honestly really sexy seeing him be that into something. Usually when we go out, we make out because we're just sort of having fun, but there was another layer of desire and intensity last night. We got in the door and just seriously were all over each other. It was like one split second . . . we were clearly both just dying to jump each other. It was intense, and awesome, and messy, and drunk, and sloppy, and great.

GAIL

Awkward morning?

LYREN

Not even in the slightest. So comfortable and normal. Not even a hint of awkwardness. We joked around playfully. Seemed fully normal when I left.

GAIL

Continual thing?

LYREN

I don't know. I mean, I don't want to fuck our friendship up. I need him. He's my social buddy. I know this is the part where I'm supposed to say it was totally a one-time thing. We had sexual tension to break, and it's been broken, so now we can continue on with our lives and all that, but I don't want to say that. I hope we do it again. I hope it becomes a regular thing. I love his attention. And I miss sex.

GAIL

Sex is good. Just don't fall for him. I mean, you can still count the number of people you've been with on your fingers. Alec, not so much.

LYREN

I know. I don't think I'm like special to him or anything. I just mean we can have fun. Why not? We're attracted to each other.

But I wonder if he'd have suggested breakfast or invited me to stay and hang out and watch the game if I were just some random girl.

Does that actually make me special?

I don't want to think about it too much. I need to keep the potential for feelings out of this.

GAIL

A lamppost would be attracted to either of you. That's obvious. Really hot people can't be friends with each other. It never works.

LYREN

A lamppost?

GAIL

Yeah, not sure where that one came from. In any case, sure you can just have fun. You're both adults. Sex can maybe be casual, but the friendship part is the part that never works.

LYREN

Well, maybe it was a one-time thing. I don't want to push it or anything. I don't want anything to change or get weird, so I guess only time will tell.

GAIL

In any case, congrats on breaking your dry spell. I know you were worried about shriveling up.

LYREN

LOL no kidding. At least that problem's fixed.

It's Sunday, and I'm wondering what to do with myself. I make some scrambled eggs with peppers, onions, tomatoes, Canadian bacon, and cheese. I start to organize the mass of mail that has accumulated on my counter, but my hangover is still not subsiding, so I decide, fuck it, and sit on the couch.

As I am channel surfing and simultaneously messing around

on my computer, Olivia messages me. I will eventually tell her I did the horizontal tango with her brother, but now doesn't seem like the right time. I don't want to make her uncomfortable.

I know she won't *care* care. Before I met him, she used to say she'd set me up with him if he weren't such a player. Now she just thinks we're weird because we make out casually and she doesn't get it. I guess I don't either, but it's working, so why not?

OLIVIA

Want to come to trivia night with the guys tonight?

She's dating one of my college friends, which is convenient for me because I actually like joining her when she's hanging out with her boyfriend's friends. I can't say the same about all of my girlfriends' choices.

LYREN

That sounds fun. I'm hungover right now, but that will change. There is only one Sunday a week.

OLIVIA

My thoughts exactly.

My mother thinks I party too much. She might be right. At some point, one is supposed to grow up and all. In less than one year, I will officially be in my late twenties. I have not had a serious relationship in four years, and since then, I have started socializing a lot more than I did even in college.

LYREN

OK, well, I'm gonna go try to be productive or something. Text me later, and I'll meet up with you guys.

OLIVIA
Sounds good, Love.

Chapter Two

I swivel around in the chair in my cubicle and glaze over at my computer, trying to process my weekend.

I work as a copyeditor for an education materials company. It's less than glamorous, but I'm fairly good at it when I'm not trying to fight the socially inept, wretched excuse for a woman that is my boss. When I'm at my best, I like to think of myself as a creative and driven person, but there really isn't a lot of room for that in my job. When you're really good at English and really bad at math, you don't have many options, and the doors in my preferred field of journalism were not exactly flying open. Instead, I read hundreds of pages of textbook material a day, checking for superfluous comma usage and correcting ambiguous pronouns. I don't have to take my work home with me; I have a nice little space in a temperate office, and I work with pretty decent people with whom I choose not to fraternize on weekends. It's not my dream job, but it covers my rent.

I ignore my work emails for a few minutes and delete fifty emails from my personal email from stores I shopped at one time. I scroll through random celebrity boredom on Twitter. I check Facebook. When I first started this job, I never did things like open Facebook on the clock, but I happen to know by now that no one is looking into it and I still get my shit done. Besides, when you hate your boss as much as I hate Claire, respecting her and being good at work isn't on your highest priority list. I do what I can to not get fired, and that's my only career aspiration at this point.

I still hope to do something that inspires me and connects back to issues I care about. Somewhere inside me is still the bright, enthusiastic, and engaged person I was in college. But for today, I'm just getting through.

I go through the usual Facebook checklist. Browse the newsfeed. Emma put up a few new pictures from her weekend. Someone is bragging about fantasy football. Alec is bitching about the cold with a picture in a scarf and hat. He looks so sexy even with the face he is making. At least three girls have commented on it already. I don't know any of them.

I shake my head, wondering if one of them is the girl he said he's been going on dates with. They met online, but I know his intentions aren't serious. Part of what I like to remind my mother every time she acts like online dating is the cure to my Single Person Disease.

I make a point to check Evan's profile. I'm not supposed to do this, but it's second nature. I can't help it. I still want to know every girl that comments on his shit. I want to know what he's doing and more importantly, *who* he's doing. He commented on some girl's bikini picture from a vacation. She's skinnier than me. I start to feel nauseous.

"Lyren, can you look over this teacher's manual? It's supposed to go to press ASAP."

It's probably good that my pointless surfing is interrupted. I don't need to sit around wondering what skirt Evan is chasing these days.

"No problem, John."

I reach over the top of my cubicle and grab the manuscript. I take one look and get bored. It's about five hundred pages long and looks like the kind of crap teaching manual I hate, where they take all the creativity away from teachers and treat them like color-by-number factory workers on an assembly line. I've had enough teacher friends in my life to understand what it's about. Instead of thinking about the manual, I wonder what I should eat for lunch.

Olivia messages me on Facebook. *Excellent. Just what I am looking for. A new distraction.*

OLIVIA
Hey, Ly.

LYREN
Hey, Girl. What's up?

OLIVIA
Making sure we're still tutoring tomorrow.

LYREN
Absolutely.

OLIVIA
Cool.

There was once a time in my life when I was socially conscious. I wanted to be a journalist and advocate for human rights and education equity. When the economy decided to crash mid-internship, I realized pretty quickly that my fantasy career was going to have to take a backseat to realistic bill-paying, and when I saw the copyeditor position on Indeed, I figured I could check it out, move out of my parents' house, make a few contacts, and pursue my journalism career in the interim. That was four years ago. The backseat seems more like it's being towed somewhere far behind me these days.

Olivia is a social worker and does a lot of volunteer work on the side. She's an unbelievably thoughtful person. We met when we both started tutoring together three years ago. We then began going to ethnic restaurants across the city to discuss politics and what was wrong with the world. Being her friend has kept me connected to things I care about. A year ago, I brought her to a party. I was meeting Evan there, and that was where she hit it off with Chris. At this point, our lives are so intertwined it's hard to tell what was whose first. Especially now that I just intertwined something new.

LYREN
I cannot focus on work to save my life.

OLIVIA
I'm on break and have to get back, but have fun. I'll talk to you later and see you tomorrow. Want to grab some dinner afterward?

LYREN
Yeah, that sounds good.

Olivia still inspires me, but lately, both of us seem to be a little more disillusioned. Our conversations are more about frustration with our day jobs, drama among friends, and boy complications than what's wrong with the world. Even though she's in a stable and healthy relationship, there's still always something.

I look back at the teacher's manual and get through the first ten pages. It's dreadful and straightforward, but I'm not noticing too many mechanical errors. You'd think anyone who writes a teaching manual in the first place should have a pretty strong handle on the English language, but it's surprising how few of these people have any real-world experience in what they are writing about.

My thoughts drift back to that bikini chick. *Who is she?* She commented about the Bears. We don't have many mutual follow-ers, which means Evan is probably banging, or trying to bang, her.

ALEC
Do some work!

Oh jeez. This is why you can't have Facebook open at work when you have the willpower of an alcoholic in a bar.

LYREN
I was trying before you bothered me.

ALEC
Yeah yeah.

LYREN
What about you?

ALEC
Just got up. Jealous?

LYREN
No. Do something with your life, you lazy bum.

ALEC
Nah, no thanks. I'll leave working to you.

Alec is a travel agent. For the most part, he works with indi-vidual clients on his own time. Because of his connections, he

gets a lot of deals and discounts in addition to a great salary and
commission. I always wondered how people managed to get jobs
like that, but one thing I will definitely give Alec is his gift
of gab.

LYREN
OK, I really do have to do some work, though, because
your sister and I have tutoring tomorrow, so I leave a
little early.

ALEC
Yeah, you guys trying to help out and save the world, one
inner-city kid at a time.

LYREN
Well, it wouldn't kill you to do something with all your
spare time you know.

ALEC
Oh I do plenty with my spare time. I order food delivery,
watch TV, show women the time of their lives . . .

LYREN
Don't flatter yourself.

ALEC
Well, I do what I can ;)

LYREN
Yeah yeah yeah. Sorry, I forgot what high demand you
are in. How's your new lady going?

ALEC
Meh. She's alright. Great body. She wants to be my girl-

friend, but I just moved here! I need to have some fun
before I get serious with some girl!

I shake my head, though I am glad it's not getting serious. I
don't want some girl to steal Alec away from me just yet. Not
when we just spiced things up. I need him for his availability and
fun energy. But now I'm worried that if we don't continue
sleeping together, our friendship will be over. How long can you
keep up casual? I guess I'll find out. I don't even know if we'll
sleep together again. It wasn't exactly discussed.

LYREN
Who are you kidding? You're never gonna settle down.

ALEC
I will. One day. When I meet the right girl, maybe in like
five years. I have too much traveling to do. Which
reminds me. I signed on because it's time to finish
booking my next trip.

LYREN
Oh for heaven's sake, where are you going now?

ALEC
Italy. Two weeks next month.

LYREN
Wow, why?

ALEC
Some extended family is out there, and I'm gonna visit
and check it out.

LYREN
Nice.

I'm more jealous than I want to let on as I look out the window at the gray sky and back down at the teaching manual.

LYREN
You staying in Italy the whole time?

ALEC
Most of it. Maybe all of it. Should be a good time. I'll have an extra glass of vino for you while I'm there.

LYREN
Thanks. Isn't your girlfriend going to miss you for two weeks?

ALEC
Yeah yeah. That's enough out of you. Go back to work.

I once asked Alec what his dream job would be. He said he wanted nothing to do with any job if he didn't have to work. There was no job that could possibly make him happy or feel fulfilled. Life was about having fun. He wanted to see the world, he wanted to make good friends, and he wanted to have a great time along the way. When he first said it, it turned me off.

Like I said, I was once more fervent about making a differ-ence. I like to think that somewhere deep down I still am, which is probably why I tutor. I won a ton of awards for my college newspaper. I graduated with cords. If money weren't an issue, I'd probably spend all of my time researching human rights issues. I could write articles and send them out to magazines or something and work my own hours at my own pace and only focus on what I was actually interested in and have something that was, I don't know . . . *mine.*

"Looks like you're really busy over here!" The arrogant, though impressively insecure, serpent of a woman, who claims to be a leader, sneaks up on me, breaking my daydream.

"Sorry, Claire. I got caught up in a thought."

"Well, I'm going to need you to do less thinking and more editing. We need that manual like right now," she says in a passive-aggressive, whiny tone.

Then maybe you shouldn't have given a 500-page manual for me to edit "right now"!

I hold back rolling my eyes and nod my head, and she gives me a catty smile. How do people with such messed-up personalities get to be in charge of anything?

Chapter Three

"Lyren, can we tutor fast today?"

"No, Jarron. We are going the full hour. Why do you want to leave early, anyway?"

We are sitting with two desks facing each other in a classroom with about 12 tutor-student pairs. The teacher, who is usually in this classroom, did her best with some bright bulletin boards, but it's hard to hide the dilapidation behind the posters. The room, and the school itself, are depressing.

"Football training is starting today."

"What are you talking about? It's December."

"Yeah, but try-outs for varsity are in January, and they are letting the guys use the weight room to get ready."

"Sorry, buddy. You're on company time. Can't let you do that. How long is it?"

"Two hours."

"You'll still make the last hour of it."

"Yeah, but I want to be good enough for varsity!"

Jarron is only in sixth grade, but all he talks about is football and making the varsity team for the junior high. He plays for the junior team, but claims that's kid stuff. I enjoy his passion for football, but it makes getting him to focus on reading and writing a little more difficult.

Jarron is my third tutee. A year out of college, while still actively searching for something more fulfilling than copyediting, I came across the after-school tutoring program at a middle school in the Woodlawn neighborhood. I figured volunteering kept me engaged, gave me some sense of purpose, and maybe I could even be useful to someone. I've liked all of my students, but Jarron has a fun personality, and although he certainly has some attitude, I generally enjoy the hour I spend with him every week.

"Well, if you don't pass school, you will not get to play football at all."

"Man, that's so lame."

"Academics come first, my friend."

"Academics don't matter. I'm going to be in the NFL right after high school."

It's nice to be reminded of what it was like to have big dreams, even if the world will eventually crush them all.

"False. You have to play for a college, and even if you're the best athlete in the world, if you are bad at school, people are going to make fun of you and say the only reason you're at school is athletics. You can be better than that. You can be the guy who is a star quarterback *and* smart."

"Whatever. What are we working on today?"

"Let's see your homework." I look over at Olivia, who is tutoring a girl named Diamond. She's a handful, but always makes me laugh. Olivia has more patience than me. Jarron's mom is on him enough at home that it makes my job tutoring him just a bit easier. He knows he'll "get whooped," as he likes to call it, if I have to call home or if he brings home poor grades.

"I have to read *Where the Red Fern Grows.*"

"That's a great book," I say as he takes it out of his backpack.

"Looks like a stupid white book." He frowns, but then looks up at me. "I mean, it looks like a stupid book."

"The point of reading and school isn't for you to relearn things you already know about, Jarron. If you read about black kids in Chicago, what would you be learning?"

"But that's real life!"

"So is *Where the Red Fern Grows.* It's just about someone else's life. Someone you don't know and whose life you don't understand. It helps you understand where other people are coming from."

"I don't care about where some kid in the country who likes to hunt is coming from. I want to read about real things."

"Like what?"

"Like, fighting and football."

"Those are real things, but there are lots of other real things, too." I say this, but make a note to bring him *The Outsiders* the next time I'm here. Jarron likes to pretend he hates reading, but secretly, I can tell he has some level of interest in school and learning about other things. I plan to exploit that interest to the best of my ability.

"Yeah, whatever. I know if I don't do well on this unit that Mom is gonna whoop me cause I didn't do so good on the last test."

"And why didn't you do so well on the last test? We studied for that test together!"

"I don't know! It was hard! And Ms. Shannon hates me."

"Ms. Shannon absolutely does not hate you."

"How do you know?"

"First of all, because I have to talk to her to find out what you're learning about in school, and she shows a very dedicated interest in your education and thinks you have a lot of promise in English."

"She said that?"

"She most certainly did."

"Then why did she give me a D?"

"You gave yourself a D. We'll just study harder for the next test. Just don't blame your teacher. She wants you to succeed. It is her career and her life to make sure that you do, so if you don't, it doesn't help her in the slightest. She'd have no reason to make you look bad."

"I guess." He rolls his eyes.

"Hey! No eye-rolling!"

"Sorry, Lyren." He hesitates for a second. I'm a little more laid back than his real teachers because I sort of feel sorry for the fact that he has to stay after school and do tutoring. He's not a bad student, really.

"It's OK, just be more careful. You have to be respectful. I know I'm not your actual teacher, but I'm still an authority figure." I'm not always so sure I can pull off being "authority," but maybe if I say it, he'll believe it.

"I wish you were my teacher. You're cooler than Ms. Shannon."

"That's only because you don't have to see me every day. Alright, enough wasting time. Let's work for at least a B on this unit, OK?"

"OK."

"Seriously, do you think we can achieve that?"

"Yeah, I guess so."

"You don't guess so, you know so!"

"Yeah yeah. You're a little weird, Lyren."

I laugh. "So they tell me. OK, open that book up and let's take a look at the work you have to do with it."

After tutoring, I walk Jarron down to the weight room with Olivia. I promised him I'd talk to the coach and vouch for him.

The archaic weight room reeks of a millennium of sweat stuck to the walls and equipment. I'm thankful I attended beautiful new schools throughout my life. No wonder kids in the inner city don't do well. How could they focus in a place like this? Not that I'd have ever found myself in the weight room of whatever school I went to.

"You the coach?" I ask a tall guy around my own age who clearly knows his way around a gym. The obvious only adult in the room.

"You got it. Can I help you?"

"I'm Jarron's tutor, and I told him I'd come let you know that he's been working very hard for school and that's why he couldn't come to the first hour of practice. He's been very devastated."

"Hey man, academics come first. Always," the coach says, looking down at Jarron. "Go get changed. We're running some laps."

Jarron runs off to the locker room.

"OK, thanks. Have fun out here," I say.

"Oh, we always do." He smiles and walks off, yelling something about drills.

"He was really cute," Olivia says.

I shrug. I very rarely notice if people are cute if I don't know them yet.

"Anyway, there is a new Indian restaurant in the Loop that looks interesting. Want to check it out?"

"Sure."

"So, what's the deal with you and my brother, anyway? While we're on the subject of men."

"Were we on the subject of men?" I raise my eyes at her. She obviously has been waiting for an opportune moment to discuss, and now I suddenly worry she'll be upset that I hooked up with Alec.

"Lame attempt at a segue. I was just wondering. I mean, you make out, which is sort of weird. And you hang out all the time. You see a lot more of him than you do even of me. Do you like him?"

"I don't *like* him. I mean, I like being around him, and we have a lot of fun together, but I don't want to be *dating* dating him."

"Have you hooked up yet?"

I hesitate a moment. But I could never lie. "Yes," I admit. *Here it goes.*

"Sex?"

"Yes."

"So you like him." Olivia doesn't look the slightest bit surprised.

"No, it's not like that. I'm comfortable with him. I don't feel like he's using me or out to hurt me or anything. We're attracted to each other, and it sort of just happened."

"It was bound to happen. I mean, I know you kept saying that it wasn't going to happen. And he, like, didn't understand you as a person because you don't just go out and have sex with people."

"He said that?"

"Yeah. Most of the girls in his life want to sleep with him right away."

"I've never even had a one-night stand. Alec acts like the only reason we took so long to have sex was because I'm friends with you, but really, it takes me a while to decide I'm into someone at all. And I had to also make sure that if it did ever happen, that I would know there was no chance of me falling in love with him. I know him well enough now that I would already love him. Alec acts like girls start to go crazy and fall because of the sex, when in truth, in most of those cases, the girl had sex with the guy *because* she already really liked him and was hoping that would keep him interested in her. And usually that doesn't work."

"Totally. But guys never understand that. They think we fall in love because of sex."

"Having sex with someone is generally an expression of your attraction and feelings, and of course there are emotions connected to it. I'm being careful."

"Alec loves you. He definitely doesn't want to hurt you. I just don't know if he is the type that will ever really be in a relationship."

"He claims he wants to be one day."

"I know he does."

"He just doesn't go about it the right way. Look, I know too much about Alec to ever love him. I could never love someone that has slept with that many people. It comes too easily for him, so he'll never really appreciate a great girl because he's too used to stupid girls falling all over him. I'll never do that. And I will never again have a boyfriend who needs to learn how to be a boyfriend. I'm not gonna be the girl to whip someone into shape. The next guy I like will already be in perfect shape."

"That I do understand." She rolls her eyes, and I laugh, thinking of some of the crap she has dealt with over Chris. "In any case, you know my parents want you guys to get married, so if they get wind of this, I'll never hear the end of it."

"They do?"

"Oh yeah. They love you and have been wanting Alec to date you since they first met you."

Something about this thrills me, though I can't really explain why. I mean, it's always nice to know your good friend's parents are fans of yours. But I wonder if they see something there with Alec that I don't. Or maybe they are just sick of him playing around and think I have my shit together. Which is comical enough these days.

"Well, that's sweet. This isn't exactly dating, though."

"No, but I'm just saying. My dad would be thrilled, none-theless. Every time you do anything, my mom points out how fabulous you are for him. She wants him to start settling down, and they both just think you're great."

"Well, if they knew what a whore I was being, they might feel differently."

"Hey now. Everyone has their needs."

THREE MONTHS PRIOR

"What would you think if you met a girl whose number was crazy high?"

"What's crazy high?" Alec and I were eating late-night burritos under fluorescent lights, random Mexican flags, and streamers at Los Tres Panchos on a September night.

"Over fifty, which is still significantly less than you. Would you date her? Would you fall for her?"

"Probably not."

"See . . . that's total and complete bullshit."

I didn't want to get into an actual fight with Alec, but my blood started boiling. I couldn't understand the audacity of men who thought less of a woman for behaving the exact way they did. If you wanted to sleep around, do that, but how could you judge someone else for having the same attitude or inter-est? And then why should a woman who did prioritize her emotional values as they connected to sex be willing to over-look your own attitude and trust that she was different?

"It's not. I'm sorry. I know it's a double standard, but it's different."

"I don't think it's different. Just because society somewhere along the line made it OK for guys to screw everyone that

walks, but if a girl does the same thing, she's ruined, it's not different." My tone was sharp, though I was consciously trying not to raise my voice.

"Yeah, but all guys love sex."

I rolled my eyes. "Girls love sex, too, Alec. Girls love attention and having a guy's arms around them. Girls want to feel like the sexiest girl in the room. Girls want a guy to hold them. And girls like orgasming, too."

"I know."

"Well, I think it's no different for a guy to have sex with a ton of girls than a girl having sex with a ton of guys. But there is nothing more attractive in a guy than if he hasn't slept with many people."

"Really?" He genuinely looked surprised.

"So I really, really liked this one guy, Evan. And one time we were talking about our numbers, and his was four. Same as me at the time. And all but one were actual girlfriends who he really liked and cared about. And the one, he said he felt guilty about it and wouldn't do that again because sex is supposed to mean something. Anything else is up for grabs, but sex is supposed to mean something. And I fell in love. It was one of the hottest things a guy has ever told me."

Too bad said bastard ripped my heart into shreds.

"OK, but just because I have meaningless sex with people doesn't mean that if I really care about a girl that it doesn't mean something."

"I disagree. I'm sorry. It's just the same if you were to say 'I love you' to every person you had a fleeting interest in; the words would never mean anything real. If you have sex with a bunch of people just because you can, it's never going to mean as much as if you kept something sacred. My ex and I fought about this a lot. He was my first. I was so pure and innocent, and I just really knew in my heart what love was supposed to be and what I wanted sex to be, and I cared about it and I

respected it. And I loved him with all of my heart. But I was his tenth. And I never could get over that. If I was his second, or maybe third, that would be OK. People that he'd dated and cared about. But it wasn't like that. And the truth is, I always felt like Jason didn't fully deserve me over it. I was too good for him because I had too strong of values."

"But you were young then."

"So ten becomes twenty. What's the difference? Obviously, as you get older and are single, that number goes up, and that's fine. I don't believe anyone should be prudes. But I started regretting how I did everything the right way. I became more jaded; more skeptical. It bothered me to my core that he got to use a bunch of women for sex and then flip a switch because he actually cared about me. He actually got really hurt when I said that cuddling with him meant more to me than sex on an emotional level. And he was like, 'But that's how we express our intimacy,' and I said, 'How can you pretend sexual intimacy is special if you do the same thing with girls who you don't care about? When was the last time you watched a movie cuddling with a girl you didn't care about? Never? Right. So that's why cuddling means more to me than sex.'"

"But you aren't jaded. You don't go around sleeping with a bunch of people or using people."

"No. And I wouldn't want to date someone who did."

"Ouch. It's not like I go around lying to girls or cheating on them. I'm always incredibly honest."

"I know. I'm sorry. I'm not saying that to offend you. It's the way you've chosen to go, and that's fine. There are plenty of people who don't feel the way I do about it. I'm just saying that you can't act like your number doesn't matter at all just because you're a guy. There are people who feel it does."

"But you make out with me."

"I like you, Alec. I'm attracted to you. But if I met another guy like you, I'd be really hesitant. I'm not saying that I

wouldn't date them. You don't know who you'll fall for. All I'm
saying is that it's a really unattractive quality. And it's bullshit
that you say you'd write off a girl for being exactly like you."

"*I wouldn't. It's just . . . an unattractive quality."*

It was as if I was the first person who had ever told him
that it works two ways. I didn't mean to hurt Alec. I just really
hated the double standard.

Now I wonder if I'm a hypocrite for sleeping with Alec. He's my
number five. I lost my virginity at age 19 to Jason, whom I was
absolutely crazy about and whom I knew was absolutely crazy
about me. We dated for three years. After we broke up, it took
me a while to warm up to new guys. Everyone I slept with after
that was someone I was either dating, or really thought I wanted
to be dating. Like Scott. God, was he pretty.

I always wanted to believe sex meant something, which is
why I was so impressed when Evan said he only enjoyed sex
with women he really cared about. I wanted to believe that there
were guys like that all over. That they didn't have sex just
because the option was available.

In any case, I think having sex with Alec is still OK because
I *do* care about him. He's a very good friend. He means a lot.

Right?

What am I getting myself into?

Would I even like Alec if he weren't good-looking and
charming and all those things that make a guy exactly what your
mother warns you about? Probably not. But a girl has needs, and
if Alec can fill some of mine, it's time I stop being so goddamn
sensitive about everything.

Chapter Four

I step into my mom's kitchen, and my nose becomes keenly aware that she is already cooking. Walking into my parent's house at Christmas time always overwhelms me with festive energy and sweet nostalgia. My mom still puts up a 12-foot real tree even though Emma and I moved out years ago. Everything seems to have a dusting of glitter and cheer. I'm immediately taken back to making lists for Santa and picking out our favorite new ornaments and puff painting sweatshirts to wear through the season.

"Hey Ly!" Matt, Emma's fiancé, comes over to hug me. They are wrapping gifts on the kitchen table.

"Shhh! Turn around, Lyren! Don't look!" Emma tries to shield the gift she is wrapping from my eyes as I laugh and hug Matt.

Suddenly, I am attacked by a snorting ball of muscle.

"Meatloaf!!!" I yell, bending down to pet my mother's insane English Bulldog, who seems as though he might die of a heart attack over all the excitement going on in the house. "Meatloaf . . . hello!!!!" I say in an obnoxious deep voice; the only appropriate way to handle such a hilarious little beast.

"How are you doing, Matt?" I ask when Meatloaf calms down and I have a chance to stand up and put my things down.

"I'm great! Looking forward to dinner tonight."

"What are you making, Mom?" I ask, walking deeper into the kitchen, making a point to still not look at Emma.

"Oh, a hello would be nice."

"Hi, Mom," I laugh and give her a hug before lifting up a lid on the stove to see soup. "Homemade soup?? YES!"

"Well, I know it's you girls' favorite, and Matt has never tried it."

"Get excited. It's an initiation to the family. You can't be one of us without loving the soup, so you better start vamping up your acting skills in case you don't," I kid.

"It might be a no-wedding type of deal breaker if he doesn't," Emma says, finally done decorating the gift and coming over to give me a hug.

"What's the big deal about this soup, anyway?" Matt asks.

"It's just the most amazing soup ever!" I exclaim, intentionally hyping up our childhood favorite.

"Oh, they are just being silly. First of all, it's OK if you don't like it. I won't be offended," my mom responds.

"She's lying," Emma says.

"Oh now! But they used to love it when they would come in from the snow at their grandma's. It was my mom's soup and one of their favorite things about winter. They'd go sledding at her house and then come in and she'd have the soup ready for them."

"Oh, that's really sweet."

"Yeah, well, the nostalgia aspect is certainly touching, but it's really all about the dumplings," I add.

"It's absolutely about the dumplings. It's a winter staple around here," Emma says. "So, Lyren, what did you bring over?"

She starts to walk over to the cake I just set down.

"It's gingerbread cake, but stay away from it! It's for tomorrow night!"

"Damn it! I don't want to share that. Your baking is the best!" Matt says, admiring it.

"I love the little gingerbread men you put on top of it. So cute. Did you make those yourself?" Emma points to the more aesthetic pleasures of my Christmas cake.

"I did indeed. They were actually the hardest part. But I sort of made up the recipe, so I really do hope it's good. Either that or that we're all drunk enough by dessert that no one really notices if it isn't."

"Likely in this family," Mom adds. "Speaking of which, if anyone would like to have some wine, dinner won't be ready for a while and it would be nice to sit and visit."

"Sure," I say, going to the cabinet to get some glasses while Emma grabs a bottle of wine.

"You guys are nothing. You should see the way my family drinks at holiday functions. Italians, we're crazy. Everyone starts to think they are in the mob and they end up in some ridiculous brawl, all to be forgotten about the very next day."

"It's so true," Emma laughs. "His family is so funny. They cook so much food, way more than anyone could ever eat, and then they just keep it going with the drinks until everyone is yelling at each other and vows they are never speaking again."

"Hey! Smells good in here!"

"Hey Dad!" We all sort of yell in unison as my dad walks in from work.

Something about the holidays always makes our family get all Norman-Rockwell-like for a week or so. The house always smells like nutmeg from my mom's speciality candles. We are all a little giddy about celebrations and dinners. Emma already made Matt fuss over the tree for a good twenty minutes. Then, a week or so later, we're back to using "dumbass" as a term of endearment.

"Matt! What's going on, son?" My dad laughs as Matt looks at him awkwardly. "Too soon?"

"Just about a year away now!" Matt shakes my dad's hand.

"Yeah, don't remind my pocketbook of that. How is business going?"

"It's good. Really good right now, with the holidays and all. We just picked up a few new clients, actually."

"Let me know if you need some recommendations."

My dad and Matt have a lot in common. Both work for consulting firms. Dad is higher up in a larger firm, Matt is just starting out in a smaller one, but he is a really hard worker, and my dad thinks he shows a lot of promise. My mother loves that he is close to his really big family, even though they are in Philadelphia. By all standards, Matt is more than accepted in the family, probably why my mom is always on me to try to meet a guy, too, so she can know that both of her girls are taken care of and that she doesn't have to worry. I give her no such comfort.

"I will absolutely do that."

"Would you like a glass of wine, honey?" Mom asks.

"Absolutely. What did you guys bring out?"

"Just a merlot. I don't know that much about wine," Emma said.

"As long as it's not from my really expensive stash. You guys aren't important enough to share that with."

"Yeah, I don't know who he does think is important enough to share any of that with. Not sure when he thinks the president is coming over." Mom rolls her eyes.

"The way he's running this country right now, I'm not even sure if he's good enough for it," Dad comments.

"Well, you better be careful or you're going to end up keeping them too long and they are going to go sour. You'd hate to be opening a bottle of really expensive wine for someone impressive or for a special occasion and have it taste like vinegar or something."

"Interesting point. So Lyren, how is your job going?" Time for my dad to start his grilling about what I'm doing with my life. One of my least favorite topics.

"Oh, it's terrifically interesting. You'd never believe how many people have no command over the English vocabulary or bog technical manuals down with jargon that no layperson could comprehend."

"Sounds fascinating," he responds.

"You actually like doing that all day?" Matt asks.

"I was being facetious. It's incredibly boring; however, I'm good enough at it and it pays the bills."

"When are you going to actually pursue something relevant?" my dad asks.

I know he means well, but we've been going over all of this for years now. Even if I had a job I loved in a field like journalism, he'd still be worried. He always wants to make sure I'm financially secure. It is really touching, but he just doesn't get why I am interested in the things I am and isn't really sure of what I'm doing in my future. Which makes two of us. But when he grills me on it, I feel like I'm letting him down.

"Who knows, Dad? It's fine for now, anyway. Maybe I'll move up in it, maybe I'll start looking for something else eventually. I don't have to figure that out now."

"You know, it's really never too late to get your MBA. There is such a market right now for people who are good with numbers. If you go back to school for computer science, that would be even better! That's where all the really good jobs are nowadays and in this economy."

"Hi Dad, I'm Lyren. Nice to meet you." I sarcastically put my hand out for him to shake it.

"I'm just saying."

"Dad, not everyone is good at technology and business. I'm

fine doing what I'm doing right now. I can always move into something else eventually, but if I went back to school, it would definitely not be for business or computer science, so there is no point. All the things I am good at or interested in are the things there are no jobs in now, so I'm stuck either way."

"I really think you should have started a bakery. You're so good at baking and those little cupcake bakeries are everywhere now. You could have had one of them," Mom says.

We've had this conversation multiple times. She knows it's something I've dreamed of, but I have no idea where to even begin, and it's not like I can afford to just go to pastry school or anything.

"Yeah, you really should have. I'd be a frequent guest," Emma adds, admiring my gingerbread cake again.

"Good to know. I really just want to be a Food Network host. Anyone know how I can get that job?" I laugh.

"Well, I think you have to start with culinary school or open a restaurant or, you know, otherwise prove yourself as a chef besides," Emma jokes.

"Hell, you never even cook for your family!" my mom chides.

"You never want to drive over to my place! I'd have you people over! But no, obviously you have to do a lot to prove yourself as an actual chef. I don't have the background at all for that. Although, I think it would be interesting to have a show where I make really good and not that hard or expensive healthy meals. Almost everything you see on the Food Network is bad for you."

"What? You mean all of those Paula Dean recipes Emma has been cooking for me are BAD for me?" Matt laughs.

"Yeah right," I respond. "We all know Emma can't cook."

"Hey! I make a badass Kraft macaroni and cheese!"

"She never helps out in the kitchen, so she never learned," my mom says.

"Great, let's all gang up on Emma because she can't cook. I have a busy job! I don't have time for cooking!"

Emma is a dental hygienist. She probably could easily make time to cook if she wanted to. She was never that interested. But at least her job and her relationship are very stable at age 28.

"Anyway, I would rather be like a cupcake show host, where I get to just invent amazing cupcakes and teach people how to make them all day. How great would that be?"

"Yeah, and I never gave up my ambition of being a rock star," Matt jokes.

"There is only one major difference, baby," Emma says, putting her arm around him. "Lyren is actually an amazing cupcake baker, and you can't play an instrument, sing, or write songs."

"Never too old to learn!" he says.

"Well, if you marry someone with money, maybe you can go to cooking school or pastry school, then you'd be able to focus on that!" my mom chimes in, bringing the focus back to me. It makes my skin crawl.

"Yes, Mom. I will redirect my life ambition to finding a rich man to wed, pronto."

I've never been attracted to people with money. My first boyfriend worked in construction, Evan was a teacher, and Scott was bartending while working on environmental activism. I was doomed to the life of poverty that comes with dating bleeding heart Marxist types.

"Can we go back to talking about soup now?"

"OK, well, the Blackhawks are on in the other room. Let me know when the soup is done guys," Dad says, grabbing his Blackberry and walking into the living room.

I sit for a second, enjoying my surroundings the day before the holidays. This part is the best. The small immediate family. Parents, dog, Emma, and Matt. And I'd be blatantly lying if I said I didn't get jealous of the way Emma has been able to bring someone not just into our lives, but into this comfortable, intimate version of our family.

Alec texts me Christmas night.

ALEC
Still have people over?

My family always has a huge party for friends, neighbors, and other family after everyone finishes their dinner obligations. It has come to the point where people arrange their family celebrations around, making sure they will be at our house at night. I had invited some friends to stop by, but Olivia was with Chris's family, and Sarah was with her own.

LYREN
Party is still going strong. Stop by if you'd like. Just walk straight in. The door is open and the party is in the basement.

I send him my parents' address, too. I've been drinking heavily and talking to friends of my parents all night, most of whom have asked me ten thousand questions about my career and my relationship status, neither of which are topics I really enjoy discussing with anyone, let alone making small talk about. It will be nice to have my own friend here. And sort of nice for maybe some people to think that I do have a boyfriend. And maybe to observe that he's ridiculously good-looking. As long as they don't actually ask me about it, the façade can't hurt.

"It's rude to be texting at a party, Lyren," my mother chides.

"Alec is stopping by. His family dinner is over."

"No Olivia?"

"Olivia is with her boyfriend."

"I see." I can feel the suspicion in my mother's voice.

"Who is Alec?" Andrea, my mom's friend, asks.

"Alec is just a friend. He's my good friend. Olivia's brother," I explain, without giving too much detail.

"Is he cute?" she asks immediately.

"Very. But it's not like that. He's just a friend."

"You know, I have a nephew who is a little older than you. He has a really good job, owns a condo in the city, and has a car. You really should meet him."

I fight my eyes' desperate need to roll. Being set up is about the equivalent of slowly stabbing myself with a fork. First of all, when I go into the inevitable phase of the relationship where I become honest with myself that I will never develop feelings for this person, that kissing him is like kissing a wall, and that he will be forever in the friend zone, I now have to deal with the fact that he's also friends with someone I know and I can't be a bitch about it. Second, none of the people who try to set me up actually seem to know anything about me or what I'm attracted to. The factors Andrea just named are the exact things I keep trying to find attractive, but will always end up leaving for some inner city teacher whose life assets are a toaster and a mattress.

"Appreciate it, but I'm really not very good at the whole 'being set up' thing."

"So how is work going, Ly?" Andrea asks.

"It's going. It's work. What is it supposed to be?"

"Well, that's true. But you've always been so smart and creative. You should be doing something with your talents, you know."

She means well; they all do. I just really have the urge to run upstairs and never talk to anyone again. Thinking about my career has that effect. When I don't think about it, I don't have time to be disappointed in myself, and can avoid freaking out about what I could do to become a person of substance like I once aspired to be. Or expected to be.

"Ho ho ho! Merry Christmas!" I turn around to see Alec walking into the house wearing a Santa hat and carrying a huge bottle of Effen Black Cherry.

"Hello Alec!" My mom gives him a hug as if she has known him forever instead of only meeting him a couple of times. Everyone's quite a few beverages in.

"Hello, Mrs. Valence!"

"Oh for god's sake, call me Lane."

"Hey you." I go up and hug him. He looks absolutely adorable in the hat. "Love your holiday spirit."

"Of course!" He takes the hat off and puts it on my head, messing up my hair and smiling at me. *God, he looks good.*

"Thanks for messing up my hair."

"I didn't realize family holiday parties were all the rage for picking people up. I'd have worn my dancing shoes."

"You can wear your dancing shoes anyway, because we've been dancing around and making merry, if you will, all night long."

"Excellent."

"How was your family dinner?"

"It was really nice. Relaxing. Always good to see the cousins and all. But most of them have kids now, so the night ends a little early, and without Olivia there, it gets boring. So, I figured I may as well stop by. You guys have a ton of people here!"

"Yeah, this has gotten crazy."

"So you do this every year?"

"For the last six or so years since we've gotten older, yeah. It's kind of a fun tradition."

"I like it."

"I see you know the way to my family's hearts," I say, taking the bottle of Effen to make him a drink.

"What do you want?" I hold up the Effen, asking whether he wants some of it.

"I'll actually just have a beer. That's for you guys."

"You didn't have to do that," Mom says, taking the bottle from him. "But thank you so much, and Merry Christmas."

I introduce him to a few people, without specifying "friend" as his title just in case anyone feels like making their own inferences. It's nice not to feel alone during the holidays.

I look over at Matt and Emma dancing together to Sinatra. They are laughing and looking into each other's eyes. It's cute. In almost exactly one year, they will be married—a thought that is still really weird to me.

"Care for a dance?" Alec extends his hand and pulls me into the middle of the basement, which has sort of become the dance floor of our house. I smile and follow him.

"Why thank you, kind sir," I say as he pulls me closer.

"You look absolutely lovely this fine Christmas. Was Santa good to you?"

"He was. I got a lot of cooking stuff, including my own KitchenAid stand mixer, finally."

"Ways to know you're getting old. You get excited about getting kitchen utensils on Christmas."

"I know. I was thinking the same thing. But I really am excited about it. I bake a lot."

"Bake me something."

"There is a little bit of my gingerbread cake leftover that I brought to my aunt's last night upstairs. You can have some later if you like, but don't tell anyone. There isn't enough to share."

"Ooh, first Christmas at the Valences and I'm already getting special treatment."

"It's only cause you're pretty."

As Alec and I dance together, being careful not to get too close as it's a family party, I can't help but notice how our relationship hasn't changed at all. We're still flirty and complimentary but not relationshipy. Not mooshy. Just nice and comfortable. Like always.

"Well, I may take you up on that cake offer in a little bit. As if I haven't eaten enough this December."

He then excuses himself to the bathroom, and I refill my drink and get him another beer.

"You weren't kidding," Andrea says. "That is quite an attractive gentleman."

"I know." I just look at her and smile.

"Your mom tells me that he is a huge player."

"He is. We're just friends."

She looks at me as if she absolutely knows better. And obviously, so does my mother. But I don't feel like explaining the friends with benefits status to adults (and I still don't know how to think of it myself). If that's even what Alec and I are. Maybe it was a one-time thing. We haven't talked about it. We probably aren't going to.

"Who wants to play Catch Phrase?" Emma has an app on her phone, and we gather round the table.

Eventually, the party fizzles out.

"So how about that cake?" Alec comes up to me after talking to Emma for a little while.

I love how he can be social with my friends and family without needing a babysitter. Like a good friend rather than an awkward date. It's the kind of natural ease Matt has around us, and I almost wish Alec and I were together. If I took away his playboy tendencies and carefree approach to his entire future. I'm starting to think the idea of carrying on a friends with benefits relationship with him could be perfect. I don't want to push my luck, though. He's been nice, playful and flirty, but nothing that alludes to wanting to have sex. And even though just looking at him sort of turns me on, we're in my parents' house after all.

I let my mom know that I'm going upstairs to get Alec a piece of cake so she doesn't get suspicious. He grabs a water bottle and follows me to where it is a lot quieter. I'm drunker than he is because he came late and drove here.

"Thanks for the invite," he says. "My house was getting boring, and you know how I feel about going to bed early."

"No worries. I'm glad you could come. Helps me avoid some of the small talk with my parents' friends."

"Yeah, that gets old." I cut him a piece of the cake, making sure to give him a gingerbread man.

"You better appreciate this. I worked damn hard on it."

"Wow, you actually made this?" His genuine appreciation fills me with pride, and I try not to beam too obviously. It's rare that I feel much pride lately.

"I did, indeed. I love the holidays. A great excuse to bake!"

"Liv told me you liked to cook and bake, but I had no idea you were this good. This is absolutely delicious."

I haven't actually shared my baking with any guy I've been interested in since Jason, who was always a fan. But with him, I was still in a trial learning phase. It was procrastination from studying, and he got to be the beneficiary. Since then, letting a man taste my cooking somehow felt even more intimate than sex. It was personal, and the stakes seemed higher. But, much like having sex with Alec, letting him try my baking is just easy. And it's not like I made it *for* him.

"Thank you," I say as coyly as I can muster.

"Seriously. Why are you wasting your time in a cubicle if you bake this good?"

"It's not so easy just opening up a bakery."

"And you yell at me for taking the easy way out."

"Yeah, whatever. Too risky."

He may be right. Maybe following your passions is something for people a lot stronger than me. Maybe I should start thinking more like Alec and see work as a means to an end instead of worrying about some larger concept of fulfillment.

"Well, you can feel free to bake for me any time you like. I'm not opposed to getting fat."

"Yeah right. Do you know how much your life would change if you got fat? You'd actually have to put effort into making girls like you rather than just standing there looking at them."

"Hey now! Give me more credit than that! I don't just stand there. I am incredibly charming."

"Sure you are."

"It worked on you," he says, lifting an eyebrow, and I can't help but blush. It's the first time in two weeks that we've actually acknowledged the change in our relationship, and I sort of like it.

"Well, it took you five months to get in my pants."

"I wasn't trying that hard. You're Olivia's friend."

"Yeah right. You were totally trying. You couldn't resist this."

"Well, it certainly did not disappoint." He looks at me all dazed and sparkly and hot.

"Don't give me that look. We're in my parents' house."

"What look? Who said anything about having sex with you? So eager you are. See? I'm great with women. Remember that you aren't allowed to get attached to my penis. We've been over this."

"Don't flatter yourself. There's nothing you can do that my vibrator can't," I lie. I quickly flashback to a particular moment when Alec pulled my hair while biting my ear as he thrust himself inside me, and I'm about ready to shove him against the kitchen wall.

"Good bye, you two!" Andrea and her family come through the kitchen with their coats on, and I immediately snap back to reality. She gives me a knowing smile as we hug.

"Thank you for coming over. Hope you had fun."

"I had a great time! Thanks again, bye!" They walk out along with a few other people, interrupting Alec and my conversation. I would sort of like to have a conversation about what we are doing, but I also know that is a terrible idea. I can't push it. And I can't get upset when he doesn't make a move, or when he goes out with someone else. We are not dating. We are not even necessarily friends with benefits. We are friends who got drunk and screwed. Once. But obviously he was into it too, or he wouldn't have just brought it up. I wish we could just be alone to talk about it. Or . . . not talk.

"This has been fun, but I should get going. It's late, and it is Christmas after all. Thank you for everything, especially the cake," Alec says.

"Of course. I'm so glad you came over."

I'm disappointed he's leaving, even though I'm getting tired. Most of our company has left. I don't like that I'm going to spend the night alone. Probably just the holidays and their incredible way of creating a void in an otherwise perfectly fulfilling life.

"I'll walk you out," I say, getting up to grab my coat.

"Sounds good." He helps me with my coat and puts his on. "I should probably go down and say goodbye to everyone. Or maybe you could just say it for me later."

"That's fine."

We walk out to his car slowly and silently. Suddenly, the playful flirtatiousness has left, and there is a rigidity I can't quite read. Are we both sexually frustrated and disappointed the moment broke? Or is he actually just tired and ready to get home?

"Well, thanks again." He looks at me awkwardly as we stand next to his car in the cold.

"Yeah. No problem."

Neither of us hugs the other, and he doesn't make a point of getting into his car. I am barely breathing, anticipating his next move. I'm not sure if I should make one first. I can't risk getting rejected, especially on Christmas. He wouldn't do it to hurt me. He's just afraid I'll catch feelings for him. I start to move, not sure whether to hug him or wave. I can't stand the tension.

"OK, well, good night then." I wave. So lame.

Quickly, he reaches his hand out, placing it on the small of my back, and pulls me in to him, and within a split second, we are kissing. Hard.

I force him back against his car and keep kissing him, pushing my body into his with all of my weight.

"Want to go for a ride?" he asks, and without hesitation, I agree.

He lets me into his car and, when he's in the driver's seat, he starts kissing me intensely. I'm hot and exhilarated, getting exactly what I wanted.

"Alec, we can't hook up in your car right in front of my parents' house. Some of the guests are still walking to their cars."

"Sounds like a good night to look at lights?"

"Sounds like a plan."

He starts his car, and we drive around the block. I really do look at Christmas lights. They look gorgeous. It's one of those perfectly still winter nights with the lightest dusting of snow covering the roofs.

As we drive, he puts his hand on my thigh and starts rubbing it. Every street still has cars on it from various parties. I can barely keep still. I start rubbing his leg up and down his pants. His breathing becomes choppy.

"Aren't all the lights pretty?" I lean over and whisper into his ear, biting it softly and still moving my hand around, and eventually, inside his pants.

"Oh my god," he whispers back. "Oh my god."

"Don't use the Lord's name in vain. It's Christmas," I whisper again, kissing his neck, massaging him with my hand.

"Oh, the Lord and I are great friends right now."

"Maybe I should stop," I tease as he keeps driving around the neighborhood.

"Please don't stop. Oh my god."

I pull down his pants as far as the car will allow. I am loving teasing him and want to increase his excitement. I lower my head to his lap and take him in my mouth.

"Holy shit," he says, barely audible. "Holy shit."

"Keep driving." I look up at him.

"Don't stop. Oh my god."

I'm amusing myself greatly, teasing him, going down on him, and finally the car stops. I look up and we are in a quiet cul-du-sac.

"Jesus Christ." He pulls me up and kisses me on the lips, pressing into me as much as he can while lifting up my dress. We can't move fast enough. Everything is clumsy as we act on pure desire and climb into the back seat.

"Get on top of me," he says, helping me get his pants down.

Seconds later, he's thrusting inside of me. Something about the lack of space in the car gives me the perfect amount of leverage to help him hit the right spot as I lift my hips to meet him. In a few quick moments, all our built-up energy is released simultaneously, and I crash back down on top of him.

"Wow," he finally says.

"Yeah. Wow."

Both of us are still wearing coats and letting our breathing adjust to normal. We sit for a second, not saying anything, but smiling occasionally.

"OK, we need to get out of here before someone notices."

"Yeah," he says, but doesn't move.

We lay curled up and entangled in our own sweat, just looking at the car ceiling. I guess we are friends with benefits after all.

Eventually, I pull my panties back up, fix my dress, and get back into the passenger seat, trying to adjust my makeup in the mirror.

"I don't know what to do to hide the way I look right now," I laugh.

"You look stunning." He kisses my cheek from the back seat and puts his pants back in place. "That was incredible."

"I haven't had car sex since I was like 19."

"I haven't in a long time either. I'm not gonna lie, it was kind of awesome."

"It was kind of awesome, wasn't it?" We are quiet as he drives me back to my house, and I keep messing with my hair. "Am I still red?"

"No, you look fine. And everyone at the party was drinking. It looks like your company is gone anyway," he says as we pull up. All the cars are gone.

"Well, Merry Christmas, Alec." I smile.

"Merry, Merry Christmas, Ly." He leans in to kiss me again, then I get out of the car.

This seems to be working out exactly as I hoped. Casual, fun, unemotional.

Chapter Five

"So have you seen him since?" Sarah asks when we are grabbing coffee at Julius Meinl, recapping after the holidays.

Sarah lives in the city, but she stays in more than me, so I don't see her as often as I'd like. She shared insights about her December and getting to spend more time with Nick's family, and I can't really imagine having a whole new family to get to know. Part of me is jealous. But I suppose there is also a good chance that the family could suck, and then you're stuck with them. I like my flexibility. But Sarah likes his parents and gets along with his brother. So far, it all seems like what you hope your in-law situation will be. So I counter her balanced, traditional holidays with my tales of raunchy drunken sex with a friend I wasn't supposed to be having sex with.

"No, I mean, the holidays are always so crazy around my house. I've been at my parents' place more than my own, and it's not like he and I are phone, or even text, friends. We only text to make plans. Things are just getting back to normal, and he leaves for Italy in a few days."

"Oh, that's right. It's crazy how much he travels. Has he ever settled down?"

"Definitely not."

"OK. I know you're not gonna be honest with your family or with Olivia about it, but as your oldest and closest friend, I feel you have a duty to me, as my maid of honor, to tell me the truth. What do you honestly want to come of this? Best-case scenario?"

"Best-case?"

"Yep. Honestly. Seriously, don't lie to me. I'm not gonna judge you."

"Oh, I've done plenty more judge-worthy things than liking Alec, and you are still my friend, so I believe you."

"Well, that is true."

"But truly, the best-case scenario is that we keep this up for a while, at least through the winter. We have fun, I don't get jealous or anything, we see other people, and then we end things amicably. I'm not an idiot. That might not be entirely realistic. I know the absolute best situation would be for both of us to meet someone right around the same time, but the honest best-case for me would be that I do, so I have someone real to replace Alec with when the time comes."

"OK, so what if Alec were to say, 'Hey, I've been thinking. We're really good together. We have great sex, we enjoy each other's company. I think I'm ready to try something serious. Let's do this.' Would you honestly say no?"

"I can't even fathom that happening."

"Seriously put yourself there though. It's not insanely unrealistic. You've definitely thought about it. And I think knowing the answer to that question means knowing your true secret hopes. Because I think you would say yes, and that you would try it out.

You might not have a ton of faith in it, but you'd try it out. And I think that means you sort of secretly want that to happen."

"Maybe you're right. I don't know. I know we would never ever work together. He just doesn't even want to be monogamous with someone right now, and although he says he wants to settle down one day, he's so interested in traveling and loves to go out and hook up with people. We never really sit and talk about things, so I can't say I know him that well as a person. I truly don't like him as a potential boyfriend. But if he actually really liked me, maybe I'd see him differently. I don't know. It's a moot point. I don't see him that way, and he doesn't see me that way. We're cool and all. I think he'd be a horrible boyfriend. He's always looking for what else and who else is out there to excite him. I think I just really like the idea that someone very attractive is also attracted to me, and we'll see what happens. At this point, we may never have sex again. We didn't really discuss it or anything. Maybe he thinks it was a huge mistake getting involved with one of his sister's best friends. Maybe he and that girl he's gone on a few dates with are actually getting serious. I honestly don't know. And honestly, as your maid of honor, on my grave, I promise that if that's the case, I will experience nothing more than a mild sense of disappointment over the loss of a fun void-filler."

"Really? No Evan-style depression?"

"If I ever go through another Evan-style depression again, I want you to slap me. Maybe defriend me. Not on Facebook. In real life. Just end your own misery."

Sarah laughs. "I will not do that, but it damn well better not happen again."

"No more Evans. I'm not being an idiot about relationships anymore. I'm not taking this thing with Alec seriously in the slightest. I'm having fun because I honestly have nothing better going on right now. And next time I do meet a guy that I take seriously, I will look for all the signs. I won't be blind, and I will *never* dangle."

"OK, good. I'm glad you're aware of all that. I just don't know that you should entirely rule it out. You're a grown up and maybe you guys should talk about it. Like hey, we're sleeping together. We have a lot of fun and are obviously attracted to each other. Are we doing this to see where it goes, or are we keeping it casual? Friends with benefits?"

"But doesn't that make it sound like I *want* us to be more? Does that sound too invested to make him talk about it?"

"Lyren, you're being ridiculous. You are just thinking about how to clarify your situation to make sure you're on the same page. Acknowledging whatever it is. You've already banged twice, and you both want to do it again. I know he doesn't think it's a mistake. Maybe next time you do it, talk about shit in the morning to keep you both in the clear for your expectations."

"Yes. You are always so wise, Sarah. I don't know why it scares me so much to push the convo."

"Maybe because Evan basically just ran away and stopped talking to you instead of having a real conversation?"

"Yeah. I walked on eggshells with Evan, I guess. I didn't want him to know I was so invested before I knew he was. And then I was just bereft when he clearly wasn't."

"It's the worst, and he's the worst. When did you last talk to him, by the way?"

"Luckily, I haven't seen him since that party in June when he half-flirted with me but then aggressively made a point to leave without saying goodbye."

"Typical selfish ass. Loved knowing you were still available to him if he wanted but not willing to be a partner."

Sarah is, of course, correct that Evan is just a selfish ass. We hooked up for the first time after one of the many parties my college friends threw at a bar. We started texting regularly after that. We made a point to meet up toward the end of the night on several occasions when we had been out with other friends. I guess we never actually even went on a real date in those few months. The signs were there if I had wanted to pay attention to them. But he did call me on the phone a few times and we'd talk for hours. I was falling in love, and I really thought he was too. We talked on Facebook Messenger throughout our work days. We'd show up at parties knowing we'd go home together. I thought it was what the early days of a relationship were supposed to look like when you're not quite at the point of ready to commit, but you make a point to talk and see each other when you can. I was waiting for the right time to have a "What are we doing?" conversation. Meanwhile, he wasn't thinking about me long term at all. And he handled that by not reaching out, not making plans to meet up even after nights out and not responding to my texts until hours or days later with lame excuses and no follow up. The aforementioned party, where he was flirty and friendly but then pretty much ran away to avoid me, made it all starkly clear.

"Yeah. I can pretend I walked away feeling strong and knowing it was for the best."

"Sure. We can pretend."

In actuality, when I realized he Irish-goodbyed me, I locked myself in the bar bathroom and sobbed on the floor for an ungodly amount of time until some kind girl waiting patiently to pee decided to pep-talk me by coming under the stall, handing me tissues, and telling me how much better I was than this guy she did not know. There really is no camaraderie like drunk girls in a bar bathroom.

Pretty sure, or very sure, I actually ended up crying in the bathroom to my girlfriends, real and barline made, about fifty-four times over the following months as I stared at my phone, willing it to light up with his name and bring me back to life. Sarah and Olivia got the brunt of it.

"So anyway, I hope that at the very least, this new thing with Alec helps you stop crying about Evan."

"So far, so good. Do I need to be like AA? It has been 153 days since I cried over Evan?"

"Well, there's no way it has been 153 days."

"You've got me there. Probably about 24 though?"

"Excellent progress."

"Agree. If anything, it's the first time in many months I feel actual excitement about anything. It's not like I get much from my job. Anyway, now that we're done talking about the wreckage that is my love life, let's discuss wedding stuff. What needs do you have for me?"

"Great question, because I was just thinking about something I do need from you. I'm gonna need help picking the playlist for my wedding, and I have a brilliant idea."

"Well, you know I can't wait to help with that. What is your idea?"

"90s music. Tons of 90s music."

"Like Backstreet Boys and Britney Spears?"

"Precisely."

"That, Sarah Caldwell, is why you are my best friend in the entire world."

Taking on a playlist is a challenge I am more than happy to jump into, and it shows how well Sarah knows me that this is the kind of task she'd assign to me. The truth is, I have to feign my interest in most things related to weddings and their planning, despite being a double maid of honor right now. I am Emma's maid of honor by default because I am her sister. I am Sarah's because I am her oldest friend. But despite my love for both of these people, neither of these are qualifications for being an actual good maid of honor. I want to be excited about their weddings. I *want* to want to talk about flowers and tablecloth colors and first dance songs and shower invitations. But I really don't want to.

Chapter Six

"Hey, how was your day?" Olivia asks as I show up at tutoring, blazingly angry and ready to drop under a pillow fort and never surface again.

As if Claire, my wretched boss, calling me into her office to talk about how I don't have enough enthusiasm for work or being a team player and how she's watching me wasn't enough, Evan has been bantering back and forth with the same bikini girl all over Facebook, Alec is rubbing it in, with his pictures with gelato and wine all across Italy, and Emma wants me to organize some lame craft for all the bridesmaids for her shower.

"Absolute shit," I reply to what I'm sure Olivia assumed was an innocuous question. "Would you want to go out and get insanely drunk with me tonight?"

"It's Tuesday," she reminds me.

"Is that a problem?"

"No," she laughs. "You'll have to tell me all about it."

The kids start filing in for tutoring, and I try to shake off my day. Jarron sits down next to me, looking somehow even more frustrated than I do.

"What's wrong with you?" I ask.

"You said if I studied for this test, I'd get at least a B!" Jarron throws a C- on the desk.

"Well, a C- is better than a D, so you're actually still improving," I say, trying to keep my irritation at bay. I'm mad at Claire, and maybe all of Planet Earth. Not Jarron.

"This is bullshit! Why do I have to come to tutoring if you don't teach me anything?! Moms says if I don't get this grade up, I can't play football. You're ruining my life!"

"Stop shouting! First of all, let's talk about this like rational people."

I'm having a hard time keeping my own cool. I know I'm the authority in the room, but I want to quit. I want to run out of the room and start crying. I am on the verge of losing my job for no reason other than that my boss is an evil self-obsessed tyrant, Evan is probably about to go to Facebook official with that girl, Alec is probably sleeping with half of Italy, and now Jarron is blaming me for his grade sucking?

Why am I even doing this?

Jarron is getting over his initial tantrum and instead turns it into a quiet protest. He folds his arms, refusing to look at me.

"Jarron, take out your work for today." No response.

Fine kid. Fail out of school.

Part of me wants to sit here and let this 12-year-old have his stalemate. His football aspirations are at least more interesting than what you get for excelling at college only to take a soul-sucking job where you're treated like shit just to make a living.

I stare at him for an uncomfortable minute. I cannot get into a standoff with a 12-year-old. *I am the grown up. I am the grown up.* I take an obvious deep breath and look at Jarron's test.

You can do this, Lyren. Right now, your only responsibility is to this kid.

"Jarron. Sometimes getting a grade up just takes a lot of practice, OK? Getting a C- is better than getting a D or an F, and you got a D last time, right? That means you are doing better! That means studying is working. You're not going to start getting A's overnight. That's what we're working toward. And if you work really hard, you will get better grades, and you'll get to stay on the football team. You have to do more work than just what we do here. You have to do homework on your own, too."

"I quit. I am stupid."

It is hard to argue with him when I share his exact sentiment regarding basically everything in my own life.

"You are not stupid! You're just not trying. Did you finish the book? Be honest with me."

"Yes." I can tell he is lying by the sheepish way he responded. "Well, most of it."

"How do you think you're going to get a good grade on a test if you don't even finish the whole book? Don't blame me or your teacher when you aren't trying. Now take out your work." I'm being short with Jarron, but maybe being patient isn't working. And I don't have the energy to be patient right now.

I look over at Olivia, who is working calmly, as always, with Diamond. Why do I seem to be the only person who doesn't have any aspect of my life together? She looks up at me and shakes her head, smiling. She can tell I am struggling with Jarron. Well, the entire room can, thanks to his outburst.

OLIVIA
Several drinks

I look over at Olivia across the room and nod.

I need about one hundred drinks. Maybe I can black out my entire existence for a while.

"So basically I feel like Jennifer Aniston's character in *Office Space*, being told I don't have enough flair," I rant to Olivia over drinks and saag paneer at Tandoor, one of our favorite spots for Indian food. "Like, for fuck's sake, I copyedit textbooks. What do I need enthusiasm for? Are the commas in the right fucking place or not?"

"She sounds like a huge bitch," Olivia supports. "I mean, you're still getting your work done, aren't you?"

"Yeah. I mean, I probably could step it up and get more done, but for what? It's not like I'm paid per manual. I'm salaried; there is no upward promise here. Well, not that I am interested in, anyway."

"I'm sure that's what's hard about having a job that is just a job. I'm always interested in my job, but it's so exhausting sometimes. No job is perfect. But I have a really supportive boss, and I think that's what matters most."

"I don't know if I'd be any more fulfilled if I had a supportive boss. But I guess I'd be less miserable, so there's that. Like, what you do? It really matters. So you get to go home from a stressful day and know that you're making an actual difference."

"Right, I don't think anyone could do my job if they didn't care."

"You mean get paid peanuts to deal with the hardest situations in humanity? Yeah, no. I think being an altruist is a top-of-the-resume requirement for being a social worker."

"It is so hard, though. I just want to take every kid home and foster them. Show them love and support. I go into these homes sometimes and see a kid just completely neglected, and it rips my heart to shreds. And what can I really do? I can check up on them. Find some basic levels of therapy and support. But I can't take them all home. One of my kids just always has this completely defeated look already at 9 years old. Like the world has already been so cruel to her that she doesn't believe in goodness. And I want to show her there is some goodness."

"I guess having to deal with so much of that shows why you're so much better at being patient with Diamond than I am with Jarron. You see so much worse. Jarron is a good kid with supportive parents and hope and ambition. But I'm just so zapped emotionally that it's hard to get into a better headspace. God, I sound so selfish. You literally use your extra time to help even more kids, and I can barely do one good thing."

"You're just struggling to find stability in your world right now. And don't be fooled. We all go through shit. I cry to Chris all the time. I'm wiped. I feel I'm not doing enough. Or I get so mad at the system that we don't have real resources. And it's not all altruism. I get pissed as hell about the pittance of a salary I make for doing this work."

"Your salary is an abomination on society. Like I make about the same as you to correct sentence structure in lame teaching guides. And I didn't need a master's degree to do it!"

"Well, I guess there are always tradeoffs. I have a job where I have purpose and fulfillment, but there's still more I'd like to be doing that I'm not doing. There always is. We all have shit to be stressed about."

"Yeah. At least you and Chris seem to be in a good place."

"He has been great and very supportive. So thanks for that connection. Sorry to have offered my brother in response."

"You know, your brother is the most exciting thing I have going for me right now, so even if it's not stability, it's something."

"Oh, speaking of Chris, you're going to Tom's party this weekend, right?"

Because Chris is one of my college friends, Olivia is now part of multiple inner circles.

"I am planning to, yes. But I'm also a little terrified."

"Why?" she asks. But then a look of recognition passes across her face. "Oh. Evan."

"Yep. There is a 90% chance Evan will be at this party."

"And you haven't talked?"

"Nope. Never even had a conversation about how we should stop seeing each other. Haven't seen him in many months. I honestly don't even think about him as much anymore or even miss him. But seeing him could be hard."

"You'll be fine. Chris and I have a concert earlier in the night, so we'll be late, but we'll be there. And you have plenty of other friends to distract you."

"Yeah. I'll be fine."

So long as I don't end up crying in a bathroom again.

I am nervous as I get ready for Tom's party. I can't not go. First of all, I really want to see all the other people attending, and second, I can't let seeing Evan stop me from living my life. He'll never totally go away as long as I want to see my college friends, and I know that I can handle him. Either way, I have to look fabulous, and I'm not really sure I can do that. It's the dead of winter, and I'm pale as shit and don't feel my thinnest. Then again, I haven't really felt my thinnest since college, so I don't know who I am kidding.

I try on three outfits before settling on a lacy tank with a statement necklace and a short skirt with a long off-white sweater and high boots. It hides my body in all the right places and is cute enough. However, when I'm walking to the bar, I realize I have to talk myself through it.

I whisper under my breath: *Be cool under all circumstances. If he's ignoring you, pay no mind. Talk to your other friends, laugh, enjoy yourself. If he's with a girl, pretend you don't notice or care. Better yet, DON'T care! If he flirts with you, make him feel stupid, but don't be obvious about it.*

As I hand the door guy my ID, I'm almost shaking.

This is ridiculous. It's been months since there was anything between us. It's over. We're adults. I can handle this.

"Well, look who it is!" My friend Peter comes over and gives me a huge hug, alleviating some of the chaos in my mind. "Let's get you a drink!"

I make a point not to look for Evan, though I try to be aware of my surroundings lest he creep up on me or I catch a glimpse of him with a girl unexpectedly.

I have enough friends at the bar to make me feel welcome and secure. I say hello to Tom, the birthday boy, and realize there is a notable shortage of females at this party. I guess that's always been the case with this group of friends. I texted Alec this morning asking if he was coming, and he was on the fence. He just got back from Italy and had to see how the jetlag was hitting him. Peter hands me the drink he got me, and we catch up for a quick moment before someone comes behind me and pinches my side.

"Nice boots."

Ugh! He wasn't supposed to catch me off guard!

My heart does that really annoying drop through the floor thing, and I wonder for a moment if I might throw up. He's not supposed to make me do this anymore. This is supposed to be completely over; though, I don't know if it ever will be. It doesn't matter how many times you're that girl crying in the bathroom over some douchebag, or how many times you tell yourself you're finally done with it, some assholes still make you melt at the sight of them.

"Hi Evan." I flash him my sweetest smile, but I hope I convey that I think he's an idiot.

You're an idiot if you think this just comes around again when you are ready for it. You don't let someone go just because you feel immature and stupid and want to act like a frat boy. When you meet someone you look at the way you looked at me, you do ANYTHING to keep it, you stupid piece of shit.

But I just turn my head, knowing there's no way he can understand what he put me through or what he gave up on. Maybe he'll realize in five years, when he's lonely and single, and every girl he's dated since has felt vapid and pointless, that how he felt when he was with me mattered and he gave up on it because he wanted time to figure things out. I hope I'm married by then to someone so much better at life than he is. Or that I'm hugely successful. Or just ten thousand times more fabulous than I already am. And I hope he regrets all of it every day of his selfish life.

I wish I knew how to stop feeling so bitter about it, but it's really hard to act cool and calm and collected when all you want to do is rip someone's heart out of their body and step on it repeatedly while you watch them cry. And people wonder why I don't like to give love a chance. Sure, once in a decade maybe you find someone who is actually a decent human that makes you all happy and giddy. But there is a whole lot of shit in between that just doesn't make it seem worth it.

"You look gorgeous," he says, hugging me too close and running his hand along my back.

Seriously? He never seemed to understand that it wasn't all a big joke. I had told him. I'd been honest with him that I really liked him and all that. He claimed he liked me too. It all hurt worse than anything I'd experienced since high school. I always knew I was being weak and pathetic, in a way I never expected I would be over some guy, but he had complete power over me. Breaking away from him took strength and guts. And now I'm acting like things are all just cool and fine, while he can't comprehend he shouldn't keep flirting with me.

"You look OK too," I laugh, being too friendly. I wish I were here with a guy so I could make him jealous or rub it in his face that he's not with me.

He pouts, and someone else comes up and greets him before we can continue our conversation, which is all well and good because I came here hoping to show him I am too good for him.

I continue drinking and pretending to ignore Evan by making merry with my old college friends around me, but can't help but notice that he looks over at me regularly, or makes a point to touch me every time he comes up to the bar to get another drink. Maybe I'm actually pulling this off.

"Hey lady!" Olivia sneaks up on me and whispers, "So how are things going with Douche Face?"

"AHH! So happy you're here!" I squeeze her. "I'm working really hard to be strong, and I'm really hoping he wants me so I can turn him down, but I think that's asking too much." I am thrilled she is here, and with a small entourage. Alec is behind her, showing the door guy his ID, and my heart skips a quick second. Then he comes up and spins me around, squeezing me.

"Hey, stranger!"

We've both been drinking, and I'm so glad to see him that I don't want to let go. He seems the same way, and relief washes over me. We catch up on his trip and my boring workweek and the concert he was evidently at, too.

"Hey, so this guy, over there? That's Evan, the one who broke my heart in seventeen pieces last year. Will you do me a favor?"

Alec smiles at me mischievously. I need not say anymore. He grabs my hand and pulls me to the floor, dancing with me closely and seductively. It's working wonders, both to make Evan keep looking over, and also to make me forget that Evan is in the room.

"You're the best friend ever," I say to him as he pulls me in and runs his hand up my leg.

"It's not a hard game to play when you look so good. God,

these hooker boots . . . they are fucking sexy." He plays with the top of the boots, which stop about two inches above my knee. "I love your legs." I'm so glad he's back.

As the night goes on, I continue to stay close to Alec. He's attentive to me and is blatantly making Evan jealous all night long. I imagine that we're succeeding. Alec is gorgeous.

By the end of the night, we're stealing brief make-outs in the dark corners of the bar. Whether or not people are annoyed with our PDA doesn't bother me. PDA is always fun when you're the one doing it. Watching it not so much.

"Last call for alcohol!" I hear this all the time now that I'm hanging out with Alec. The idea of leaving a bar before it closes is absurd. The lights go on, but I'm not ready to go home.

Somehow, Alec is even prettier in the light. I stare at him a little too long and find myself hoping he wants to go home with me.

"Well, what's the deal?" Peter comes up and asks as we all start to gather our coats.

Olivia and Chris come up, and the group is trying to figure out what's next as bartenders and employees are literally shoving us out the door. Evan chugs his beer.

"What's still open?" Evan asks.

Why is he lurking?

"We can go downtown. Hangge Uppe?" Chris suggests, but all of us know that's an expensive cab ride.

"The line is going to be insane," Peter says as we walk out into the freezing cold. "I don't want to go home, though. I mean, we can just get food."

"Yeah, but that's no more drinking," Olivia reminds us.

And they said you have to grow up one day . . .

"Hey, I mean, I know this isn't really exciting or anything, but I live down the street and I have a ton of beer at my place," I suggest. It's the most sensible solution I have.

"I am really hungry, though. Can you help with that?" Alec asks.

"I have some shit you can throw together, I'm sure."

"Done," Evan says.

I try to ignore the deliberation with which Evan has lingered. I assess the group of people following me to my place. My post-college obsession, my sex buddy, his little sister and her boyfriend, and Peter, a good friend from college. This ought to be interesting.

It becomes clear after a while that all of these people are going to be spending the night at my place. After a couple of beers, Olivia and Chris cuddle up on the futon.

"Ew!" Alec shouts as they walk over, but Olivia just dismisses him. "Don't make me kick your ass!" But he's laughing as he says it.

"Yeah, no funny stuff while we're here!" Peter adds.

"Like I could succeed in any funny stuff this drunk at 4 a.m.," Chris responds, and Olivia playfully pinches him.

The night is a drunken mess. People are slurring their words, we're blasting rap music, and eating random shit from my fridge that doesn't make sense together. I'm surprised my neighbors haven't knocked on my door yet.

"You have had a fucking frozen pizza in here all this time and you haven't even told anyone?" Alec acts astonished as he struggles to open the packaging.

"I didn't even know I had that in there. Way to look through my entire freezer. If you want to make that now, we have to stay up for another like 40 minutes."

"I'll do anything for pizza," Alec says, throwing it in the oven without preheating.

"I mean, I'm all about pizza, but I don't think I'll do *anything* for it." Evan laughs.

"I guess this means we all grab another beer?" Peter goes to the fridge and takes one of the last beers.

I can't believe I'm still drinking. If it were summer, the sun would already be coming out.

"I'm gonna pass out," Evan says as I'm talking to Peter and Alec, and it takes me a second to notice he heads for my room.

I look at Alec. "Did he really just go in my room?"

"Yes. Are you going to follow him?"

I can't read Alec's reaction. Is he jealous? Concerned? Generally curious and here for the story?

"Of course not. We have a pizza in the oven." Do I want to follow him? Did Evan do this on purpose because he was jealous of Alec? Is he hoping I come in there and we hook up, or is he truly just drunk and crashing out on my bed seemed like the most logical destination?

"Good answer. Pizza cures all. Even ex-boyfriend drama." Alec is smiling at me, but not judging. I realize this is the kind of situation Alec has found himself in plenty of times before, only he would have no qualms about hooking up with the ex in his bed.

Peter says nothing. He always knew what was going on between Evan and me and stayed out of it, being a true friend to both parties and never allowing me to trash talk his friend or give me real advice on the matter.

The oven dings, and Alec goes to take it out without grabbing a mitt. "OWWW!" he screams, dumping the pizza upside down on the oven door.

"Are you fucking serious right now, you idiot?" I should be concerned, but I'm laughing. He's running his hand under water. "Are you OK?"

Peter grabs a towel and picks up the pizza, and whatever he can salvage of the cheese that is now melting to my oven door.

"Yeah, I didn't grab it that hard. I really only touched the pizza."

"You are such a drunken idiot."

"No shit. Cut up that pizza."

"Well, most of it is now on my oven door, thanks to you. That's going to be a real joy to clean up."

Peter slices it up, and I eat one while Alec babies his hand.

"Well, you boys are free to stay up all you like, but I'm exhausted and have a situation to deal with." Alec watches me for a second, maybe recognizing we won't be hooking up tonight. Even if I didn't go to Evan in my room, Olivia and Chris are on the futon and Peter has to sleep somewhere.

"Good luck," Alec shares with only a mild hint of disappointment.

If he were actually into me, or this, he would care. Instead, he's being supportive. I need to keep things in check here with him.

"Don't give me that look. He's passed out. There is nowhere else for me to sleep since you guys will take the couch and chair."

"Yeah. OK." He nods in almost approval. I don't actually like it.

I leave them to finish the pizza and find Evan passed out in the middle of my bed, on top of the covers, still in his clothes.

I shouldn't be thrilled about this, but I am. I don't want to change with him in my room and to be honest, I'm so drunk that I don't care what's going on, so I pull the sheet down around him until he wakes up enough to move under it with me and I lay down in all of my clothes with him. He wraps his arms around me, and I instinctively curl up into him. I know this is exactly what I'm not supposed to be doing. I'm letting him win again . . . but he feels so fucking good. His arms are amazing, and his sweatshirt smells like memories. He kisses my head, and I look up at him. He brings his lips to mine and they feel soft and familiar.

Oh my god. Evan is in my bed. Not Alec. Evan. I love Evan. What the fuck am I doing???

Every part of me is screaming at myself to stop this. To tell

Evan to fuck himself. To make him get a cab and go home with his erect dick in his hand. To be the bigger person. Why is that impossible? Why does his hand in my hair undo me? Who am I? I've lost all my brain cells. I am just a body responding to movement. Hands and lips. Liquid and parts. What does it really hurt if I give in one last time?

No . . . no, I have to stop this.

"Evan . . . don't. Stop." It takes all of my might.

"What's wrong?" This jerk. All night he tries to flirt with me. I try to ignore him, and now the bastard is winning. Sneaking into my room. Ignoring that time I told him I loved him, or the fact that I unfriended him on Facebook because it was literally killing me to see him happy without me. (I refriended him like a month later. It was killing me worse not to see him at all). Or that I once lay on the floor hysterical in my coat and shoes with the door wide open, sobbing uncontrollably and texting all our friends that I didn't know how to hurt him as bad as I was hurting. Well, he probably didn't know about that. But still. *Goddamnit*!

He kisses me again. It's perfect. He's so perfect. He starts running one hand up my back, turning me on in a way it seems only he knows how. The other pulls my hair. *NO!* I push him away gently.

"This, whatever it is we used to do, it's not happening. I'm done with this, with you. This doesn't go beyond cuddling." I'm proud of myself. There is nothing in the world I want more than to rip his clothes off him.

"OK. Whatever you want," he says and wraps me in closer. And that's that. I wish this night could last forever exactly the way it is right now. Because right now, I'm ignoring all the times I hated him, the times I cried, the times he made me feel like a piece of shit. All I want is for him to want me. "Lyren . . . I really am sorry I hurt you."

"I know. That's not the point. I just am not going to keep doing this with you."

"OK."

I am dying to keep talking about it. I want to ask him why he didn't love me back. Why he could love talking to me and flirting with me and hooking up with me and not want to be with me. But I know he can't give me answers. And it will only make it worse.

We had talked about real things. It wasn't like my friendship with Alec where we joke around with each other and drink and screw. It was real. We talked about our pasts and our insecurities, things that were important to us in the world and things we thought about humanity. I'll never understand how it's possible to feel that much for someone who doesn't feel it back. I didn't have a choice. What I felt was chemical. I couldn't not feel it— so what caused it? Shouldn't there be some law that your heart will only do that when it hits a real counterpoint?

I wake up foggy and dizzy and almost confused. How did I let Evan end up in my goddamn bed? But I'm also proud of myself because I stopped it from going anywhere. I could have had sex with him again. I could have had what I thought about every damn day for months. But I respected myself. That's good, right?

We're still wrapped tightly together. He's one of the few people I can say that has ever happened with. Most of the time I fall asleep cuddling but wake up on the other end of the bed. It's nice. It's secure. And probably really stupid. This bastard could take my heart back with one swipe, and I'd be a ruined fool again. Everything I worked so hard to achieve would be for nothing.

"Last night was insane," he says.

"God, I don't even know what happened last night."

"You had anal sex with me."

"Yeah . . . that I know I didn't do."

He laughs.

I wonder for a minute if Alec is still here. If this situation were reversed and Alec had some girl in his room, I'd walk home barefoot in the freezing cold before taking second place on the couch. The fact that Alec was cool about it is an indication of how casually he really sees this thing with me. I wish he had tried to convince me to stay on the couch with him and just cuddle even if we couldn't hook up. But friends with benefits aren't supposed to cuddle, I don't think.

"Ugh, I have so much grading to do today," he says, looking up at the ceiling. "I feel like I'm gonna die."

"I'm sorry. That's very unfortunate for you. I think I'll probably spend my entire day sleeping. I might eat at some point."

"I hate you."

"False."

He starts to get up, and I'm disappointed he isn't staying longer. I was really loving curling up against him. When I think about it, it only happened for a few hours. It's 9 a.m.

"Let me walk you out." I stand up and realize how out of it I really am. It will be nice to have my bed to myself and stretch out for a few hours, actually. When I step out of my room, I walk into chaos.

"What the fuck?" I whisper.

There are beer cans absolutely everywhere. Pizza remains. Pillaged hummus and pita. That must have been Olivia. Peter is in a chair. Alec is on the couch, but he's sleeping straight up and still has a beer on his lap, although a good deal of it has made its way to his jeans and my couch. I remember the melted cheese burnt to the inside of my oven.

"Wow. We really did a number on this place. Well, have fun with that," Evan says as I open the door and hug him goodbye. He looks at me for a second. I am thinking about five hundred things as he turns and walks out the door. I close the door after him and stare at it for a while.

What the fuck just happened?

Glancing around my place, I can't decide whether to crack up or cry.

"What the fuck?" Alec groggily wakes up and looks down at his wet pants.

"Nice going," I whisper back. "If you pissed on my couch, I will seriously straight up murder your ass."

He smells the couch where there is a clear yellow stain. "Nope, definitely beer."

"You're lucky." I continue walking to my room and realize he is following me.

"Who says I want you in here?" I ask.

"Hey, I just slept straight up on the couch, swimming in beer, so you could be with your whatever. You owe me a comfy space."

We both get under the covers, and even though he smells like beer, I'm glad he's there. We pass out cuddled up together for a few more hours. Maybe friends with benefits are allowed to cuddle after all.

There is nothing better in the entire world than cuddling. Food? Sex? Whatever. Cuddling. Greatest part of life.

"Hey you, get up. We're going to the pub." Alec is poking me, and I groan.

"What? What are you talking about? I am not going drinking, Alec. I'm fucking hungover."

"Suck it up, you pussy."

"Yes, I am a pussy. My head is killing me."

"A beer is the best cure for that. Come on, game's on."

"What the fuck game are you talking about?"

"NFL Playoffs! It's a big day!"

"I don't watch football."

"I don't care! You're coming with me!" He starts tickling me.

"I'm going to fucking kill you, you nut job," I say through laughs and squirms as he keeps tickling me.

"You are not. You'll be fine."

"Are there other people still here?"

"Fuck should I know?"

"What time is it?"

"1:30."

"Oh Jesus," I say and flop back down on the bed. It reeks of beer.

"You don't have a choice in this matter. I'm not going to the pub alone, and you don't have sports channels here."

"Don't you have some girlfriend now? Drag her ass to the pub with you."

"She's not my girlfriend. She's some random chick I'm screwing that wants to be my girlfriend. And you're cooler than her."

That's all he needed to say to win me over.

I can't believe I'm even contemplating this. I feel like death. We were up until after 5 in the morning, I have been a complete cuddle whore the past few hours, and I'm actually considering going drinking. My place looks like I had a hundred-person party, and I don't even know who is still here.

"You're already dressed and everything."

"I'm not wearing this. If you're dragging me to the pub, I'm wearing sweatpants."

He grins. He won.

I put on sweatpants and a big t-shirt with Ugg boots. It's almost like I am putting effort into looking like shit. I can't believe I'm about to go out in public. "Are you seriously going out in that beer-soaked shirt? Here. Have one of my t-shirts."

"Thanks, friend!"

We step out of my room, and everyone has left. No one made any effort to clean my place, and truthfully, I don't think I could clean anything either. An hour or two at the pub for a Sunday Funday could be enjoyable. I can't sit here in this disaster, anyway.

"I'll have a Bloody Mary," I say, plopping myself in a chair at McCragen's Pub.

"Make that two, please," Alec echoes me. "See, aren't you glad you're not at home now?"

"No." I'm laughing when I say it, though. "So what's the big deal about this game?"

He explains the teams to me and why he likes who he does, and though I am only half listening, the truth is, I am thrilled to be here. I have grown accustomed to spending Sundays on the couch, watching mindless TV. It's nice to have company.

The pub is a little Irish dive, and the only other people inside on this cold January day are a few other football fans coming out to cheer on their teams. They go in and out as we stay. Each game takes a few hours, and we're sitting through two.

"So you must be directly from Ireland," I say to the bartender, who after a few hours, got used to the idea of Alec and I sitting in his bar. We clearly aren't going anywhere. I have tried almost every beer on tap and have settled on an interesting darker ale. Alec sticks with Guinness.

"I am. I've been here for seven years, though. I go back at least once a year. It's beautiful."

"I've been to Ireland. I absolutely love it."

Alec starts telling stories of his experiences in Ireland, and I share how much I want to go one day. I guess a huge plus to dating Alec for real would be a permanent travel partner. Someone with real enthusiasm to see everything. And as a travel agent, someone who could do it at a discount. I haven't traveled anywhere with a boyfriend unless you count that time Jason and I took a weekend trip to Milwaukee to see a Brewers game and hit up some breweries. Not exactly a jet set to Europe. It sounds nice.

Every time we finish a beer, we order another one, and I'm wondering if he has any intention of leaving at a reasonable hour. I don't care. There is no place in the world I'd rather be.

"Let's pick out some tunes." Alec nudges me over to the TouchTunes. We have the bar almost exclusively to ourselves by now.

"Zeppelin!" I insist.

"OK, you get one Zeppelin song, but I'm putting on Metallica."

"Cool with me." I keep flipping through the choices. After we've loaded up enough classic rock with the occasional rap thrown in to last the rest of the evening, we return to our seats.

"I still can't believe you think Zeppelin is the greatest band in the world."

"OK, well, I didn't say they are my favorite band. I think they are the best as far as talent goes and the way they put songs together. They are amazing."

"OK, but the Beatles are better."

"The Beatles are amazing. Don't get me wrong."

"Yeah, I'm not saying that Led Zeppelin isn't good. I just get bored of them after a while."

"Cause you just don't understand good music."

"This is coming from the girl who loves Eminem?"

"Don't you dare diss Eminem. He's the best writer ever. I love him."

"Yeah . . . you want to have his babies."

"That's a stretch. But I would absolutely perform actions that could potentially result in the having of a child."

"Sick. I can't believe I'm your friend."

"You love how ghetto I am."

"Oh yeah, that's you. Straight from the hood."

I pretend to look gangster, and he tickles me. My phone rings, and I see it's Olivia. "Hey Liv, where are you?"

"Just left Chris's. Thinking about going home but seeing what you are up to."

"Oh, well, I'm drinking with your brother. You should join!"

"You're drinking again??"

"Yeah, blame him."

"Whatever, you love it," Alec chimes in beside me.

"Well, maybe I'll come by for a minute. I have to go home at some point."

"Is she coming?" Alec asks when I'm off the phone.

"I believe she is."

"Cool."

I hate admitting it, but part of me almost doesn't want Liv to join. I absolutely love Liv, but I've liked having Alec to myself all day, just giving each other shit, talking about music and travels. Anyone in the bar would assume we are in a long-term relationship. It's comfortable. I like playing house knowing I still have the freedom to go out and flirt with guys and make out with strangers and get phone numbers and not consult someone before making plans. This thing I have going on with Alec is absolutely perfect.

I suddenly think to myself that when it's all over, this is what I'm going to miss most. Stupid Sunday Fundays just hanging out with a friend without any added pressure of impressing him.

I'm sitting backward on my stool with my legs over the back when Olivia arrives. It's 7 p.m., and we've been there for hours. I have a pretty good buzz going.

"What have you done all day, love?" I ask as I give her a hug.

"Chris and I just hung around doing nothing. I'd have preferred us to have come here with you, but you know Chris. He's like an old man and can't handle going out on Sundays."

"Well, I can't say our day has been very exciting. You missed Patrick, the amazing bartender. They just switched shifts."

"Damn."

"It's nice you joined the party," Alec joins in. "Welcome. Let's get you a beer."

Olivia stays for about an hour, taking pictures, dancing along to our songs still playing throughout the bar, and starting conversations with random patrons.

"How are you going to work tomorrow? You haven't slept all weekend," Olivia asks me.

The thought has crossed my mind as I have ordered beer after beer, but it doesn't deter me in the slightest. "Oh, I'll get my shit together one way or another. It's probably gonna be rough, but I can handle it one day. I work to make money to live my life. Not gonna pass on a fun time so that I can be 100% at a meaningless job."

"I'm rubbing off on you," Alec says, high fiving and then hugging me. "Screw the man!"

"Well, you don't have to get up until 10 a.m. I need to be in my car by 6:30."

"That sucks."

"I'll be fine. I can handle myself."

"Don't get fired. I don't want to lose my favorite drinking partner because she is poor," he says, putting his arm around me. We are tipsy to the point of hanging on each other in a way that isn't normal, even for us.

"Don't you worry your pretty little head."

"You guys are weird," Olivia adds.

"You're weird!" Alec sticks his tongue out at his little sister before heading to the bathroom.

"I have to say, Alec is really cute with you," she points out when he walks away.

"What do you mean?"

"I don't know. He's flirty and attentive with you. It's nice to see after some of the stuff I've seen from him."

"He's really nice."

"He can be."

He returns, and I start to think about what Olivia said. Whether it means anything that she sees the way he treats me as special. I like knowing I'm not just any girl.

"Well guys, I'm gonna head home. I have to drive, and it's almost 9. If either of you has any sense, you'll go home as well," she says and gets her coat.

"Bye, you pansy," Alec says, giving her a hug.

"Call me tomorrow, dear," I say, and she leaves.

"We have like five songs left at least!" Alec exclaims. "Two more beers, please, Anne!" The new bartender is not quite as interesting as Patrick, but she has also taken a liking to us and has kept our pints full and our spirits up.

"What are you supposed to do on a January day? May as well spend it in a pub with good people," I say.

"Damn straight!"

"I LOVE this song! I don't remember us putting it on!"

"Separate Ways" has started over the speakers, and I immediately get up with my beer and start dancing around. Alec laughs a second and then joins me, beer in one hand, my hand in the other. He starts twirling me in and out. We look ridiculous, him wearing my t-shirt and me in my sweats, but we can't stop laughing as we spill our beers and dance around like fools, singing at the top of our lungs. Even our new friend Anne joins in when she is done laughing at us.

Around 10, Anne says she wants to start closing up. There is no one else in the bar, and it's a Sunday night. When we get the tab, it's over $100.

"I can't believe we just spent $100 at a dive bar on a Sunday," I say.

"The saddest part is that they actually took a bunch off of it," he laughs. I start to get my money out. "Don't worry about it. I dragged you out with me today, and I had a great time, so whatever."

"Alec, this is a huge tab. You don't have to get it. I've had a great day."

"Seriously, it's no big deal. You can get me a few beers next time we're out, OK?"

"Sounds good."

"Well, kiddo, what now?"

"Well, it's after 10 p.m. on a Sunday, and we've been drinking for eight hours. I think it might be time for bed."

"Let's keep hanging out. I'm not ready to end the night yet. It's early."

"OK, but we're hanging out at my place so I can pass out. You can wake up way later than me."

"Sure. We'll just watch a movie or something."

I can't believe that I'm saying yes to this. It's a terrible idea. I should get some sleep so I can maybe not be that hungover for work, but I'm in too good of a mood to go home alone. And there is a lot of promise in the idea of Alec coming home with me after this much alcohol consumption.

"Hey, Sleeping Beauty," I say to him, poking at his side. I've already brushed my teeth and have my underwear on and am trying to figure out what the hell to wear to work. A part of me thinks I'd rather die than go to work right now. My head is killing me, and my hot sex friend is naked in my bed after a steamy night, and it's freezing out.

He groans, not opening his eyes. "Mmm, what?"

"I need to leave for work. You are welcome to stay here and sleep longer and just cab it home, or I can drive you, but then you have to get up now so I'm not late."

"Um, I should probably go home and go back to sleep in my own bed for a while."

"OK, then you need to start getting up," I say, sitting down on the bed next to him. I play with his hair, and he reaches up my back and starts scratching it. It feels amazing. I need to be getting dressed for work, but how can I do that when I'm in ecstasy?

"Don't go to work." He's still groaning; his eyes barely open.

"I have to, but you don't have to stop," I say. He rubs harder, and I lay down next to him again.

Fail. I really need to get going. I cannot afford to be late.

His hand runs from my back to my stomach, and I move my body closer against him so we're spooning. I let him continue to caress up and down my stomach, then his hand is down my underwear.

Fuck.

"What are you trying to do?" I whisper, but I'm smiling.

"I'm trying to wake up so you can get to work on time. What?"

"Oh, nothing," I gasp.

He pulls my hair up and starts kissing my neck, while still working me with his other hand. I'm groaning. Can't stop this now. If I'm late for work, screw it. He feels like magic curled up from behind me. All of a sudden, he's inside me, and it's the hottest thing I can imagine right now. I lose remembrance of my hangover or my career.

"Aren't you supposed to be getting ready for work?" he asks, thrusting in and out.

"Shut up."

"You're making it really difficult to get ready."

"Yeah . . . I'm bad like that."

"How do you want it?"

"Keep doing exactly what you're doing. I'm going to explode."

"I certainly hope so."

Fifteen minutes later, I'm red and sweating and supposed to be in my car.

"God . . . you," I say, shaking my head and putting my panties back on, even though it's about the last thing in the world I want to do.

He smiles at me and starts looking around. "Where are my clothes?"

"Probably in the living room."

"Oh, I forgot we fucked on the couch last night."

That happened somewhere between turning the TV off and relocating to the bed. I can understand why the memory is not front and center.

"We christened my couch last night."

"Victory!" he announces.

"Congrats."

"You christened my new couch, too."

"Well, aren't we just so cute. Seriously though, that was amazing, but get your shit together. I'm gonna be so late for work."

"I'm working on it." He puts his pants on and slaps my ass as I slip into some black pants and a button-down. "Look at you. You almost look like a professional. If only they knew . . . "

"God, no kidding," I say, grabbing my coffee.

"Thanks for making me some."

"Shut up, you bastard. You can make your own damn coffee when you wake up for work in three hours."

"I have no idea how you're gonna work all day."

"Me either. And I hate you right now." He grins.

We get in my car and barely talk. I'm exhausted, but in a good mood. I get to his house and we hug, no kiss.

Friends don't kiss goodbye. I think about Sarah saying I needed to talk about this with him the next time we hooked up. The rules or goals or whatever. *Whoops.*

Chapter Seven

As I'm driving down I-94, I realize I shouldn't be. I'm 100% against drunk driving, but I am left with few options. I can't help but keep shaking my head to myself while blasting Queen in an effort to wake up.

I have to park in the farthest lot because I'm so late, and I try to shield myself from anyone who might catch a glimpse of me. I'm a screaming train wreck. Keeping my head down, I walk past the cubicles, toss my bag on the floor, and flop into my chair.

I start my computer and put my head on my desk while it loads. Looking up, I have thirty missed emails. *Joy. I can't handle this.* I take another sip of coffee, put headphones on, and open Pandora. Technically, I can get yelled at for this, but I really don't care. Just one look at this manual makes my head spin, but I'm behind as it is. My job might not be life-changing, but it's also not one I can do well with half a functioning brain.

"I'm not gonna lie, Lyren . . . " John starts and stops, laughing to himself. "Lie, Ly . . . " I roll my eyes up at his face over my cubicle. "But anyway . . . you look like you just stepped out of a night with Guns N' Roses circa 1987."

"I imagine Slash has felt like this a few times, yes."

"Don't worry. I won't tell Claire."

"I appreciate that." Just the thought of my self-absorbed bitch of a boss reaming me out for my less than professional state at work is enough to make me want to throw up.

"So anyway, I know you probably don't want to think about this the way you're feeling right now, but my friends and I are going out this weekend, and you seem like the kind of person that can hang."

"Ha, yes, hang I can," I laugh, thinking of the insanity that was my weekend.

"I mean, if you don't have anything else going on. We're a pretty cool group of people. And I think you'd like my girlfriend. She's a lot of fun. Plus, there are a lot of single guys around in case you are looking . . . "

"Well, thanks for that. Anyway, keep me updated on it, but it sounds like a good time."

"Bring whoever you want. And let me know if you need Tylenol or something."

"I'll live. Thank you."

Tylenol might have been a good idea, but for some reason I feel when my headaches are self-induced, I need to suffer through them properly.

I look at the manual I'm supposed to be editing and decide to check Instagram instead of getting started. There are just too many ready-made distractions available at any moment. I see that Taylor Swift is letting the world know that she baked cupcakes. They are cute.

I haven't baked since Christmas. Most of my weeknights I am exhausted from this mind-numbing excuse for a job, and on weekends I'm obviously either drunk or hungover. No time to do things that others might consider productive. Part of me feels bad about it, like I should have my shit together. But I am also having a lot of fun, so why should it matter?

I start to feel sick and make my way to the bathroom quickly, trying not to draw attention to myself. I get there in time and just hope that no one walks in as I am gagging and coughing and spewing the contents of my weekend into the toilet.

This is lovely, I think, and kind of smile when I get it together again.

I laugh, staring up in the mirror as I splash water on my face and wipe away the fallen mascara, still reminiscent of Saturday night. Four years ago, I would not have recognized the person staring back at me. Just four short years ago, I was excelling in college, planning to marry Jason, and ready to set the world on fire.

JUNE 2007

"I just don't feel like we're on the same page anymore," I said to Jason when we met up for coffee a few days after the break up. I'd been crying for days, but somehow knew it was the right decision.

"How are we not on the same page? The only page I've been on for three years is that I love you and I want to marry you and spend my life with you. I don't understand how all of a sudden we're not on the same page. What changed?"

"Maybe it's what I want? I don't know for sure what changed. I know that I believed that for years, too. At least for the first two."

"Two? So you're saying you've wanted to dump me for an entire year? You really could have saved me a lot of trouble trying to make you happy. That's just awesome. Fucking awesome."

"I didn't know I wanted to end things, Jason. If I had known, I would have done it."

"So what do you mean?"

"I mean that for the first two years, I had no doubts. For the first two years, I was living in some kind of cloud of love and thriving in college and everything, and I don't know, I didn't doubt anything then. I just knew everything was right. And now? Now, I don't know. Now, there have been a million signs along the way that I've tried to ignore and put aside and work past, and I'm to a point where I realize I can't do it anymore. We don't belong together. I love you, but we love each other in a vacuum. You don't like my life, and I don't like yours, and you're changing the person you want to be just to make me happy."

"I've made a few sacrifices along the way. I wouldn't exactly call that completely changing. That's what you do in a relationship. I imagine you compromised a few times as well."

"Finishing college for someone isn't a compromise."

"Yeah, but I know that it's technically better for me. I know that you're pushing me to be a better person. So it's never been a problem."

"It's a problem if it's not what you want. If you are changing the course of your life and your career and what you really want just because you are afraid that I'm going to leave you. Your priorities just seem to be in a very different place than mine."

"Explain."

"Jason, it doesn't take a CSI investigation to look at the amount of partying you do and notice that you're not really on a straightforward career path right now. You talk about traveling, you talk about starting some company, you talk about not bothering to finish. I'm not saying it to hold it against you. You can go ahead and travel and not finish your degree. But I finished mine in four years, and I want to start my life without *waiting around for you to grow up. Your frat boy days are over, Jason." I was being harsh with him, but at least it was the truth I was trying so hard to ignore for so long.*

"So basically you think I'm some idiot party boy that doesn't have his shit figured out enough to be with you? Who do you think you are?"

"You're absolutely not an idiot, Jason. You know I don't think you're an idiot. That's why I get so mad when you choose to go to toga parties instead of studying. That's why I don't get why you let yourself fail classes and get behind over a semester. Jason, I hope you figure it all out, but I can't do this anymore. I can't wait around for you in hopes that you'll want what I want or want to be around the people that I want. This has been a great relationship in so many ways. We've done a lot together. But in the beginning, the chemistry we had, we don't have that anymore. We were on the same page then. We were both in college. We were both figuring things out. But we haven't grown together, and we haven't grown in the same way."

"This is really eye-opening, Lyren. You know, you may have a few things figured out, and you may have all of your ducks in a row and all that shit, but I've learned a few things through the years, too."

"Jason, stop taking offense. I'm just being honest. You like to surround yourself with people that are just not like me. You want to impress the people who have a chip on their shoulder against success. You want to be so cool and unaffected. You don't challenge yourself, and the people you look up to don't either. I'm not saying they're bad or wrong, but we're too different. Your friends think I'm a stuck-up snob. I think your friends are assholes, and they bring out a side of you that I just don't like. And the more I see it, the more I realize that's the person you want to be. And that's fine, Jason. That's totally fine. I'm not judging it. I just don't want to marry it. I'm not* *gonna be the wife that sits at home with the kids after work while you go have a few drinks with the guys at a local bar."*

"Who said that's what I want?"

"Look at all the older people you prefer to associate with or look up to. Most of your friends have already dropped out and have no idea what they want to do. They are already living in their parents' basements, smoking weed all day, and you don't judge them for it. You don't judge the people who have grown up and settled for mediocrity. That is what you want. And that's fine. But it's not me. I want a career. If I become a mom, I want to be a mom who enjoys spending time with my kids and going to family and neighborhood parties. And I want to go to those family parties and not worry that my husband is making a statement by wearing jeans with holes in them and a high school band t-shirt."

"Oh for god's sake, we're still not over that?"

"No, no, we aren't Jason. Because that was a clear sign of something to me. That wasn't just one t-shirt and a horrific pair of pants at a doctor's deck party. That was a sign that you have absolutely no desire to ever fit into a world where people expect anything of you. And your constant need to fight it is exhausting. I know you hate the thought that people are judging you, but they are. They are judging your every move. And you can keep hating it and keep fighting it, but it's not going away. You learn to adapt. The funny thing is, you worry more about your friends judging you than any other figure. You shouldn't have guilty pleasures you hide from your friends. You should have jeans you hide from respectable people. How you present yourself to the world counts for a lot, Jason. Sorry."

"I'm sorry that you chose to see things so superficially."

"I see things realistically. Appearances count for something. Look, it's not like I'm breaking up with you because you don't know how to dress at a nice party. It's that you just don't want to adjust to any setting except the ones you want to be in,

and that's not realistic. I don't know what the point of explaining it is. We're on different pages, we value different things, and that's all there really is to it, Jason. I'm tired of fighting or being disappointed when things don't go the way I think they should. I'm tired of feeling like you're doing things for the wrong reasons. I love you; I love so many things about you. You have been an unbelievable boyfriend. The best. I think you're a great man, and you will make someone very happy one day. You'll be a great husband and father. It's just not going to be with me."

When we walked away, I was sad. For months. You invest a lot in a three-year relationship. The person you are changes. The things you want change. You come out a little unsure of yourself without that person in your life. Sometimes it takes a while for a new reality to take shape. But you move on. You get a new life, and you make new friends, and you accept yourself. I never looked back. No matter how sad I was.

Now, looking at myself in the mirror at work, I'm some sort of cross between hungover and still drunk. I look like absolute shit. It's not a new thing or a one-time thing. I've done it before. I woke up naked with a friend in a relationship that is based entirely on sex and alcohol. I've given my heart to another person who never wanted it and I can't get a hold of myself. I have a job. It's not a career.

What am I doing? Who am I?

I go back to my desk and think about what would have happened if Jason and I had stayed together. If I hadn't wanted something different than him. It would have been seven years. We'd be married. I could even have a kid. Would I have been happy?

Maybe. Maybe if things had stayed the way they were in the

beginning. When I was confident in us. But I've turned into a hypocrite. I ended a relationship over his immaturity, and I was more mature as a 19-year-old than I am now. But I think of how much fun I'm having with Alec, and I smile.

"You know, Gail?" I say on the phone later that night. I'm so happy to be in sweats on the couch. "I think I know why I'm partying so much."

"Because you're lacking in responsibilities at the moment and Alec is hot?"

"Besides that," I laugh. "I lived my whole life doing the right thing and knowing what was good and making a point to act on it the right way. Good grades, never caused trouble, and when I did something my parents wouldn't approve of, I went through such extensive lengths to never get caught. I just really never took risks. Quiet, sweet, wanted people to like me."

"Yeah, me too."

"Well, deep down, I was always a little jealous of the kids who took risks. The kids who didn't always worry about their grades or what their parents wanted them to do or what some authority figure was going to think of them. It looked fun to break the rules. Because that's what high school and college kids do. Sometimes they act like idiots, and it's OK. Your whole life doesn't always end because you act the fool a little bit growing up and learning. But I was so afraid. Of what? Being yelled at? Getting grounded? Letting a teacher down for ten seconds? How seriously would I have messed up my future by letting loose a little? And what future? I'm not doing anything. Most of the people who messed up all the time are in just as good a place as I am, if not better ones. As a construction worker, Jason is making three times what I'm making. My life is no better because I got straight As in college and had a loyal, sweet relationship and ran productive social groups."

"So you're letting out your inner high school rebel?"

"Maybe."

"You are doing well, though. You are awesome at maintaining friendships and your family ties, and you have a real job and pay your own rent and your car payment. You're doing perfectly well in life."

"I know. I'm not depressed about it or anything. I just think I had to do this whole irresponsible party thing. I just want to do what everyone else always did. And you know what? I was right. It *is* a lot of fun."

"Well, that's fine, Ly, but just don't lose your job, get knocked up, or turn into a shallow bitch."

"You have my word that I will try my hardest not to do any of the above. So how are you doing?"

"I'm OK. Just sitting around waiting for Brad to propose. I'm starting to wonder if it's ever going to happen."

"It will happen. When you're both ready."

"I'm ready! I've been ready for an eternity. All of my friends have kids already, and I feel like every day I'm just getting older and losing more time."

"You're not old though, Gail. I know that it's a little different not being in a big city, but still. You have tons of time to get married and have kids. What's the rush?"

"The rush is being with the same person for five years and for at least three of them already having a career and a home and wanting to move on to the next steps of my life. I did party in college. I had a great time. And now I'm ready to have babies, and my stupid boyfriend has the mental maturity he did when he was 21." Gail is lying. She really didn't party in college. Partying was never really her thing. But some people don't need that phase.

"Well, you can't force him to marry you, but you can make it clear that you're not going to just wait around forever for him to grow up. You're way too good for that. It's your life, and you should have more say in it."

"Yeah, but what am I supposed to do?"

"Tell him you want to start seeing other people if you aren't going to be moving forward with him. You'll regret it if another two years go by and you're in the same place you are now."

"Oh my god, I will seriously just die. Like watch you get engaged before me or something. I'll kill someone. No offense."

"Gail, then you need to do something. He's not showing any signs that that's not the case. Maybe he's truly just not ready to grow up. He's in love with you, and you will ruin his life if you leave him, so he needs to learn to step it up. Don't let him dictate your life for you."

"Yeah, but I don't want to be that crazy girl with an agenda. Am I crazy for wanting to get married and all that? Is it weird? Brad acts like every one of our friends who gets married is absolutely crazy and that we're all way too young for that still."

"No, Gail. You're absolutely not crazy. You're almost 27. That's not just out of college or something. You both have jobs. You have been together forever. I'd probably stab someone for putting me through what you're doing, to be honest. If someone claimed to love me and wanted to spend their life with me but just dragged me around for five freakin' years? Gail, I like Brad, but he needs to get his shit together yesterday."

The truth is, I liked Brad when we were in college. He was good for Gail then. Funny and sarcastic. We all hung around together. The problem is: Gail has grown up, and Brad has stayed the same. The thought of it makes me shudder. If I am totally honest, I want Gail to dump Brad. She has outgrown him. But you can't just say that to a good friend. She needs to figure it out on her own.

"Ugh, I just don't know what to do. I love him. I want him to be the father of my kids and all that. I really do. I just don't know why he's not ready to get married yet."

"I'm totally the opposite. I'm so afraid of marriage. When did I get so immature?"

"You're really not immature, though. You know what you want."

"Do I?"

"You just said it. You want to experience what you feel like you missed out on when you were being a good kid and doing the right things all the time. You're not taking it so far as to mess up your life. As long as you're careful, I think it will be OK. It's like a young life crisis."

"Maybe. But why don't I want what you want? And what Sarah wants and what Emma wants? Why does the idea of being in a relationship just sound so stifling and exhausting and limiting to me? I'm at the end of my mid-20s. Aren't I supposed to be getting baby fever? Be freaked out that my biological clock is ticking and I'm still single? Be worried that I'll end up alone with cats?"

"You're allergic to cats."

"Yeah, fuck cats."

"You'll meet someone who will change your mind on all of that."

"But I hate that sentiment. I know you're not doing it to annoy me or anything, and I know that you and everyone who says that says it out of the goodness of their heart, but why do I have to meet someone? What if I want to stay single? What if I never want to be married or have kids? Listening to Sarah and Emma talk about their weddings? It freaks me out. People think I should be jealous. I'm not. I'm repelled by it all. All the formalities and the expectations and the social graces of it all. Having to buy the same stupid dress and shoes as a bunch of girls who I have nothing in common with as far as style, and walking up with flowers and watching people follow traditions that have nothing really to do with them as a couple. Will people forever assume something is wrong with me if that's not what I want ever?"

"You're going to change your mind on it. I'm not saying it's not fine if you don't. It is fine. If you get your career going and you find other things in life that make you happy and all that. I think part of your problem is that you hate your job."

"Yeah, but what can I do about that? I can't quit it. I have bills."

"I know. It sucks."

"And all this about people saying I just haven't met the right guy. No one is attractive to me. Honestly. No one. I mean, Alec is because he's fun and easygoing and it's safely not going anywhere. He's not going to encroach on my independence. I'm comfortable with it. But real guys who could potentially put me in places like all of my friends? They repulse me." I'm sort of laughing, but sort of serious.

Is there something wrong with me that I don't want the things other people my age seem to put such a high premium on?

"Oh, Lyren. You will figure it out. Everyone wants something different. I want to be married and settled down. Going out drinking and dating is of no interest to me. It never really was. I can't wait to spend my life with Brad, making babies and staying at home. If that ever happens."

"Ew."

"Thanks for the support."

I laugh. "You know you have my support. All you crazy marriage-prone bitches in my life do. I just need to go hang out with college kids or something since that seems to be who I'd fit in with better these days."

"Well, don't worry. I obviously have a lot to figure out too. What if Brad isn't the one for me? We're still young. Like you said."

"Remember that. You can still have babies in your 20s if it

isn't with Brad. You'd replace him in two days. You're gorgeous and smart and you know what you want. There are a million men who would die to marry you and get you knocked up."

"Thanks."

"Ugh, I still feel slow. I may be partying like a rock star, but I certainly don't have the liver of one. I don't know how Alec has been doing this for so many years straight. I think my body would have given out by now."

"Alec has rock star blood. They don't get sick the way us mortals do. I mean, look at Keith Richards."

We laugh about it for a while. How different everything is in the real world. You go to college and you succeed and you just assume you'll get a steady, decent job and work toward moving up and moving out and getting married and having kids and because it all seemed so far away, I guess I was OK with it then.

I hang up the phone and look at the dishes piling up in the sink. They can wait another day.

Chapter Eight

"Lyren, it's your life and you can do whatever you want to do. You're an adult. But I'm worried about you in this relationship. I just really think you like Alec. I always have."

My mom made stew and invited Emma and I to stay over and avoid an impending early February blizzard. My dad is out of town for work, and Matt couldn't come, so it is another opportunity to discuss bridal shower and bachelorette prep for the all-consuming wedding. Well, all-consuming except for the breaks to take jabs at my sex and lack of love life.

"Mom, it's not like that. I've told you a million times that Alec just really isn't my type."

"Well, I just don't think girls are capable of having sex and not developing an attachment to someone."

"Mom, that is kind of an old-fashioned way of looking at it, though," Emma adds. "Things really are different now. Girls have a lot more power in these situations than they used to."

"Right. You met Dad really young. You never became a single 26-year-old. I'm in control of my emotions in a way I definitely wasn't when I was 22, like you were when you met Dad. Then, yeah, I agree, I don't think I was comfortable enough with my body or with men to have a casual relationship at all. But the thing is, that was more about trust. I used to feel that if a guy was getting sex at all, the girl was being used. I don't feel like that anymore. I have needs and interests, too. While I'm sure it would be better to be with someone who actually meant a lot to me, I don't have that so Alec fills a really nice void, and I have enough friends and family to fill other voids left by my lack of a relationship. To be honest, other than my shitty job, I have to say that I don't feel anything is really missing from my life right now."

"Yeah, but I do feel like Alec is using you. Alec is a player. He needs his ego boosted. The second you're not around, he's hitting on girls and sleeping with other girls. How can that not bother you?"

"Well, it's not like he's doing it in front of me."

"But you know he is."

"Yes, and I don't care what he does. He needs sex and attention, and I need sex and attention. I don't care what he does other than that, Mom. I assure you Alec does not have the ability to break my heart, for he does not have anything close to my heart. How can he be using me if I'm using him for the exact same thing?"

I love that I can be so open with my mom and sister. We've always been close about everything, even things most people find weird or awkward. But it is hard to make her understand some things because she was just so different about dating.

"Well, why do you like sleeping with someone if you don't actually like them then?" my mom continues.

"I *do* like him. I like him on some level. A very physical one. We have a great time. He's really nice to me. He makes me feel good about myself. He makes me feel confident and sexy and wanted, and when I'm bored and all my lame friends are with their boyfriends, he's up for doing fun things. But you know me. I need a guy who inspires me and challenges me. Alec doesn't have the things that interest me in the long run."

"It seems like no one interests you in the long run."

"Well, not at the moment anyway."

"You just like guys that you can't have," Emma chimes in again.

"Also not true."

"The last guy you liked didn't like you back."

"Yeah, OK. The situation with Evan was bad. I fell without a warrant. It was stupid. But he was everything I like in a person. Smart, tall, passionate, interesting, funny, sarcastic. He had it all. He just was getting out of a serious relationship and the timing was bad. It's not that he didn't like me. He did like me. He still likes me. Just not enough. And whatever, that's over and done."

And it never helped that all of my friends were always all like, *"Oh, well, he* totally *likes you. It's obvious. He is just busy with work. He just needs time to get over his ex."* My mom was the only honest person about him, which was awful to hear at the time, but in hindsight she was entirely correct. *"If he liked you, he'd be with you. Done."* So true. So hard to accept when you want something against all logic.

"Well, you're right. I don't know what it's like to have causal relationships the way you crazy kids seem to find so normal these days. And I'm not against it. To be honest, people of my generation were too bottled up about all of that. Sometimes I wish I hadn't been so careful all the time. I'm glad you're confident and comfortable with your body and all that. Really, I am. You're a confident, independent woman, and that's all I could ask of my daughters. But what worries me is that Alec is so comfortable to you. You like being out with him, you have so much fun with him, and he's filling your other needs, so what incentive do you have to go out and meet someone else? I worry that you'll pass up going out on dates because the idea of being with Alec is more appealing to you."

"Well, I guess that's the first real concern you may have. Because I hate dates. Dates are awkward, and I choose to hang out with friends over them all the time. Actually, I might choose doing laundry over dating."

"Why? I think dating seems so fun. That's the one problem with me and Matt. We've been together so long. I don't even know what it would be like to date," Emma explains.

"Ugh. It's so not fun. Two people putting on airs, trying to impress someone else, meanwhile trying to assess whether they have any interest in the other person. And then guys are super visual, and I'm not visual right away, so they want to get physical, and I have no desire. It's just ten thousand shades of awkward discomfort on so many levels." Meatloaf comes snorting up. "You know dating's not fun, don't you, Meatloaf? Don't you?"

I wish they'd just drop it. I love how close we all are, but sometimes it's hard being nagged about my relationship choices and experiences.

"How are you ever going to get to know a good guy that way? You just have to power through that awkward a little bit. I mean, I wasn't crazy about Matt on the first date. You have to give things time."

"I don't think it's that crazy that I want a faster connection with someone. I know you and Matt are great now, but I have no interest in spending months trying to get feelings. I think you should just have them. And if I don't have them, can't I just be single and not be some pariah of society for not forcing myself to get feelings for some mediocre guy?"

"Ouch. So you think Matt is mediocre?" Emma looks legitimately hurt.

"That's not what I meant, Emma. I mean, if I think a guy is mediocre and I don't have feelings, I don't think it's worth pushing through to hope I develop them just so I can prove to society I'm a 'regular' woman. New conversation, please? I can't stand how my dating life is always the topic around here. I'm good. I'm having a great time. I'm happy. I assure all of you. And when I meet someone, it will be natural, and it will happen. And if I don't? I'll be perfectly content. Maybe I'll adopt a baby from Africa when I turn 35."

"OK. I just really think you should get on It's Just Lunch or one of those more exclusive dating sites," my mom says without looking up at me.

"I'm going to walk out of this room in ten seconds."

"Hey, did anyone listen to Carrie Underwood's latest album?" Emma blatantly changes the subject, and I laugh.

"Thank you."

Going out with John's friends is a welcome change for me. Away from my girlfriends and their serious relationships and wedding talk, away from my job, and away from Alec for once.

"Hey, Lyren!" John greets me immediately, and we hug.

We've always been cool at work but haven't done much consorting outside of it. I am forcing myself to step out of my comfort zone, and part of me wonders if it's just to prove my mom wrong. I *won't* always turn back to Alec. Then again, I have no idea what Alec's doing this evening, and I don't like it.

"This is my girlfriend, Trisha," John introduces.

"So are you gonna go up there and rock out?" I ask Trisha and John.

We're at a karaoke bar, which helps lessen any tension that may arise with me not knowing anyone. Laughing at people who attempt to sing is always a good icebreaker.

"Oh, hell yes! I do a mean 'Sweet Caroline'," John says as

Trisha rolls her eyes. "I'm glad you got here in time to see the amazing performance."

John introduces me around, and I make no note to memorize people's names, which is always a problem when I'm supposed to address anyone later.

The group is fun and easygoing, taking turns on the mic, dancing around and choosing mostly inappropriate songs. I've never been socially awkward or anything, but I'm surprised that I'm actually having fun. John's friend Steve approaches me a few drinks in.

"OK, you haven't gone up there all night. What's the deal?"

I haven't paid much attention to Steve in particular. He's one of the many. But now that he's singling me out, I wonder if he's interested. And in return, wonder if I could be. I am supposed to be proving to myself that I do not just wait around for Alec and that I'm cool with both of us seeing other people.

"Oh, I don't know. Stage fright? Not drunk enough yet?"

"How about I go up there with you?"

"OK. That sounds like it would be better. I don't want to break anyone's eardrums or anything. What will we sing?"

"Well, there's always 'Summer Nights'," he suggests.

"Yeah, but come on. That's so cliché. We can do something better than that, I think."

"Hmm, the silent karaoke girl seems to have strong opinions. What would you suggest we perform?"

"Let's do some Bon Jovi. Get the crowd going. I mean, if we're gonna pretend to be rock stars, we should really pretend to be rock stars."

"You got it. 'Livin' on a Prayer', it is!"

I go get another drink as he requests the song. Steve is actually kind of cute. He's a lot taller than me, even in my heels, with dark shaggy hair and big brown eyes. Not cute in a take-your-breath-away manner, but in the way that you could definitely see yourself making out with him and not being ashamed the next morning. I feel a buzz in my purse and check my text messages.

ALEC
Where you at Chica?

I chastise myself for the heart flutter and sigh of relief that follows. It's *just* Alec!

LYREN
Redmond's at the moment with some coworkers. And yourself?

It's supposed to be an Alec-free night, but it certainly can't hurt if we meet up later. We'll at least have spent some amount of time with other people.

"So, Lyren, you work with John?" Steve asks when we both return to the table.

"Yeah, unfortunately," I laugh.

"Um, it's actually very fortunate for you! You'd be fired ten times over if it weren't for me covering your ass!" John joins.

I laugh. "That was one time! I've seen you looking a bit Lil' Wayne on the occasional Monday yourself, Mr.!"

"It's true, it's true. I mean, you have to do something to ward off Claire. If you don't kill those brain cells, I firmly believe that the memory of your day will truly destroy your veins."

"No kidding. She's wretched. I know that you have this girl-friend, and she seems really sweet, but I'm sure she'd just under-stand if you took one for the team and would let her blow you already."

"Disgusting." John makes a face, and Trisha looks interested.

"Our boss has a huge crush on your boyfriend. She hates everyone who is friends with him. She doesn't know you, but she really hates you." I laugh.

"Good to know." Trisha almost looks concerned, so I assuage her. "No need to worry. Claire is disgusting. As much as the entire company would probably benefit from John just letting Claire have her way, I think his dick would literally recoil if she got near."

"It's true. However, her crush on me is benefiting me, so I'm gonna go with it. I get all the easiest shit at work, and she never cares if I miss my deadlines. She never even looks over half my shit. Also, it's really entertaining to watch how much she hates you."

"Yeah, glad everyone can have a good laugh at that. I'm just waiting until she finally makes up some reason she thinks is good enough to give me my walking papers."

"That bad, huh?" Steve asks.

"Yesterday, John and I were talking at the end of the day, and she came up to ask him a favor while literally twirling her hair like a high school student and smiling. Didn't even acknowledge me until she walked away, when she honestly gave me a dirty look and left without saying a word." I imitated the standard-evil bitch look Claire had given me. You expect to see it in a typical high school prom queen, not in a managing director at a company.

"No way!" Steve cracks up.

"She really isn't kidding. That exactly happened. It's ridiculous. I hope you don't get fired, though. What if she replaces you with someone who totally sucks?"

"If she really fires me, she's an idiot. Even when I'm hungover, I'm still really good at that job."

"That's true. She very clearly has no real reason to dislike you. She's intimidated by you."

"Well, that's pathetic. I'm not out at a nightclub with her. What is she competing for?"

"I don't know. You women are so weird with all of your competition."

"Oh, and men don't have alpha-male dick-measuring competitions on a regular basis?" Trisha adds. "Like you really needed to make sure your car was just a little faster than Bob's?"

"Totally different," John laughs, though realizing it's true.

"So what do you do over there?" Steve, apparently feeling left out, gets back into the conversation.

"Oh, I run the entire company. With my amazing editing skills."

"So you're an editor?"

"Well, when you say 'editor', it sort of insinuates some sort of position of authority over content. I grammar-edit. Literally just making sure that the general syntax and punctuation is correct."

"You lost me entirely at syntax and punctuation. Living the dream?"

"You know it."

"What brought you into that business?"

"I want to be an editor or a writer eventually. Maybe move up into content editing, but not for an educational materials company. It's rather boring. But I'm good at English and grammar, and there really aren't a wealth of opportunities in the world for these things. Unfortunately, this civilization is much more in need of computer scientists and other number-type people than writing people. What about you?"

"I'm one of those number people you don't like."

"Computer science?"

"No, no. Actuary. It's a good job. I like what I do. It pays well, which is always a good thing."

My dad would love him.

"Steve and Lyren, you're up!" the KJ calls over the loudspeaker.

"Oh god, here we go," I laugh, taking a huge swig of my beer.

The world is getting a little fuzzy, and I'm glad to have a

quick break from the conversation. We get really into it on stage. Singing loudly, if you can call it that, and dancing. The bar sings along. I'm surprised by how much fun it is to be on stage.

"You're a lot of fun, Lyren," Steve says as we walk down from the stage.

"Thanks. You're not so bad yourself."

I check my phone again when we get back.

ALEC

Bar Celona. Thinking about heading to Red Ivy in a bit. Meet me out! I'm way more fun than your work friends.

It's still early enough that I don't have to consider this a total booty call, right? 10:30. I mean, that's my sort of unwritten rule with Alec. We only have sex if we've been hanging out together and actually enjoying each other's company. There has to be some sort of buildup to turn me on in the first place. I have to feel sexy and wanted. Always. It's never just a booty call.

LYREN

I'll meet you there in a while if you're still out.

I put the phone away. He can wait. I'll hang out with John's friends for another half an hour. I've done my good deed by hanging out with other people. It didn't have to be all night.

"OK, everyone, this has been so much fun, and I'd love to hang out again!" I stand up at 11:07 (a time I chose specifically because it's less likely that I was waiting until exactly 11).

"You're leaving already?" Steve looks disappointed.

"Yeah, I'm gonna meet some other friends down the street." I don't invite Steve or anyone from this group to join me.

"Have a good time!" John says, and I wave to everyone.

Steve follows me. "So, uh, any chance you want to hang out again?"

I was expecting this, and I'm not opposed to the idea. I have enjoyed talking to him, and after checking him out again, he's definitely a decent-looking guy. I have no immediate attraction, and I'm glad he doesn't awkwardly try to kiss me or anything, but he's worth a number exchange.

"Yeah, definitely. Here, I'll give you my number." He takes out his phone, and I dictate my number to him. He immediately sends a text back with his name. Gone is the age of giving someone a fake.

"Awesome. Have a great rest of your night. I'll give you a call later this weekend!"

"Yeah! Good night!" I walk out the door in a great mood.

"Well, hello, sexy." Alec drunkenly wraps his arm around me the second I walk up.

I wave to his friends and note none of them are talking to any women. I wonder if Alec has been rejected yet, or just chose to text me rather than investigate. I prefer the latter, regardless of the fact that I already got a phone number tonight.

"Hello Alec. How is your night?"

"Oh, it's good. Started at 5. We watched the game, and I am quite intoxicated."

"I see that."

"Where were you?"

"I was out with a coworker and his friends, actually. It was a lot of fun. We karaoked. I sang Bon Jovi."

"Nice! Any hotties?"

"I did get a phone number, actually. Thanks for asking."

"High five!" We high-five on it, and I laugh as he grabs my hand and leads me to the dance floor.

The night goes as usual. We do a few shots, taking our beers onto the dance floor. We are anything but graceful. I'm completely at ease in his arms as he twirls and dips me around, whispering how good I look into my ear whenever I get up close to him.

"I want to rip that dress off of you."

Done.

He pulls away, smirking as he does so, twirling me away, and I feel my blood rushing, wanting to meet his face again. When I spin back up to him, he quickly kisses my neck. It's tortuous and so sexy. The anticipation of sliding up close to him again, the pulling away and dancing, the stolen, brief words. Finally, he spins me around to face him, pulls me close, and starts to kiss me, and I realize why Mother said what she did.

Who would trade feeling like this for an awkward date?

"Hey, guys! Get a room!" one of Alec's friends shouts at us.

Our making out is getting more intense and more inappropriate to the extent that strangers are giving us dirty looks. It makes me want to do it more. Alec blatantly squeezes my butt and lets his hand slowly move up my skirt. The dance floor is crowded with people behaving similarly.

"You guys might want this," a very drunken stranger comes up and hands us a condom. It makes us both laugh.

"Hey, thanks, man! Free stuff!" Alec laughs, then continues kissing me.

The guy might have done it as a joke, but we don't take any offense. Anyone who doesn't have what I have right now should be jealous. Everyone wants this feeling. I don't care if it's not going to be real anymore tomorrow. Right now, I have a gorgeous boy making me feel like the only girl in the world. And that is the best there is.

It's 2 a.m., and the bar is about to kick us out.

"So, do we continue this party at a late-night bar where we can keep drinking or should we just go back to my place where I can fuck your brains out?"

My body tingles at the words. "I think the latter sounds like a great plan."

We hail a cab and make out as the driver leads us to our destination. After a few minutes he pulls back.

"Ly, I do want to say something." I don't like the look on his face.

"What? Right now? Are you serious?" All I want is to devour him, and the cab feels like it's taking forever to arrive at our destination.

"I just . . . this . . . we're doing a lot of this."

"And the problem is?"

"Well, it's not that there's a problem. Trust me, I'm really enjoying all of this, and I always do. But we're friends, and this is just becoming sort of really regular. Like every time we go out together, we end up going home together."

I suddenly want to punch him. *Is he serious right now? What the hell is the problem with us going home together?*

"I don't see how that's such a problem."

"I just mean, this isn't going to turn into anything else. If we see each other and go home together this often, it seems like it's going somewhere else."

I feel a sort of drunken rage. *What the hell does it matter what it turns into if we're enjoying it?*

"Alec, you texted me tonight. In case you had forgotten. I was having a perfectly good evening with friends who are not you, flirting and getting phone numbers, if you don't recall. If you didn't want to see me, you shouldn't have texted me. I didn't realize that going home with me was a bad thing."

"It's not. It's an awesome thing. I texted you because you're a lot of fun. I guess I'm just afraid that we're seeing a little too much of each other and that it's getting really comfortable."

"Don't flatter yourself. All you're doing right now is killing a perfectly good moment. If you wanted to push me away, you've been doing a really shit job at it. But if you want to stop fucking me, just say the word. I could replace you in ten fucking seconds, Alec."

"Don't be mad at me. I didn't want to offend you."

"Then you shouldn't be so fucking offensive." I get extra ornery when I've been drinking. I guess we're having the conversation. This is not how I wanted to have it.

"Damn it. I'm sorry. I am drunk and overthinking shit. I just don't want this to end ugly. This isn't the first time I've had a casual relationship, and it always ends badly. And usually, I'm just a lot better at keeping a healthy distance."

"Shut up. You're an idiot. I don't want to be with you, Alec. Get over yourself. Just because every stupid girl you've ever screwed may want more, it doesn't mean I do. You just don't have high standards. Maybe this is all a huge mistake."

Half of me wants to get out of the cab and slam the door in his asshole face.

What? I'm not good enough to go home with because I'm not new and exciting now? Who the hell does he think he is?

He rubs his hand across my leg, and I hate that it turns me on. I want to stay mad at him. I should just get out of the cab, go get a burrito, and go to bed.

"Lyren, I definitely didn't want to offend you. This whole thing we have going here is really, really awesome. But while I've done this thing with friends before, the fact that you're Olivia's good friend and you're mine at the same time is just complicating things for me. I'm afraid it's going to end with us hating each other if it stays this intense."

"You're way too drunk to be having a serious conversation with me. You're not even going to remember half of it in the morning, you know."

"I know. I'm being a dumbass."

"I should just go home. I'll have the cab drop you off at your place and then take it back to mine."

"No. I don't want that. We don't have to have sex if you're

that mad at me right now. Just come over. We'll hang out. We can have another drink and watch TV or something."

"Whatever."

I want to kick myself for not being stronger about it. Going home is the right thing to do. I'm mad at Alec for killing a good moment. I'm mad at him for assuming I'm going to be the one to get jealous and crazy. And I'm mad at him for thinking it would be such a freakin' terrible thing if it is a regular thing, or if we do start liking each other. Though, I don't think it's going to happen. But I'm thrilled he wants me to hang out. I'm terrified of losing him as a friend and as more. I said I could replace him in ten minutes, but I know it's a lie. Sure, I could find someone attractive to have sex with. But he wouldn't be Alec. There is just something about him.

When I wake up the next morning, I am wearing his t-shirt and we are cuddling in his bed with the TV still on. I recap the night in my head and recall that we did not have sex, which might make it worse that we are cuddling.

We didn't talk about things anymore. We came back, had another drink, watched mindless television, and went to sleep. I put on his t-shirt and shorts while he was in the bathroom. Remembering how badly I had wanted him when we were at the bar, I feel sort of unsettled and very unsatisfied with the way the night turned out. What was Alec trying to tell me? That he doesn't want to see me anymore? That he wants to see me and not have sex with me anymore? He's the one who was making all the moves!

I look at him sleeping. He has such a pretty face. Kissing it is so easy. Are there real rules to what we're doing? In the movies, when people have friends with benefits, they establish rules. No cuddling, no fighting, no talking about serious things related to the situation. We're breaking all of those. What really creates the dividing line between friends and relationships? Is it just the sex? Is it just a trust issue? How do you make that boundary between "we are just friends who are attracted to each other" and "we are just people who like each other and want to be more"? Jason and I were dating *without* benefits for three months before we kissed. We were good friends; we were afraid to admit we were in love. So we just hung out every day. We talked all the time, and we cuddled. And finally one day, he got the balls to kiss me.

Alec breaks my train of thought by shifting his position in his half-sleep. We fall into a relaxed spooning, and I try to fall back asleep. Alec tends to sleep longer than me, but I don't want to get up. I'm sort of thrilled when he shows me that he's more than half awake by running his hand up and down my body, making me crave what we missed out on last night. We don't say a word, but my reaction to him is obvious. Having sex can make all the other issues go away.

In an hour . . . things will be back to normal for us.

Chapter Nine

I'm sitting at tutoring, staring into space, remembering how Alec and I didn't really resolve anything after our dust-up in the cab the previous weekend. Do we really go home together too much? Is it too easy and too comfortable? Do I care that he doesn't want to be comfortable because I like that it's comfortable, or am I sorry he doesn't want it to be turning into something . . . more? I should pull away from him to show that I'm not trying to be clingy or dependent on our situation, whatever it is. I did get Steve's phone number and agreed to go out with him. Alec and I have only been hooking up for two months. It's not like a long-term commitment.

Maybe Alec is just being too sensitive. But then why does it bother me? Maybe because I like things the way they are right now. Fun and sexy. Not super clingy. I mean, yes. We go out drinking a lot, and we go home together pretty much every time. But it's not like we're trying to be part of each other's day to day. We never just hang out without drinking. We don't grab lunch or a coffee or talk on the phone. So what is he so worried about? Is he just getting bored with having sex with me and trying to create some space?

Why did things feel so different with Evan even though we technically weren't in an official relationship? Is it because we spent hours talking on the phone and getting closer to each other, talking about our truths and our insecurities and our hopes for ourselves in the future? Having deep conversations about things we cared about? Evan is a teacher. It was great talking to him about how much he cared about his students and how messed up the system was. I talked to him about tutoring being a thing that grounded me back to my idealist self. When I was around Evan, I was inspired to be better, to reach for more, even if I was still stuck and settling. It didn't feel as rooted as it does now, a year later.

Why does my shitty job bother me so much? Is it because I'm just not feeling inspiration anywhere at all anymore? I used to love being around friends who I felt inspired by, but now half the conversations I have with my girlfriends are about planning wedding invitations and tablecloths. I just can't relate and, worse, I don't care. Does it make me a terrible friend that I truly do not give a fuck about flower displays?

"Hey! Lyren!" Jarron jolts me back to reality.

"I'm sorry, Jarron. What's up?"

"What are you doing?"

"I'm just thinking about something. I'm sorry, what are you having trouble with?"

I'm even a half-assed volunteer. It's like I'm too exhausted lately to try to be a better person. I've given Jarron a worksheet, and it's honestly lazy as hell. I printed it from some website. I'm not being thoughtful or creative here. I'm suddenly just checking a box during the thing I used to be motivated by.

"I don't understand this one."

"OK, let's take a look at it." I refocus to help Jarron and glance over at Olivia.

She's so diligently helping Diamond. They are working through a creative project where Olivia has Diamond recreating a character's experience as a journal entry. She never just gives her stupid worksheets. I really need to step up my game here.

"OK, so what does the verb do in a sentence?"

"It's the action."

"Good. So every sentence needs a verb. Something needs to happen in every sentence. When you're writing a sentence that doesn't have a verb, that makes it a fragment. So which of these sentences have no action?"

It's hard for me to concentrate on what Jarron is working out in his head when I have so much going on in mine. I keep going over what Alec said. That wasn't just alcohol talking. That was obviously something he felt sober and didn't know how to say. Vodka gave him the power to admit it. He didn't like how much sex we had because he was afraid it meant we were going for something more. And obviously, he was strongly against going for something more.

Am I? Why is it really so offensive? Am I so sick of being alone that it's nice to wake up in someone's arms? To have someone you hope is out, or hope texts you, or hope hugs you just one second too long. It's so nice feeling adored. And Alec may not be 100%, but it's the closest thing I have right now.

"God, I'm even getting lazy volunteering," I say to Olivia as we walk out into the dark of Chicago cold.

"You're just feeling a little blah. It's probably because it's winter."

"Yeah, maybe that's it. So dismal and gray. I wake up when it's dark. I get home when it's dark. There isn't pretty snow, just melting ice and sludge. It's hard to be excited, I guess."

"For sure." Olivia doesn't seem nearly as affected by the

dismal Chicago winter, though. In fact, she seems to be carrying herself just fine and getting all of her shit done without whining.

"I'm going flower shopping with Sarah on Saturday."

"Oh, that will be fun!"

"Yeah, it will be. Except I'm not really good with all of this wedding stuff. I don't really think of cute things. I'm gonna have to plan the bachelorette party, and while I'm very good at going out drinking, I am not good at thinking of sweet wedding-related things. I'm a terrible maid of honor."

"You are not. You will be fine. Just be supportive and make sure it's all about her whenever you're planning wedding stuff."

"I'm getting married in a field if I ever get married. In a maxi dress. And then I'm going to spend a bunch of money traveling the world. Hopefully, with my husband or something." I catch myself as I realize how aligned Alec is for that vision.

"Good call."

"I'm sorry I bitch to you about weddings so much. I know you and Chris will probably get engaged. I don't want you to feel like you can't talk about your wedding with me. I'm just in a bad place to be dealing with making other people's perfect day with their perfect person more special. I need something that is my own to be excited about before I can really help anyone else with something they are excited about. Basically, I'm just insanely selfish lately."

"I get it. It's hard to plan other people's weddings when you're not in a great state yourself. How are things with my brother?"

I can't be honest with her. I can't complain about the fight we had. I have to work very hard to make sure I'm not making things uncomfortable for her, even though I want to analyze it down to the minute details. It's hard to do with Sarah because of the juxtaposition between her asking wedding advice and my misery. Olivia has been my go-to, and now, I'm in a relationship I can't analyze with her. And I don't even know what is wrong. I just know I can't accept that Alec and I, whatever we are, are ending.

"It's fine. Keeping me entertained. But it's not the same as love, or knowing someone really cares about you. At all. That guy Steve actually texted me. The one I met out with my coworker a bit ago?"

"Oh yeah? Are you going to go out with him?"

"I think so. I may as well. He's out of town next week, but he's mentioned wanting to hang out. I've been noncommittal."

"Sounds like a nice change of scenery."

I shrug. "I guess so."

I wake up on Saturday to Alec's phone buzzing. We aren't cuddling, and it's all well. I'm dying and wish he had a fan, though. Last night we were all out for a friend of Olivia's birthday, and Alec and I fell back into our regular pattern. At some point in the night, we were paying attention to each other, flirting, and he turned me on enough to make me want to go home with him. We didn't discuss anything. Again.

"What's up, Liv? Yeah . . . you can come over. Sure. I'm not getting up to check on your car right now . . . No . . . Sorry. Whatever, just get here and take care of it."

"Liv's coming over?" I ask.

"Yeah, she left her car parked here overnight, and it's probably ticketed. I totally forgot."

"I'm sure it's fine."

If Liv's on her way, this means we aren't going to have morning sex, and I'm OK with it. I just wish my head would stop throbbing.

Alec gets up to grab a glass of water and comes back, letting me have a sip.

"Should probably make myself look presentable since my sister is coming over."

"Yeah. Do you have a t-shirt or anything I can throw on?"

"I'm starting to run out. You have half my shit."

"Well, if I ever see you not out drunk, I'll try to remember all of it. I have a special Alec pile in a corner in my room."

"Excellent. Here, you can throw this on."

I wish I had a toothbrush at Alec's place. I stay here enough that it would make sense, but that's a girlfriend thing to have. I go to the bathroom and put the toothpaste on my finger. It will have to do.

There's a knock at the door.

"Goddamnit! I got a ticket! I totally forgot to move it." Olivia is bitching as Alec lets her in and she makes herself comfortable on the couch.

"That totally sucks," I say.

"You have to be really careful around here. I totally forgot that you parked it here. How'd you get here?"

"Chris drove me. He's got some game he's watching. I sort of just want to hang out and chill. Do you guys want to order some food?"

"That sounds awesome," I say.

Alec looks hesitant, then says, "Well, we can get food, but let's get something kind of quick."

"Why? You have a hot date?" I ask.

"Actually, I sort of do. I'm taking this girl to the Bulls game later, and she's coming here first for drinks. I want to have time to pick the place up."

I wasn't expecting that, and it feels a little biting.

"Oh, don't worry, Your Highness. We'll get out of here in time for you to make a grand impression," I say sarcastically, but I can't help but feel insulted.

Alec is actually kicking me out of his place to entertain a real date. A date he is taking to a Bulls game. I took him to a

Blackhawks game I got free tickets to, but I'm aware that favor will never be reciprocated. I'm too easy. All he has to do is go out with me when I'm drinking to get me naked. No effort required.

"Yeah, yeah. Just make it something quick."

I laugh, but I wonder if it's obvious how fake it is. Even when Liv and I leave, I can't admit it to her because she can't know how much it actually bothers me.

As far as she knows, everything is casual. I don't care about Alec at all.

Is that even true? I don't do one-night stands. Because if I'm honest, sex isn't about the actual feeling of a man sliding in and out. That's nice for about 30 seconds.

It's about everything else. The build up. The flirting. The feeling sexy and powerful. The kissing. The touching. The way he moves his hand on your legs and your back and your stomach and the way he kisses your neck. The way you feel just knowing that someone is as close to you as a person can possibly be, yet you are trying your hardest to pull them closer. Sharing the same air in the same space while they try to consume you. And cuddling. Curling up in someone's perfect arms, smelling their leftover cologne and knowing that the entire world is in place because this person adores you. Right now, this person thinks you're great. And then you wake up and you feel loved. And even though it may not be real, and that jackass may have another date, one he cares about way more than you, when you're lying there in those early moments of morning, it makes it all seem so worth it.

———

"So what are good flowers for an August wedding?" Sarah is asking the salesgirl at the florist.

This is our first florist, though we've already spent time

going through linens, color patterns, and bridesmaid dresses. I'm ready for all of it to be over.

"Well, it's summer, so you probably want something really bright. What are your colors?" It's weird to think about summer in late February when everything around us is gray and icy.

"Red and orange."

"Oh, that is just perfect! We have sunflower setups that are just stunning."

We look through hundreds of flowers, settling on a really gorgeous arrangement.

"OK, I'll bring someone over to go over the basics and next steps with you," the salesgirl says and walks away.

"Those are going to be so beautiful, Sarah. Your wedding will be absolutely perfect."

I'm trying really hard to put on a smiling face and be supportive, but I just can't get into the whole wedding thing. I just don't get them. I don't care about what goddamn flowers are going to adorn someone else's perfect little wedding to a perfect man. Even if she's my oldest and closest friend. And I don't get why it's "normal" that when someone gets married, all of their friends have to spend thousands of dollars on them because they are choosing to spend their life with a man. I'm starting my life too. Why don't people have to spend thousands of dollars on me just because I am doing it alone? That's harder! Falling in love isn't an accomplishment. It's luck. Why is it so celebrated?

"Thank you. I'm really excited. Stressed with all the planning, but excited. What are you up to tonight?"

"Well, I don't have plans, but to be honest, I really sort of want to go out and get totally slutted up and drink a ton. I'd sort of like a random make out night." If Alec can get some from someone else, so can I.

"Hmm, Nick is not going out because he has to work tomorrow. I'd maybe be down to play wing girl for the night. I feel like it's been forever since we've had girls' night."

"I agree! Let's go downtown or something for a change."
Something non-wedding related? That exists??
"Sounds like a plan."

I'm excited to go out, but wonder if Sarah is even going to be any fun. I love her to death and always have, but it seems Liv is my only friend who really ever wants to go out for more than wine and dinner anymore. Everyone around me is growing up. Adulthood is skipping me entirely.

Sarah and I are having a great time enjoying free pitchers of beer with some enjoyable men, though I'm not feeling into any of them in terms of a make out. That is until I receive a text from my high school crush.

SEAN
You out this evening?

Suddenly, I have a brilliant plan.

Sean Tractyn was my first high school crush because he was the first guy to make me feel attractive. I was a scrawny freshman with braces, and he was a sophomore with too-curly hair. He taught me about bands, he called me late at night, and he always told me how pretty I was. He fell in love with someone else at some point that year, and my sophomore year was spent heartbroken. I hadn't really talked to him much until I ran into him at a party recently and found out he lived nearby. We've seen each other at a few bars and events over the recent months, and there has been a definite undercurrent. But as I had already turned him down once before, meeting him at 1 a.m. seems like a great idea. He's a sure thing. And tonight, I need a sure thing.

We do a cherry bomb immediately, and it is clear he is even farther into his drinking than I. At some point, Sarah leaves, seeing that I have accomplished my mission. We start making out. We do more cherry bombs. Is this romantic? Nope. Is this sexy? Nope. Am I getting the attention I am so desperately seeking? Absolutely. And when we stumble back to my place, the world seems to be working exactly as I'd hoped.

The night is a blur. We are too drunk to have actual sex. We do a lot of making out. We take off a lot of clothes. I spend a good chunk of the night with my head in the toilet. I'm pretty sure he's doing the same in my kitchen sink.

"What the fuck happened last night?" Sean asks as we start to open our eyes.

"Oh my god."

All of my pictures and one lamp have made their way to the floor. One is broken. Sean's face is cut up.

"What happened to my face?" He rubs his hand over it.

"Oh my god, I don't know, but you're going to have a hell of a time explaining it at work Monday."

His eyes widen. "It's that bad??"

"Oh yeah. I'm pretty sure you fell at least six times on the four-block walk here."

"Why didn't you help me walk?"

"I'm sure I was too busy laughing at you. It was really icy out."

"Did we have sex last night?"

"I don't believe so. Actually, no. I know we didn't," I clarify.

"Why not?"

"I don't think it was really an option." I eye his nether regions.

"Hmm." He reaches his hand down on himself. "I don't think I'm still having that problem."

We sort of laugh and then start kissing. It's the sensible thing to do since he's already naked in my bed.

"High school me is so proud of myself right now."

"Whatever, high school me is probably kicking myself. Or high fiving. Depends on when you asked me," I reply.

"Why?"

"What do you mean, why? You were such a jerk to me when you started dating Leah."

"Oh, I don't remember being a jerk to you. I remember thinking you were really cute."

"And then you started dating Leah and forgot I existed."

"Well, what was I supposed to do? I wasn't going to cheat on her!"

"You were supposed to want me! Jerkface!"

We laugh, and I start touching his chest. "I want you now if that makes anything better. I'm not exactly holding a 10-year grudge on this." I kiss him again.

"Do you have condoms?"

I guess we may as well go there. We've gotten this far. I had assumed he would have left at this point. God knows what the rest of my place looks like if my room is this bad.

"Yeah, they're uh . . . " I lean over the bed to pull them out of the drawer and start laughing.

"What?" he asks, but leans over to see what I am laughing at. My box of condoms is in the middle of my floor. Not from last night. But from whenever Alec was here last. Clearly, living alone has caused me to let go of a few things.

"I live alone!!" I defend. It sort of kills the mood. Which is good, because as I lean back over, I notice something else on my floor.

I flash back through the night for a second. *No. This can't be. Is that what it looks like?* Of course it is. But it's not mine. There is no way it's mine. I didn't black out. Things are blurry, but I remember. I remember making out. I remember vomiting a lot. I remember not having sex. I would remember this. I wonder for a second if I should call attention to it or just hide it, but no. I have to.

"Seriously? Seriously, Sean?" I exclaim as I point.

"Oh my god, is that??"

"Yes, Sean. That is. That is shit. Literal human shit on my floor."

"You don't have a dog?"

"No, Sean. I don't have a dog. And I did not shit on my floor. This is all on you."

"Wait a second. How can you be so sure it was me? We were both wasted. Why couldn't it have been you?"

"Because you blacked out. I didn't."

"Yeah, but since I blacked out, there is no way we can be sure."

"Sean, if there was the slightest hint of a possibility that I shat on my own goddamn floor, I would hide it from you with whatever it took rather than let you know it. This is all you."

"Well, this is a first."

"Sure. You probably go around shitting on people's floors all the time." I don't know whether to be laughing or just plain horrified. There is seriously shit on my floor. I hooked up with a guy who shat on my floor. My life has hit an all-new low.

"I swear to god, I have no recollection of this."

"Well, I happen to know that I occupied my bathroom for most of the night. I do remember that. And I know that at one point when I came out, your head was in the kitchen sink. Apparently, you also decided to pop a squat."

"I do not remember popping a squat. But I'm also not entirely sure I'm ashamed. This is hilarious."

"And seriously gross. You are not leaving here until you have cleaned the shit."

"What am I supposed to do?"

"What the fuck do you mean, what are you supposed to do?

You are going to get a paper towel, you are going to pick up the shit, and you are going to flush it down the toilet. You are then going to return with a new paper towel, and you are going to clean where the shit was." I'm laughing hysterically at this point. It is unreal. This is the kind of thing that doesn't happen in real life, and yet here it is, happening to me.

Sean cleans his shit, his literal actual shit, and then leaves my home, I'm sure never to talk to me again.

Well, I went home with someone. Wasn't that what I wanted? To prove that I could also get some and that Alec is not alone in being a player? I wonder if Alec's date shat on his floor.

I send a text individually to Olivia, Gail, and Sarah.

LYREN
I woke up naked with my high school crush. There was shit on the floor. These are facts.

GAIL
OMG.

OLIVIA
Wait, what?

LYREN
Shit, Liv. Literal human shit.

OLIVIA
Bahahahaha OMG. What? How?

LYREN
I'm not really sure of the exact logistics. I am assuming that at some point in the very drunken night, Sean Trackyn, of high school crush fame, removed his trousers, squatted down, and pushed out a turd. A small

turd, but a turd, nonetheless. We did not have sex after this point.

SARAH
Brunch?

Sarah's response is the obvious winner. I am dying of a hangover, but brunch is a fabulous idea. I sit in a chair, throw my head back, and let my arms hang before the waitress comes up to take our drink order. I order a Diet Coke, but we are in a bar.

"Can I buy you pretty ladies a shot?"

I look up. At the table next to us are two rather attractive gentlemen. This cannot be real.

"Hello there," I said, deadpan. "I had someone shit on my floor last night. The last thing I need in the entire world is a shot."

And with that, both guys are sitting at our table, ordering four cherry bombs. Yes, cherry bombs.

"Is this real life?" I ask Sarah.

"Yes, yes, Lyren. I believe right now, this is your real life."

"OK, so I'll need this story immediately."

Shots turn into more shots and more drinks and suddenly, we are full on day drinking and telling stories with two guys who are completely enamored because I woke up to human poop on my floor.

"So what do you ladies do?"

"I am a starving artist, and Sarah is a spy."

"Sounds intriguing."

"It is."

It's clear early on that Jimmy, as he informs us his name is, and his friend Todd, are very successful with women. Most of our conversation revolves around disgraceful Las Vegas trips and awkward sexual encounters.

"Never have I ever video taped a sexual act," I say, sort of out of nowhere, but our conversation has been racy so far, and I have no plans of really getting to know these guys. It's noon, and I am enjoying free drinks and a Sunday Funday with Sarah for once instead of Alec. Plus, Jimmy is very sexy.

"Oh, this is going to get interesting now," Jimmy says as he and Todd both drink.

"Never have I ever had a fivesome," he says next.

"Who the hell has had a fivesome, except maybe Tiger Woods?" I ask.

"Well, this game isn't easy for me. I spend a lot of time in Las Vegas." Jimmy leans in close to me. "I've done everything," he says slyly.

I'm not sure why it turns me on. He doesn't attempt to hide that he's a bastard. I like his straightforwardness.

"Never have I ever had an STD," I say, and Sarah looks at me in shock. Jimmy and Todd both take a drink. *Sick.*

"OK, I have to explain this now. I don't have AIDS or herpes or anything. I just had whichever one it was that you have to take a pill and it goes away. Minor annoyance. Nothing major. Cleared up many years ago."

"Sick."

"It was a few years ago, I promise."

"What about you, Todd?" I ask.

"Same."

"What, you guys screwed the same girl? Did you have a threesome with her?" Sarah asks, getting more emboldened as I show no hesitation in asking ridiculous things of these guys.

"What happens in Vegas stays in Vegas." He smirks.

"So why do you go to Vegas so much?"

"Why not?" Jimmy responds. "I'm a man with the means to have an amazing time in Vegas."

"Lots of hookers?"

"Oh, I don't need hookers. I do just fine on my own."

This is obvious. Within minutes, I could tell that this guy

doesn't hear the word "no" a whole lot, and I'm surprised by how attractive I can find something technically so repulsive.

So this is how people end up in one-night stands.

After a while, he goes to put his number in my phone, which is lying on the bar. "How do you work this thing?"

"First of all, how do you not know how to work an iPhone at this point in time? And second of all, what's the point of giving me your number? I'm never going to call you. You're old." He is 37.

"Ouch."

"I'm sorry. Were you falling in love with me?"

"Maybe."

"Yeah, OK."

"How many people have you slept with?" he asks me.

"Six," I respond, in all honesty. Sean does not have to be added to that list, thank god.

"Bullshit."

"Dead serious."

"You cannot have slept with only six people and had one of them shit on your floor. That's a law."

"I did not actually have sex with the floor shitter. We just hooked up. And this is not exactly typical behavior for me." But I can see how one might be deceived. I'm almost shocked that my number is only six. Anyone would look at my weekend and assume I am a complete nympho freak. Or at least just really easy.

"I'm going to be your number seven." He looks me straight in the eyes.

"Oh, is that so?"

Somehow, I already know it might be true. I have no idea how this work. I just know that I am not repulsed by the idea of sleeping with him. In fact, I am loving every second of his ridiculous attention.

"I really love the bartenders' shirts here." I change the

subject, not really believing I had said what I did. Sarah is laughing.

"They sell them."

"They do?"

"Do you want one?"

"Yes!" I say. I can't believe I'm being this blatant about using a guy for drinks, a shirt, and a make out, but isn't that what guys do all the time? Lure women in just for sex? He goes off to find my shirt with Todd.

"Lyren, what on earth are you doing?" Sarah asks, but with humor and not judgement.

"I have no idea. Being a player? Having fun?"

"It's cracking me up. Are you going to go home with this guy?"

"I don't know. Maybe actually. He's sort of charming."

"He sort of probably has an STD."

"Yes, I seem to have an attraction to dirtbag men who sleep with hundreds of women these days. In any case, between Alec being on a date last night, and my attempt at diversion being an epic fail, I need redemption."

"The truth comes out."

"Yeah, whatever. Why does he get to have all the fun? Girls can be players, too."

"Just make him wear a condom."

"Doesn't he look like Bradley Cooper?"

"He has incredible blue eyes and Bradley Cooper hair, yes. He's very good-looking. Which is what makes him such a great player."

"It's like Bradley Cooper in *Hangover.* His best look."

"Yes, I see it."

"Will you judge me?"

"Have I ever? I'm not judging you. I understand why you need attention and how you're annoyed with Alec going on a date after sleeping with you. We can't discuss that when these guys are about to come back, but I'm going to make you talk about it eventually."

"Yes, boss."

"But no. I'm not judging you as long as you're safe here."

"Hey, they don't have the one you like. Do you want a different one?" Jimmy comes back.

"Oh no, it's fine. I just really like the saying on that one." I pretend to pout, but I am impressed he went and looked. It's cute.

He then leans in to ask the bartender something and goes back over to the shirts. The next thing I know, the bartender is in a corner taking his shirt off, and Jimmy is handing him a new one.

"I'd wash this before wearing it if I were you." Jimmy comes back with the shirt off the bartender's back, and I am in awe.

"You seriously just bought me the shirt off some guy's back?"

"I seriously did, yes."

"Wow. That's sort of amazing."

"You're sort of amazing."

"What do you say we hit up some place else?" Todd interrupts.

And just like that, Sunday Funday continues in full bloom. Todd and Jimmy pay for all of Sarah and my drinks, and a rather expensive dinner later where Sarah grabs the menu and pretty much orders the entire left side. Kind of funny since she's getting married and all and has no intention of touching Todd, much to his dismay.

The day turns into night, and we are still drinking. Somehow, we have not gotten bored of each other. Sarah and I can't stop staring at each other, wondering how all of this is really happening.

I wake up to the sound of my alarm. It is 6 a.m. on Monday morning. I am naked. There is a naked stranger in my bed next to me. There are no sheets. I remember that I had to throw them in the wash before brunch because god knows what other havoc Sean may have wreaked in my life, but then I never came back home to finish the job. I breathe a sigh of relief when I see a condom wrapper on the floor.

"Uh . . . Jimmy?"

"Hey you." He smiles and pulls me in.

"Yeah, this is nice and all, but I need to go to work."

"Oh my god, it's Monday."

"Yes, it is Monday."

"Jesus Christ."

"My sentiments exactly."

He starts to put on his clothes, and I reach for something, anything, to wear to work. My hangover is insane. Or am I still drunk? Hard to tell.

"Where are we?" he asks when we are outside.

"You live that way." I point and walk over to my car.

I don't care that I will never see him again. And just like that, I have experienced my first one-night stand. Hey, at least it was more of a full-day stand.

Chapter Ten

"Lyren, come into my office." Claire comes by my cubicle as I'm packing up to leave. I can tell from her tone that I am in trouble, and my stomach drops below the floor.

Two weeks after my one-day stand, my work performance is continuing to sink.

"What's up?" At least I am sober for this meeting, though it's still hard to pretend I look like I care.

"Lyren, you have not been doing high-quality work lately."

"Explain." This is the best attempt I have at trying. I don't give a shit.

"You used to turn in multiple manuscripts a week. Now it's down to one, and they need to be checked again because we have found additional errors." She holds out my latest manuscript, which has a few highlighted points to showcase my slacking. Maybe this is it. Maybe I am being fired right here.

I'm tempted to look at Claire and say, *"Of course that manuscript has errors. I had maybe two functioning brain cells that morning and they were both trying to process the fact that I had a trifecta weekend including sleeping with my best friend's brother, hooking up with a high school crush who shat my floor, and then screwing some Bradley-Cooper-lookalike on my sheet-less bed until the wee hours of Monday morning. What do you expect, Dragon Lady?"*

"I'm sorry. I have a lot going on right now." It's the best I can do.

"We're going to put you on a performance evaluation plan. If your numbers don't go up in the next month, we will have to let you go." I know what she is saying. These are the first formalities of being fired. "Do you understand?"

"Yes." *Yes, Claire. Yes, I understand.*

I walk to my car stunned. Sure, my job totally sucks. In fact, I completely hate it. But I have rent. A car. I cannot get fired. It is my fault for slacking off and not caring about anything but sex and drinking, but suddenly everything hits me. Not just my job. But *everything*.

I sit in the driver's seat and sob hysterically. When the hell did everything go so wrong? When did I last feel I had everything so under control? A boyfriend I loved, a plan for the future, the credentials to be dumb enough to think made me deserve it. I did everything right! I got the grades. I did the volunteering. I interned. I didn't fuck around. And where did it get me? A dead-end job I'm failing at. An ex half-relationship that still haunts me and leaves me wondering if I'm even capable of loving someone anymore. At least not of someone who could actually love me back. Am I so unlovable? Am I just a toy for men to flirt with and then cast aside when it's not shiny anymore?

I am sobbing for Alec, wondering if he gives a shit about me or if he's bored, or if I care because I *care* care or because I'm bored too. I am sobbing because I am a hypocrite for sleeping around and judging other people for doing everything I am doing now. I hate all my friends for pairing off and settling down and having their shit together while I'm stranded and a failure. Fuck all of their stupid boyfriends and fiancés that actually call them when they are supposed to and who show up when it's not just fun and who are there even when they aren't getting laid.

And fuck jobs where you are respected and paid and get a sense of purpose or fulfillment. And fuck Claire. And fuck Evan. And fuck Alec. And fuck weddings. And fuck fuck fuck everything.

Three nights later, my mom, Emma, and I are out for sushi to discuss her bachelorette and shower plans. I'm feeling miserable about my entire life and can think of nothing I want to do less than talk about a fucking bachelorette party. Not showing my misery is taking up every single ounce of energy I can muster.

Despite my irritation, I have taken my performance plan seriously and stepped it up at work as much as I can. They might still fire me, but I can make it harder by showing I'm good.

"I don't want to do anything huge like a big trip to Vegas or anything. It's more important that I have as many of my friends there as possible, so I don't want to make it too hard. What about just a fun Michigan lake weekend? We could rent a house and some jet skis, maybe. Or a boat rental?" Emma is going through her ideas. None of them are bad. I just don't want to talk about it.

"That sounds fun. How many friends are you thinking about inviting?" I feign support.

"Well, there's of course the six bridesmaids, and then you can bring some friends, Mom, so you have something else to do if you don't want to be part of all the activities."

"Oh, while I would be happy to invite Andrea, and she'd be happy to come, we certainly wouldn't stay in the house with your girls. We'd get a hotel room so we could do our own thing and not spoil your wilder fun," Mom adds.

"Whatever you want! But OK, in addition to the bridesmaids,

there's Lisa, Katie, I'd want to invite Maggie, even though she lives out of state and might not come in . . . "

I'm barely even listening as Emma rattles off all the friends who will drop everything and spend their time and money to celebrate Emma being chosen by a dude.

"So how many did you just name?" I ask, thinking about how big of a damn house she's gonna need. So great, I can spend the next month trying to research party houses.

"If Mom and Andrea get a separate room, I think that's 12, including you?"

"I mean, I can stay with Mom and Andrea. It's not like I'm part of your friend group."

"Don't be ridiculous! You're my maid of honor! You have to be part of everything!"

"Plus, you have to plan most of it," my mom says.

I'm trying not to break down and snap. "OK. Where in Michigan?" I am asking questions, but I'm not effusive about it.

"I dunno, maybe Traverse City? Saugatuck? Or even just Forrest Beach? Pretty close?"

"Isn't Forrest Beach still really expensive?" I ask. I'll probably be unemployed by summer, when I have to plan this for.

"That's why we do some research. Not expecting people to pay a ton."

"Yeah, that's good. Some of us are poor," I add a bit dramatically.

"You're not poor!" my mom chimes in.

"Kind of. But whatever. OK, what else? Boat rental? For all 12 or 14 with Mom and Andrea? Like a sailboat? A catamaran? A celebrity yacht with a personal chef?" I'm trying to be funny and remember that I have a personality. That I'm supposed to be happy for my sister, and that planning bachelorette parties is supposed to be fun.

"Yes, the last one, please."

"Noted. Will add 'win lottery' to my to-do list."

"Geez, I was kidding, Lyren. No one expects you to pay for everything."

"Well, that's good because if I'm paying for everything, you're getting 14 Big Macs and the party is at my apartment."

"Lyren, you know I'm going to help pay for stuff, and all the girls will pay their own way. Stop being so dramatic," my mom snaps at me. She's right. I'm being an asshole. I don't want to be here. But she doesn't know that. Emma doesn't know that either.

"I'm gonna run to the bathroom." Emma gets up and walks away.

My mom turns to me with a serious look on her face. "Lyren, while she's out of earshot, I just want to say you're being really rude and not a very supportive maid of honor. Your sister is getting married, and instead of being excited and helpful, you're acting like this is a chore. You're hurting her feelings."

Before I even start to reply, the tears begin. "Mom, has it occurred to you that my life is a mess? That maybe focusing on someone else's happy ending and being all cheerful for them while you're falling apart is impossible?" I choke through tears.

"I have no idea what it's like to be attracted to a good, stable man anymore. I'm hooking up with my best friend's brother, who doesn't give a fuck about me, just so I have something. Oh yeah, and I'm on a performance plan at work. So, I'm sorry if I'm hurting my sister's feelings by not being a perfect maid of honor. What, does she care that my life is a disaster? Do you? All you guys care about is that her party goes nicely. Do you know how annoying it is having to fuss over someone else's love when your heart is fucked? Do we make all of our unemployed friends spend all their money and focus on us when we get a promotion? No. Just weddings. And I know I'm not being enthusiastic. It actually has taken every ounce of my energy not to break down, so thank you for setting me off, because now I have to stop crying before she gets back." I look away from her, trying to get my breathing back to normal.

"OK, OK. I'm sorry. What do you mean you're on a performance plan? What happened?" My mom suddenly realizes she started a scene.

"I don't want to talk about it right now! I wasn't going to bring up my shit. I'm trying to be a good sister. But I'm not. I'm not a good sister or a good friend. I hate this shit. Call me bitter if you want. I am bitter. I am bitter that I have to spend my money and attention celebrating everyone else while nothing in my life is going right."

"Lyren, I did not know you were feeling all of this. You said things with Alec were just fun and that you didn't need a boyfriend. You said you didn't care. What happened?"

"Nothing. It is what it always was. Casual friends with benefits. But it bothers me more than I admit when he goes on real dates. And I've tried to do the same and just have some casual fun, but it doesn't bring me any fulfillment. Nothing is right. I was supposed to be a writer. I was supposed to be doing interesting, meaningful work, and now I'm desperately trying to cling to a shitty job just so I don't end up homeless."

"You will never end up homeless. You have us, and we will always be here to support you. So stop that. And maybe it's time to start thinking about what else you can do so you aren't stuck. And start dating guys you don't already know are nonstarters."

"OK, Emma is going to come back, and I don't want her to know you yelled at me for being a bad sister and I started crying. I'm gonna go to the bathroom for a second and fix my face." My mom takes a deep breath and collects herself, and I get up and pass Emma while trying not to be obvious about wiping my eyes. It's dark enough in the restaurant that maybe she won't notice.

"Hey, sorry, now I have to pee!" I say fake cheerfully as she keeps walking.

I have no idea if my mom will say anything to Emma while I am away. I only have a few moments in the bathroom, and I can't dwell on my feelings. I have to clean up and reset.

I breathe a sigh of relief that I let some of that out. It actually was nice to know it was all so bottled up and I was hiding it from my mom. That being said, I don't want her advice about dating or jobs. I KNOW everything she was trying to say. How do you just get a new job and boyfriend? If it were that easy, I'd have done it already.

But when I get home, I text Steve back.

Olivia and I meet up with Alec and his friend Dan at a bar the following Saturday, because even though my work performance has gone up, I'm still petrified of being fired and obviously need to drink to make myself feel better about it.

The three of us had gone out for Bloody Marys earlier in our sweats, and Alec went out straight from there.

"You don't need to change. You look fine!" he'd said.

"Alec, girls can't go out at night in sweats," Olivia informed him.

"Why? Who are you trying to impress tonight?"

"I happen to be meeting someone later tonight, for your information," I responded, even though it felt weird to mention this to Alec. Even if we are just friends.

"Ooooh, who's this?"

"New guy. Met him a few weekends ago. He's in the city tonight, so I'll probably meet him for a drink later. Not that it's any of your business."

Steve returned a few days ago, and we've been texting a bit. I've been trying to be excited. Maybe he'll be great! Something new to get me out of this funk.

"That's great! Good for you. Alright, well I'm gonna go meet Dan. See you girls in a few. Don't take an eternity, or we'll be shit wasted when you get there."

I love telling Alec when I have a date because he goes out

with girls all the time and I have to pretend I don't think about it. It is never acceptable for me to look jealous, but I have to wonder if Alec is the slightest bit jealous that I am meeting a guy out later. If he is, he certainly doesn't let on.

Our break from drinking was much-needed, and in half an hour, I look like a new person. I put on a low-cut black dress that accentuates all the right places and black platform pumps. It's amazing what a hair straightener and a little makeup can do.

"Wow, look at you!" Alec says as we approach. He gives me a hug and kisses me on the cheek. "What are you drinking?"

"Oh, I'll have a vodka soda."

"Two vodka sodas," he says to the bartender and takes a sip of his beer. He hands Olivia and I our drinks.

"Thanks," I say, then take a sip.

"How much have we missed?" Olivia asks.

"Oh, you know. Just a few beers. I'm a bit drunker than you last saw me. You girls look more sober. And more delicious. That was only directed at one of you, by the way. Olivia, you look, uh, nice." Alec grins at me while Olivia rolls her eyes, and I'm very glad I went home and changed. Alec's attention doesn't falter from me. I don't know how to put my finger on why. Maybe it's just relief to not be losing it yet. Maybe I can fall in love with Steve and be the first to leave this situation.

"So, Olivia, how have you been? I haven't seen you in a while," Dan asks.

"Oh good. Working mostly."

"Still doing social work?"

"Yeah, I manage a caseload and I tutor with Lyren at a junior high on the South Side once a week. Keeps me busy, I guess. How are you?"

"Wow, what a good person you are. So different from your brother. It makes no sense at all."

"Hey! I'm a great person! I'm the fun one, and you all need

way more of that in your life. We need to take this party to the dance floor." Alec takes my hand and leads the way.

The four of us start dancing obnoxiously to some new hip-hop song, and I laugh at Alec's lack of rhythm, though he takes it upon himself to pull me close and start grinding. We have no moves, but we really don't need them. We're looking plain silly, but Alec wants me, so I don't mind. I never used to love dancing all that much, but with Alec, it always has a way of making me feel desired, regardless of how stupid we may look to onlookers.

"You guys are so gross," Olivia says from where she is standing nearby, talking to Dan. It's probably wrong to be grinding on Alec in front of his little sister but he only stops briefly to talk to them, and we're right back at it.

"I'm gonna get another drink. Want one?" Liv comes up and asks.

"Thanks, love!" I keep checking my phone to see if Steve is on his way yet. I haven't quite forgotten that I'm supposed to be meeting him.

"You texting your boy?" Alec asks. Apparently, he hasn't forgotten either.

"Maybe." I text Steve the name of the bar I'm at and tell him to let me know when he's close. I certainly don't need him to see me all over Alec if he walks into the bar unexpectedly. Not that it's stopping me.

"Put your phone away," Alec says, taking my hand and pulling me into a spin that winds me against him again. He lets himself get too close for a while and runs his hands down my legs.

"Now you're just being naughty," I whisper, moving into him and making it easier for him to continue in his seduction. *Why is this so easy for him?*

"Mmm, that's what I do best," he whispers back, kissing my neck.

By the time Steve texts me that he's at the bar, I'm

completely, grossly, drunkenly making out with Alec in a dark corner. I have no idea where Dan or Olivia are at this point, and I quite frankly do not care as long as Alec's hand keeps easing up my dress, causing me to push it away and pretend like I'm not loving every second of it.

"I have to go," I say, pulling away and moving his hands.

"Noooo."

"Yes."

"You're evil, you know," he says.

I smile. "You already knew that."

I'm fuzzy and can't figure out any way to exit the bar very clearly. Meeting up with a guy I met only once, especially a friend of a coworker, is probably a terrible idea. It's midnight, so my only hope is that he's in as bad a state as I am so I can't make too big an ass of myself. I'm not even sure I'll recognize him.

I step outside of the bar, but it's really crowded on the street. I note to myself that if Alec did to me what I just did to him, I'd probably hate him for it, and I'd be really upset. Maybe he is somewhat bothered by it more than he is willing to let on. I kind of hate admitting that I hope so.

"Lyren!" I turn around when I hear my name. Luckily, my date apparently remembers what I look like. He's cute and taller than I remember.

"Hey!" I hug him. If I were sober, I wouldn't have made such a bold approach, but he doesn't seem to mind.

"Well, where do you want to go?" he asks.

"Um, not here. I'm sick of it," I respond. The last person I want to be around with Steve is Alec. "Probably somewhere late-night because it's already well past midnight."

"Good call. Sorry I'm so late."

"No problem! Just try not to judge my level of intoxication too harshly."

We go to one of the few late-night bars around and find a seat. It isn't too crowded yet because late-night establishments

never get very busy until almost 2. Even so, the music is pierc-
ing, and it will be difficult to have a conversation here.

"I hate this bar but options are limited," I comment.

"What?" he shouts, and I repeat myself, shouting back.

It's no mystery that I'm not going to be able to talk tomorrow. But we laugh about the noise, anyway.

"So you're an actuary, you said?"

"Yeah, for an insurance company."

"Awesome. How is that going?"

"Well, it's not always exciting, but I really don't mind it, and
I'm thankful to have a job at all in this godforsaken economy. It
is very financially rewarding as well. You're an editor?"

"Copyeditor," I correct. "Just saying 'editor' almost makes
me sound cool and important or something." It's hard to have a
normal conversation over the music, but I like that we're trying.

"Then I'm just gonna refer to you as the 'editor chick' whenever anyone asks about you. Cool?"

"Sure thing," I laugh.

He has a nice smile but big lips. I have a weird thing about
not liking guys with big lips. They are messy kissers. I like nice,
neat mouths and sharp jaws. Like Alec has.

"So tell me about yourself."

"Hmm . . . I love classic rock, rap, peppers of all kinds, *Law
and Order.* I'm a Social Democrat. I think that black is the best
color because of the statement and power it makes. I wrote a
paper on it in high school. I tutor once a week on the South Side,
and I want to make a difference in the world, but never will
because I'm too busy drinking and watching the *Food Network.*"

"Wow . . . that was a lot of information to come off the top of
the head of a supposedly drunk person. So who's your favorite
band?"

"Ever?"

"Yeah."

"Guns N' Roses. Hands down," I say.

"What?"

"What?"

"I just wasn't expecting that is all. I mean, they are cool. 'Sweet Child O' Mine' is a great tune."

"Yeah, yeah. Too obvious. 'Estranged' is a great song. 'Rocket Queen' is great. What is the best band of all time in your opinion?"

"Well, DMB."

"Oh god, you're one of *those.*"

"What? One of what?" He actually looks upset about my disapproval.

Sign of weakness. Strike one.

"Dave Mathews Band is so annoying. He sounds constipated when he sings."

"What? No way. This coming from a GNR fan? Come on, Axl sounds like he has a rod up his ass, nevermind constipated."

Getting his balls back. Good. Earning back some credibility.

"Axl has passion and energy in his voice. Anyway, here's the real reason I don't like DMB. DMB fans are the most annoying people on the planet."

"What? That's bullshit! First of all, I'm a DMB fan, and I'm absolutely awesome. Second, how can you judge a band by its fans?"

"They ruin it for me! The same way that Bengals fans suck. I hate them. Therefore, I wish their team eternal failure."

"Not fair. And what do you have against Bengals fans?"

"Their god awful cheer and the way they shout it. 'Who-Dey think gon beat dem Bengals?' First of all, everyone, because the Bengals, in fact, suck. Second, you sound like a gorilla. That cheer is not English. Use your words, people! And third, their helmets invoke regurgitation. Seriously, how does anyone watch them with their horrid dizzy stripes running around?" I am far too drunk to care about being charming.

"You hate a team for the helmets!?"

"Yes!" He laughs at me. "And 'Da Bears' isn't exactly grammatically perfect."

"'Da Bears' is awesome."

"Anyway, what's so awful about Dave fans?"

"Well, for one thing, the fact that you all call him Dave. You are not his friend. You don't go hang out on Tuesdays after work. It's a whole band, not one guy. You're not on a first-name basis with him. You've never even met him."

"Maybe I hang out with him all the time. Maybe he comes to my house on Christmas and eats ham with my family."

"Then you can call him Dave. But only when referring to the person, not the band."

"OK. What else?"

"DMB fans all think they are so cool and chill all the time. Walk around worshipping an artist because he wrote three good songs."

"Three? What!? Are you kidding me?"

Steve is being nicer than me, but picks up on my sarcasm and cynicism enough that I'm not bored. There is nothing worse than someone who takes offense at a joke or who tries to be sarcastic and then backtracks to show they mean no harm. I can't stand when people pretend to be sarcastic. You have to mean it.

"'Stay or Leave', 'Crush'." I try to remember the third DMB song I like. "'Grace is Gone'. Those are three lyrically beautiful songs, so I can get over the irritation of Dave's voice."

"You just called him Dave." He smiles.

"Not the same!"

"There are a lot of other great songs. You really should give them a try. I'll get you to listen and understand."

"Yeah, right. Think you're the first fool who has tried to convert me?"

"Well, I'm incredibly charming." He smiles. "You can try to convert me to GNR. I could be persuaded."

I didn't offer.

"You don't need me to convert you. If you had any sense of awesome, you'd know. There are other contenders for greatness that could be easily argued, and I'd listen. DMB? No way. No real passion. A great song to me is one where the artists are vocally and instrumentally competent and write a song where the musical aspect backs up the lyrics, creating a complete overall *feeling*. That's why I love 'Estranged'. The song is about being lonely and desperate, and the music actually *sounds* lonely and desperate. Very few songs really pull it off. That's why I give those three Dave Matthews songs some level of credit. Overall, they can't even compete as a band."

It's not fully true. I just like challenging people and seeing what they back up their opinions with or if they just throw shit out there to say it with no relevance or meaning. He doesn't defend this last point. I win.

"Whatever." He laughs and smiles at me.

For lack of anything better to do, I kiss him. I remember why I don't prefer big lips. He's sloppy but not bad in general. I like how large his stature is as a whole. It makes me feel petite. But his hands are sort of sausagey. Not a huge fan of that. It's just a kiss, not a make out, and then we pull away.

"Well, I certainly wasn't expecting that."

"I can't say I planned to do it."

He grins, and I let out sort of a cackle laugh as I tend to do when I have no other response. I wonder if this is yet another man who will let me walk all over him within a few dates, thus boring me to tears. I never like nice guys. I hope, for both of our sakes, that he is not one of these people.

"I'm not a very predictable person. Oh, and I've been drinking."

"You're really something."

He's doing that thing that I hate. When a guy I don't know yet gets all sparkly eyed and complimentary, and because I am crazy, it turns me off. But I'm trying not to be overly critical, and there are enough positives about this guy to warrant giving him a chance. He's good-looking but not stunning, which is perfect, masculine, has a job, is smart, and isn't super cheesy and sweet. Quite frankly, he's a perfect on-paper catch.

We stay for another drink, joking about foods we like, and talking about other people in the bar until I realize I'm about to pass out.

"Think it's time to go," I say.

He agrees and asks if I'd like him to walk me home. A perfect gentleman. While it's a nice offer, I'm tired and would prefer to hop in a cab. We kiss goodbye one more time and agree to see each other again. I'm not in love, but I give myself a few ounces of credit just for being open-minded about a date.

"So, am I a total and complete whore for last night?" I ask Olivia at Clark's Diner the next morning.

She's having her typical egg white omelet with chicken breast and veggies while I stuff my face with pancakes. Having a 24-hour diner within walking distance of my apartment is great and terrible all at once. I keep reminding myself I want to lose weight, but that I can start eating healthy maybe Monday.

"You mean for practically having sex with my brother in a bar? Kind of." She laughs.

"I'm sorry."

"Oh, I don't care . . . that much. But don't you ever bitch about being a third wheel with me and Chris ever again."

"Fair enough. I'm sorry. That was pretty gross of me."

"I didn't pay attention. I left to meet Chris once you guys started getting really nasty. I was very drunk myself and had needs of my own."

"Understandable. But I meant the whore thing, not so much because I was practically having sex with Alec in a bar, because

I actually have no regrets regarding that situation at all. Which, I suppose, says a lot about my moral compass in the first place. Because I left practically having sex with your brother to go meet a new guy that had been texting me all night."

"I can see how one might feel like that is rather whorish behavior. You're kind of on a whore kick anyway." I laugh. Olivia knows I would never take offense to her confirming my assessment. "But whatever. You didn't know the new guy, and he was out before you and met you out late, too. It's not like he knows you were doing it."

Alec must have gone home with someone else to alleviate the situation. I don't like the thought of it.

"Well, whatever. Steve was nice."

"Do you like him?"

"Mreh. He's cool. Pretty cute. Somewhat sarcastic, which does help his cause."

"Did you make out?"

"We kissed a bit. I think I kissed him mostly out of boredom. He has really big lips."

"Some people are really into that."

"I'm not. Kind of sloppy." I make a face, showcasing a reaction to a messy make out, and she chuckles.

"Are you going to see him again?"

"Yes, we are supposed to go on a real date next Saturday, actually. He's taking me to Tuscany because I mentioned that I love Little Italy. Evidently, he actually listens when I talk."

"How dare he do such a thing."

"Right?" I laugh.

"Try to keep an open mind. He seems like a good guy with his shit together, which is what you always claim you want. It wouldn't kill you to like a nice guy for once."

"I know."

"So, Chris asked me to move in with him," she says, deadpan, waiting for my reaction.

"Holy shit!" I gasp. "I'm sitting here blabbing about the multiple people I made out with last night, and you're keeping this major information away from me? Details!"

"Well, it's weird. I guess I hadn't really thought about it much before, but it does make sense. He's getting his own place soon, and he wants me to move there."

"When is soon? Are you going to?"

"Yeah, I guess so. We've been together for two years. It makes sense to start moving forward. He's moving in about two months. Big changes."

"What do your parents think?"

"I haven't run it by them yet, but I think they'll be OK with it. I mean, considering the way Alec lives his life, they don't really have a lot of room to be judgmental about me moving in with my long-term boyfriend."

"Good call. Do you guys talk about getting married?"

I know they'll get married, but god, please give me a damn year.

"Not too much yet. We have some conversations about it, but nothing too serious. He's just starting his job, and I really want to take some time and do some serious volunteering still. Not that I do anything to move forward with that process. But I don't want to do that once I'm settled down. We're not in a serious rush, but I guess this is a big step."

"This is a huge step! I'm so excited for you guys!"

I'm not lying. I *am* happy for Olivia. I *do* want Olivia to be happy. And Emma. And Sarah. And Gail. I just wish they could all be happy with their stuff, while I also were happy. About anything.

"Thanks! I hope it works out."

"It will. You guys are great together."

Another one bites the dust . . .

Chapter Eleven

S teve is picking me up at 8. My intention is to be sober, but
I'm meeting Gail and Brad for brunch because they're in
town. He travels a lot for work, and this time she decided to join.
I mean, it's just a Bloody Mary.

"Sorry we're late," Gail's friend Judy says, pulling up a chair
as her boyfriend Sam puts his arm around her.

Gail didn't tell me Judy was meeting us out. Judy and her
boyfriend drive me insane. She smiles at him, and he starts
rubbing her leg. I'm not against PDA. Obviously, considering
Alec and I can't stop touching each other in public. In fact,
sometimes I think it's sort of cute. But they are so extra. They
are so mooshy about it. Also, they look awkward together.
Something about them is just wrong, and it makes watching
them kiss disgusting. But that's just mean. Either way, I puke in
my mouth a little as they stare at each other for three solid
minutes as if they haven't been together for the last 24 straight
hours. Gag. Barf. Fart. I don't know how Gail stays friends with

her. Maybe it's just because they don't live in the same city, so she doesn't have to put up with it that much.

"No problem, we already ordered our Bloody Marys," Brad says casually.

The difference between Judy and Gail's relationships is worth noting. I have to admit I like Gail and Brad a lot more together, when he's not totally disregarding her needs as a person, that is.

"I just love this place! I'm so glad Sam introduced me!"

I get that she loves Sam, but putting his name into each sentence she says isn't necessary, especially when he's actively pawing at her. Also, "this place" is down the street from me. It's not like it's some great little hide out that Sam discovered once.

And I'm being a bitch.

"So how was your drive in?" I ask.

"Not too bad. I was really tired last night, though. We pretty much just ate and went to sleep," Gail laughs as she says this.

I make my 93rd mental note never to become an old 20-something. It's possible to be in a relationship and still maintain a healthy social life. I swear I've seen it done a few times.

"What did you do?" she asks.

"Just went out with a few high school friends in the South Loop. Nothing too major. Was in by 3." I had made an appearance out with Sarah and my old friends. Luckily, Sean wasn't there. Probably don't ever need to see floor-shitter again. I smirk to myself.

"I can't even remember the last time I was out that late," Sam interjects. "Probably college."

"Not true," Judy adds. "You go out with the guys late sometimes. You always drunk-text me."

"Well, not very often. I have a job."

"So do I," I laugh. *Well, hopefully.* "I'm just not old. What are you all up to tonight?"

"Going to dinner with Rick and Lane. Maybe gonna watch a

movie afterward if you want to come over and just chill," Gail explains.

Couples are always doing couple things together with other couples. It's the only thing that sometimes makes me wish I were a couple. OK, maybe not the *only* thing.

"Oh, I'm going on a date, actually. He's picking me up at 8 and we're going to Little Italy."

"Who is this guy?" Gail asks.

I haven't had time to catch up with her, although I can't really put my finger on what exactly I've been so busy with.

"New guy. Met him a few weeks ago. This will be our first legit date."

"So fun! We should totally crash their date!" Gail says to Brad.

"That would be pretty awesome."

"Yeah, I'll kill you," I respond. Gail just might do that if I let her think for one second that it would be acceptable. "Anyway, we were wasted the last time we hung out, so I don't even remember half of what he said. He was very cute about planning this date though, so we'll see how it goes."

"That's so exciting! I love beginnings!"

"Don't get ahead of yourself. It's one date. Do you know how many guys I go on one to three dates with and then get totally sick of?"

"True. It *is* you."

"Right. Glad we have that established."

Sam starts ordering whiskey halfway through brunch, and it becomes clear that Saturday Funday is officially in session. Most of the conversation centers around Sam's job and Judy's new dog's potty training escapades. Brad starts bragging about something, and Gail stays relatively quiet. I feel bad admitting I'm bored with the banter and am seriously in need of a change in scenery. It's just that my own career is far from interesting or anything worth talking about, and if I'm going to spend my

Saturday day drinking, I want it to be more about having fun than talking about the stress associated with jobs and dogs. I blatantly check my phone at the table even though it's rude.

ALEC

Where you at, boo?

Alec is clearly drunk. He'd never address me as "boo" sober. It makes me laugh.

LYREN

Watching the Cubs spring training game. Where are you?

I love that the Cubs are on because it means that summer will arrive shortly. I don't love that the Cubs are getting defeated, though.

ALEC

Watching a real baseball team. Meet us out!

"Who are you texting?" Gail asks.

"Oh, Alec. He's out around here with some people watching the Sux. Do you guys want to go meet up with them?"

"We can for a little while."

I'm thrilled with Gail's response because if she said no, I couldn't abandon them, but the idea of being in a bar with real music and baseball and more people is really appealing now that I'm a few drinks in. Brad and Sam are already toast. At least with more people around, we won't be talking about depressing shit anymore.

"OK, cool."

"Are you gonna be OK for your date later?"

"It's only 2. I'm fine. I've got hours."

This might have been true if I were just staying out with

these four, but meeting Alec and his friends is dangerous to my level of semi-sobriety.

In any case, we pay our bill and relocate to a bar where the music is too loud to talk to anyone without screaming. It's perfect for what I want right now, although Gail doesn't agree and Brad is having difficulty standing. Judy and Sam are already dancing, staring awkwardly into each other's eyes.

"Hey girl!" Alec gives me a big hug, and I say hello to his crew. Everyone is dancing, and I join right in while Brad gets drinks. "I thought you had a date tonight," Alec adds, spinning me around.

"I do. He's not picking me up until 8."

"Oooh, classy. Real dinner?"

"You know it."

"So, are you two like a real thing yet?"

"Psh!" I wave my hand. "It's our first real date. I'm seeing where it goes."

"Good news for me." He smiles, and we keep dancing. It's cute he cares. Clearly, he's not mad that I left him the last time we hung out.

"Hey, Lyren, I think we're gonna go. Brad is falling over, and I need to deal with that. It's been fun hanging out, though!" Gail gives me a hug.

I feel sort of guilty for not having paid more attention to her, but we weren't really doing much of anything. I knew they wouldn't last long if I brought them here. We can always catch up on Sunday, maybe just the two of us.

"OK, have a good day and night!"

"Enjoy your date later!" She leaves, and I'm left to dance with Alec and his friends, ordering drink after drink.

"What time do you have to leave?" Alec asks me around 4.

"Well, I should probably get a nap in before my shower, so at least 6. Yes, 6, the absolute latest. I need a nap to sort of at least pretend to sober up. God, what has gotten into me? I am never sober anymore."

"Some people think that's a problem."

"Some people are wrong." I laugh, but I realize the chances of me being sober on this date are slim to none. Maybe my mom is right. I *do* sabotage my dates before they can even happen. I'm not doing it intentionally. My being out right now has nothing to do with whether I'll enjoy this date or be my normal self on it. It's just that I'm having a really good time dancing with Alec and hanging out with his friends, and I really don't feel like leaving yet just because I know that it's the right thing to do.

At 6:10, my phone is dead, and it's beyond time I head back home. I almost hate that Alec wishes me good luck on my date. I want him to hate that I'm going out with another guy. I want him to be sitting there wondering if I'm going to get all pretty and wondering if he's going to make me laugh. I want him to miss me when I walk out the door, and I want him to wish he were walking out the door with me. But I know that none of those things are even remotely true, and I'm stupid to be thinking them.

I wake up an hour later and jump in the shower, never bothering to charge my phone. I'm running late as usual and have no idea what I'm going to wear. Everything is spinning in the shower. *How the hell am I going to pull it together?* I blast Rihanna to try to wake me up, but this is generally the music that puts me in the mood to party, rather than sit at a nice, respectable dinner with a nice, respectable man.

Shit. It's 7:40 p.m., and Steve has probably texted me a hundred times. I wonder if he's assuming by now that I've stood him up. I'm going to be really annoyed if I mess up my date and thus left my friends for nothing. Sobriety is slowly coming into focus as I plug in my charger and dial his number.

"Hello stranger!" He picks up.

"I'm so sorry! My phone died, and I hopped in the shower without even thinking of charging it!"

"It's OK. I was beginning to wonder if you were ditching me. I got worried."

"I'm so sorry."

"Well, hopefully you're about ready because I am on the way."

"OK, great. I'm gonna finish getting dressed and all. My phone is charging now, so you can text me when you're here." I'm impressed that despite not hearing from me, he still started driving over.

"Sounds great. I can't wait to see you."

"Ditto," I say, even though I'm relatively indifferent to the entire situation. I can't imagine admitting to a guy that I couldn't wait to see him. Maybe because I've never actually been on a date with a guy I couldn't wait to see. Not since Evan, anyway. And we never went on a real date.

I throw on a dark gray pencil skirt with a peach peplum top and a big statement necklace. I don't have much time to fix my hair and makeup, but I think I do an alright job before slipping into my stilettos and grabbing a coat.

"Do you like calamari?" he asks me when we're settled in. I've always loved Tuscany. It's a restaurant in Little Italy with an upscale but authentic vibe. Minimal decor. A good buzz of energy. Every table is full but not too loud. I feel like I'm doing a good job of hiding how much I'd been drinking earlier.

"Sure. Their bread and olive oil is absolutely fantastic though, so I need to try not to fill up too much on this stuff or I won't eat my dinner." I'm hoping some of the bread absorbs the alcohol.

"Eat as much as you want. I won't be offended if you don't finish. So what have you been up to the past week?"

"Well, work. Tutoring."

"Yeah, you never told me much about that."

"I didn't realize it was that exciting."

"I'd love to hear what made you want to do that."

It's a good question. Honestly, I'm almost confused about being with someone who's asking questions about my actual interests. It's nice.

"I studied a lot of inner-city school issues in college. I guess everyone has something political that they are sort of passionate about or whatever, and education was my thing. I was a journalism major."

"So why aren't you a teacher?"

"Too much external bullshit. State standards and all that. Parents up your ass constantly. And I have absolutely no patience. Let's be honest. You've seen me—do you really think I should have the fate of America's youth in my hands?"

"I think you'd be really good at it. You're so passionate."

"I'm passionate about the issues. Our education system is going downhill rapidly, and I just don't think our country is doing enough to stop it. Anyway, the more I researched, the more I cared and wanted to continue doing the research. I didn't really know what I could do with it, so I figured I'd get a job at a magazine or something and try to write articles. I'd love to do work sort of like Jonathan Kozol."

Talking about my past passions almost makes me miss myself. It's been a while since I've done anything close to topical research. Maybe I should start again just cause.

"Anyway, out of college, I wasn't really sure what to do, and I'm great at grammar, so I saw the job at the educational materials company and applied. It's easy enough, and they send me paychecks every two weeks. I was supposed to be working on writing articles in my downtime, but it turns out, having a full-time job can be really draining. A lot more draining than college was. So I never did. But I started volunteering because I wanted to stay in touch with schools and figured I could use it as a foundation for some of my research, but I can't say I've done too much of that, either. It's a nice thing though, and I enjoy it, and it's how I met my friend Olivia, so obviously that part is really important to me. She's one of my closest friends and one of the best humans I've ever met. Truly. She would do anything for anyone. Kind of funny how different she is from her older brother, actually." I'm babbling, and I'm not sure why. It's almost like I'm clearing my head rather than making conversation with a new guy.

"Wow, your passion is intoxicating."

"What are you passionate about?"

"That's a really intense question."

"I'm a really intense person." I sort of like that this guy is bringing this out of me. Hopefully, Steve can continue the conversation.

"I mean, I guess I'm pretty into sports." He shrugs, pondering whether there is anything else that really sparks his interest.

"Every guy likes sports. What do you really care about?"

"Like issues in the world?"

"Yes. Like the way I care about education and writing and stuff."

"I don't know if I care about anything that much, to be honest. You've caught me a bit off guard. My job takes up most of my time and energy, and I spend a lot of time helping out with my family. I have two dogs."

"Dogs are good," I respond, although I'm disappointed in his response.

It's time to lighten up the conversation, but that's the last thing I want to do when I'm into someone. I love talking to people who have real interests because they bring me back to my real interests. It's been forever. Since at least Evan. I remember going on a date with a guy who had read my Facebook profile. In the "About Me" section, I had written, "I still haven't found what I'm looking for". When he asked me what it meant, I went on a long tangent about all the things I hoped to one day get out of life to feel like I truly accomplished something or came close to it. He just stared at me and said, *"I was hoping you'd say 'the man of your dreams' or something."* I almost regurgitated my dinner.

"Yeah, I do love my dogs," he says, and the conversation goes back to being lighthearted.

I'm not having a bad time, but I'm not having an amazing time, either. Maybe I'm too sober now. I keep drinking in hopes that I'll feel more relaxed. Maybe that's why I'm always relaxed around Alec. We're always too drunk to really think about anything. There is truly nothing wrong with Steve. But something just isn't quite right about him.

We make out at the end of the night, and it's obvious he's smitten with me. I feel nothing in response. I'm not sure if I should continue dragging this out and see if another date or two will make me like him more. Emma always reminds me that she wasn't sure about Matt for a few months and now they are perfectly blissful.

I just want to believe in: *When you know, you know.*

Chapter Twelve

G ail messages me out of the blue two weeks later.

GAIL

So I'm having a party April 27th and you should come out!

*Ugh, you want me to drive out to Wisconsin for your barbe-
cue? I have to figure out an excuse.* April 27th is only three
weeks away. Perfectly feasible that I have something to do.

LYREN

Um, maybe. I have to figure out what's going on that
weekend.

It's rude of me not to want to go to Gail's party. Every time I
have seen her in the last couple of years, she's come to Chicago.
I think I justify this by the fact that Chicago is better than
Nowhereland, Wisconsin, but that's not right. It's not the

Wisconsin thing. It's the fact that Gail has nothing to talk about except her relationship and wanting to get married and Brad not being ready. And the other people at the party will all be there with their children and their husbands, and they will all want to go to bed around 10 p.m. after spending the day fussing over every shit the babies take. And they will all act like I am a leper because I am single. I just can't stomach it.

GAIL

Oh come on. You haven't been out to Wisconsin to see me in two years!

LYREN

I know, I know. I'll try to come.

GAIL

Good. You'll have fun. There are a lot of fun people going and you haven't even met most of my friends. Brad will be there too, obviously, and you know him. We can hang around in the town the next day. Just a weekend trip.

LYREN

Yeah, definitely. I will look into it and see if I can take off work that Friday or something.

GAIL

Especially since I barely saw you the last time I was in Chicago.

LYREN

Yeah, I'm sorry about that. I was really hungover all day on Sunday. I drank a lot with my date.

GAIL
Yeah and with Alec in the afternoon.

LYREN
True.

Judgment is brewing in her. That was the day I let them go home and be boring while I stayed out with Alec, but I can't help it if Alec likes to dance and drink and be out socializing while they like to have sit down dinners and have people over at their hotel or on Sam's couch while I want to gag watching him and Judy be all in love.

GAIL
How was your date?

LYREN
It was nice. He was thoughtful. I'm trying to give him a chance. Conversation was good but not great. We made out a little. I saw him again two weeks ago on St. Patrick's Day. He and some of his friends were out and me, Alec, Olivia, and the crew met up with them. It was kind of nice having a date around in front of Alec just since he's always flirting with people and is openly dating others.

GAIL
So you basically are using Steve to make Alec jealous?

Now I'm feeling open hostility through the Messenger window. But also, maybe?

LYREN
No. It was just a nice bonus. Steve and I got burritos, just

the two of us, and then he came over and watched a
movie. We cuddled on the couch and made out and I sent
him home because I didn't want more.

GAIL

That's nice though. Keep it slow. Maybe you'll decide
you like him. When are you seeing him again?

LYREN

I invited him to Emma's birthday party next week. Which
I may regret. Meeting my sister as my official date feels
like a big step. It just sort of slipped out.

I'm already wishing I could uninvite him, but I don't even
know why. We're just going to bars with Emma's friends. It's not
some major family function.

GAIL

I'm sure it will be fine. Emma can talk to anyone.

There is a pause in our conversation.

GAIL

So Marcy is pregnant.

LYREN

Oh, good for her!

Marcy is a friend of ours from college who Gail stayed in
touch with.

GAIL

Yeah. Good for her.

LYREN

You don't seem very happy.

GAIL

It's just . . . why isn't it me?

LYREN

Well, honestly, Gail, if you want to get pregnant, you technically can make that happen.

Here we go again. I roll my eyes and sigh. I'm glad this conversation isn't happening where she can see or hear me.

GAIL

You know I don't want to get pregnant and make Brad marry me. He has to want to do it on his own. I'm just so sick of waiting.

I take a deep breath and weigh whether to be honest with her or just keep placating her whining.

LYREN

Gail, maybe Brad just isn't ready to marry you.

Boom. There it is.

GAIL

So what am I supposed to do? Wait until he is ready to marry me?

LYREN

Well, either that or dump him and start over. You'd find a new guy. You could still get married and have babies with someone other than Brad, you realize. You're still very young.

GAIL

Yeah, but you're saying that like it's just picking out a different apple at the grocery store. This is my life. My future. It's kind of a big deal. Brad is a good guy and we're happy.

LYREN

Are you? Is he? No offense, but you don't sound very happy. And you never sound very happy lately. Because it sounds like you want to be married and start a family, not goofing around with him. And it sounds like that's the opposite of what is happening. So are you happy?

GAIL

I don't know.

LYREN

I just sort of think he's being really immature about the entire thing. You've been together since college. He needs to man up. And if you're not willing to leave him over it, he has no reason to leave. Right now, he gets to have his cake and eat it too. He's got a beautiful girl-friend who he can have fun with and he can still go out with his buddies and not worry about his finances or starting a family. What incentive is there really for him to put a ring on your finger at this point? And you don't want to force him to grow up because then he'll just resent you and you won't be happy together. Or you just wait for him. What is the big deal about getting married right now anyway?

GAIL

Because I'm just ready for that. I don't want to go out
and party. I don't want to put my life on hold. I want to
start a family. Everyone around me is married and having
kids and I feel like I'm left behind.

LYREN

So dump him. You can't force him to marry you, and
you've already given him all the signals. Either leave or
deal with it.

GAIL

You think I don't know all of this? It's easy for you to
say. Sure, just dump him. Move on with your life. It's
easy for someone who is perpetually single and doesn't
give any guy a chance to just say walk away and find
someone new. But that's not what I want.

LYREN

I didn't say it was easy, Gail. I know you guys have a lot
of history. But you aren't really happy right now. And I
know I'm single, so thanks for reminding me that I'm
relationship challenged.

GAIL

You're not relationship challenged. You're just too busy
partying all the time to see a guy for his real qualities. If
he can't outdrink you, you don't seem to want to be
with him.

LYREN

What is that supposed to mean?

My irritation with her and her dumb relationship is now

becoming actual anger, and I want to retaliate. The last person I need an attack from is the girl who gave up her entire life and personality to wait around for a frat boy to put a ring on her finger. I feel nauseous waiting for her response.

GAIL
Lyren, you've just been partying an awful lot. I know you're in this phase where you want to get it out, but you've been really selfish. I feel like I've needed you so much in the last year trying to figure out my relationship and all that and all you want to do is drink and screw Alec. You can't even spend time with me when I'm in town. I know you just plain don't want to come out and visit me. I'm sick of trying to make my friendship with you work.

Fuck her! I can't even type as fast as the words want to come out. My hands shake while I attack my keyboard to respond.

LYREN
Maybe you're right, Gail. Maybe I just think you're being needier than I can handle. You act like your relationship struggles or the fight you got in with Brad over your dog is the worst situation in the entire world. You're not dying of cancer. You have relationship drama. We all do. Everyone. So I'm sorry if I don't think you need to tell me about it every single day. And you're talking about it to a person who doesn't even remember what it is like to be in love or have a real career or an understanding of her future. So yes, I party a lot. Maybe I'm being really selfish. I need to be right now. I need to screw Alec because it makes me feel better about myself. I need to party because I need to feel normal and it makes other problems go away. I'm sorry that there is an error in

your relationship, but I'm sick of giving you the same goddamn options. Either dump him, or settle down with the idea of not getting married for a while. That's all there is!

GAIL
I didn't want to offend you.

Sure she didn't. She clearly has been holding that in for a while. But I guess so have I.

LYREN
I didn't want to offend you either. And I'm sorry you think I'm being selfish. You're right. I'm not psyched about driving to Wisconsin to spend the weekend with a bunch of people and their children who are going to go to bed at 10 and then I'll be up and bored and lonely after they spend the night asking why I'm single as if it's a disease. I'm sorry my life is just a lot different than yours right now. Maybe we don't have anything in common right now as friends and that's why we are annoyed with each other. I'm sorry I haven't been there for you. I just really can't relate to your situation right now, and I feel like you're whining.

GAIL
I feel like you should get your shit together.

I am incensed. I slam the computer shut without saying anything else. She'll see I've just gone offline, and I don't give a fuck.

I haven't been in a fight with a girlfriend since maybe high school, and even that was just Sarah and I distancing for a brief time. I never felt the need to call someone out before. Gail is definitely right that I'm being selfish and not supportive, but I also don't feel bad about it. I'm sick of being supportive of her relationship drama and giving her the same answers. I'm sick of talking to someone who acts like marriage is the end all. I'm sick of listening to my friends talk about planning weddings like it's so stressful. It's a fucking party. A fucking party you're throwing because you're in love, that you want the entire world to worship you while you rub it in everyone's face how you're in love and they aren't.

I don't move for a while, staring at the closed laptop. *Do any of my other friends feel the same about me being selfish and not having my shit together? Am I pushing everyone away? Or actually, maybe they are all pushing me away because I can't relate to their couples clubs and they don't know what to do with me.*

I can't be mad *at* my friends for doing the things everyone says you're supposed to do. But I am still bitter that I don't have anyone around to actually relate to. And Gail feels about dead last on that list right now. So fuck her. What do I need that shit for? So I can talk about more wedding shit with yet another friend?

Chapter Thirteen

"So, Steve, what's your most embarrassing moment?" Emma asks while pouring everyone a drink at her and Matt's place.

I kind of avoided hanging out with Steve again over the past two weeks, but we've texted and talked on the phone, and I didn't uninvite him to this party, so I guess I'm still trying to like him. Emma is always good at helping people fit in, and I'm sure she's thrilled I have a date besides Alec at something.

"Oh, this is a good one," Steve responds, delighted.

I can't quite put a finger on why I'm not feeling more into him. Steve is great, but little things are really starting to annoy me. Like the fact that he tagged himself with me on Facebook: *Out with Lyren for Emma's birthday!* As if he were in with the family or something after a couple of dates.

"Babe, did you put the other bottle of Effen somewhere?" Matt asks, coming into the kitchen from the living room, which distracts Emma from her conversation with Steve.

He is getting along with Emma's friends, which is helpful

because there is nothing I can't stand more than having to babysit some guy just because he's out with me. Steve follows Matt back out to the living room to try to get to know him a little. I guess that's a nice thing.

"He's cute!" Emma says to me when Steve is out of earshot. "I like him. He seems really nice, and he's funny too!"

"He's alright."

"Oh, come on. What's wrong with this one now?"

"I can't quite say yet. But I'm trying to give him a chance. I invited him here, didn't I? That's a pretty big deal considering I knew you were going to love him and give me shit about it."

"Well, if you knew I was going to love him, why aren't you sure about him? You must know he's a catch."

"He's a catch. I don't know." I shrug my shoulders.

"You're just annoyed because he already likes you too much."

"Maybe."

Is that it, though? Do I not like him because he likes me? Or is it something else? I wish he weren't here with me.

"See!? You always do that. As soon as a guy really likes you, you start to avoid him and be mean to him. Why do you always have to do that?"

"Emma, it's not like that. He just doesn't know me well enough to like me that much. He knows a few things about me, and he is already buying me presents based on stupid little things I say in conversation. We've only been on a few dates, and he's acting like we're in a long-term relationship." I had mentioned liking to take pictures, and he brought me a disposable camera to bring to the party for the "nostalgia factor".

"There could be worse things than a guy listening to what you have to say, Lyren. I mean, especially considering how much you talk," she adds in the jab to keep it light. But I'm getting sick of hearing from her about how I always like the wrong guys.

"I'm trying."

"Good."

As the night goes on, I like Steve less and less. Every ten seconds he puts his arm around me again or makes some gesture to remind everyone in the room that he is with me. Maybe I should be flattered, but he is just annoying me. None of the other couples are all over each other. I don't want him all over me.

While everyone in the room is playing Taboo, he leans in and tries to kiss me. I instinctively back away.

"What's wrong?" he asks.

"Nothing, I just don't like this PDA stuff," I say, catching myself in my own lie.

What I mean is, I don't like this PDA stuff with you.

"One kiss is a public display of affection?" He's keeping his voice down, but we're in a room with about twelve people. I don't need to get into this with him here.

"No one else is kissing or being all over each other, Steve. Just cut it out. It's making me uncomfortable." I am being really harsh and short with him, but what I can't understand is that the meaner I am with him, the more all over me he seems to want to be. The more space he tries to take away from me, as though he is fighting my declaration of independence. I'm more and more stifled by the second.

All night he makes comments about how he knows me so well when all he knows are a few little details about things I liked or cared about that I've shared with him. He doesn't know anything. *Why am I feeling so angry toward him?*

By the end of the night, I can't wait to get in a cab and get the hell out of here and get home to my bed. ALONE. I have to dump Steve immediately. Not tonight, because it's Emma's birthday and that would be awkward. But soon. Very very soon. I feel it in every part of my bones. I can't be like Emma and hope that if I date a nice guy long enough, I'll suddenly want him touching me. I just need to go get a cab. And then, of course, a deterrent.

"Shit! I don't have my house keys! I must have lost them in the cab on the way over here. I had too much stuff in my hands!"

I'm furious with myself. It certainly isn't the first time I've lost my keys. I am a really moronic person on a regular basis. But it probably is the most inconvenient of the times.

"Just stay on the couch. It's no problem," Emma says.

I have no real problem with staying on Emma's couch. We are meeting my parents for a birthday lunch tomorrow, and my mom can bring my spare key with her.

"I should probably stay, too. I've had so much to drink." Steve leaps at the chance. Apparently, he didn't even think he needed an invite. Had he thought he was going to be staying over at my place tonight? Assumed? Hoped? If I tell him to go home, I'll have to break up with him right now, and I don't want to have to do that and come back and talk to Emma.

"It's no big deal at all. Anyone who needs to stay can stay," Emma mentions to a few remaining friends.

A couple of them take her up on the offer. At least I won't have to ward off any potential advances considering we'll all be in the living room. But it does mean that I have to share a couch with him.

I try to take up as little space as possible to keep some room between us, but it isn't easy. He puts his arm around me and cuddles me closely. I want to scream, but I try to sleep. I can't. It is too hot. I feel like I am going to burn up. All I wanted was to have the couch to myself. Now I have this man's hairy arms around me, suffocating me.

I look down at the floor. It looks so much freer than where I am at the moment. If only . . . yes! A free blanket! I grab one of the pillows from the couch and head to the floor when I am convinced Steve is asleep. The floor has so much space. I am thrilled. I don't care that it is hard as a rock. There are no alpaca arms around me.

Half an hour later, Steve curls up next to me on the floor.

What the fuck?? What hint have you not fucking got tonight?
Every fucking time you have tried to kiss me, I have resisted.
Every time you put your arm around me, I have squirmed away. I
chose to sleep on the goddamn floor rather than share a couch
with you! But I don't say anything. I force myself to calm down
and try to sleep, once again wriggling out of his grasp. I've never
felt so possessed, and I hate it.

In the morning, I couldn't wait for him to leave. I was short with
him, didn't walk him out, and barely hugged him goodbye. I
wanted to explode by the time he left when I explained I had to
shower at Emma's place and figure out what clothes of hers to
wear to get lunch with my parents. He finally took the hint he
wasn't invited to stay and hang around.

"So why were you being so rude to him?" Emma asks when
it's finally just the two of us, having coffee at her counter.

"Oh my god, I can't stand him for one more second."

"I will admit he was really all over you last night. It was so
obvious that you weren't into it."

"Yeah, and somehow that seemed to make him even more all
over me. Like, if I say I want space, you seriously have to give
me some fucking space, not stifle me!" I'm so worked up feeling
like I was in an incinerator.

"Well, he just really likes you. You shouldn't be so mean to
him."

"I'm not mean. I didn't say anything I was thinking. But it's
time to end this. This is why I hate dating. Because I went
through all these awkward dates hoping to feel something, and
all I felt was suffocation and irritation, and now I have to have a
horrible conversation with a guy who is crazy about me. I know
I'm going to make him sad, and I just feel like a bad person. But

I'm not you! I can't keep dating a guy cause everyone says he's nice when all I feel is trapped. This is why!"

"I'm sorry," Emma says. At least she seems to finally understand and hopefully is ready to get off my back about it.

When Steve DM'd Emma two days later to finish his cut-off story about his most embarrassing moment, it made me feel more asphyxiated than ever. As if she really cared about his pointless story that much. Since the party, I've been sort of short with him and only respond to approximately one in four of his texts, but he clearly hasn't gotten the hint. I was hoping he'd just go away instead of me having to do the actual breaking up. I mean, we only went on like four dates. But he won't stop writing to me.

So when he asks me three times in a row, on three different mediums, what I want to do next weekend, I realize I have to end it officially. I can't avoid it anymore.

I do it on Facebook, the last medium he tried. Because we've only been going out for less than two months, I am not going to lie to him and agree to see him just to break up with him, or worse, make him call me so I can do it that way.

LYREN
Steve, look, I have to be honest. I think this is just going somewhere for you that it isn't for me. I don't think we should see each other anymore.

I press send and hold my breath. There. Like a band-aid. Quick and to the point. None of this "it's not you, it's me" bullshit. It's us not being compatible. And that's that.

STEVE

What? Are you serious?

LYREN

Why wouldn't I be serious? I'm sorry, Steve. I keep
trying to make this work to see if there is anything there
for me because you're a really nice guy and all that, but I
can't. It's just not there for me. I'm sorry.

STEVE

Wow. I really thought we were heading in a different
direction than that.

LYREN

I know you did. That's why I had to be honest about it.

STEVE

Well, I guess I appreciate your honesty. Sucks though.

LYREN

I'm sorry.

STEVE

I just don't get it. I feel like you never seem like you
don't want to be out or anything.

LYREN

Steve, I'm a grown woman. I know how to keep things
I'm feeling inside rather than hurt someone else's feelings. I wanted to test it out. I tried. It's just not happening. I'm sorry.

STEVE

What if you waited it out a little longer? I'm a pretty great guy. I think we're good together.

LYREN

I know we're not. I'm sorry. I can't force it. And you shouldn't want me to. Come on. You're better than that.

STEVE

I mean, can we still hang out? Even if it's not as more than friends? I really do enjoy the time we spend together. It doesn't have to be more than friends if you're not feeling that.

LYREN

Maybe in a while.

I lie. I have no desire to remain friends with Steve, and I don't know who he's kidding, thinking that'll somehow work in his favor.

STEVE

OK, I'll give you a call later. Bye, Lyren.

At least he didn't cry or something. Well. That I could see.

A few days later, Olivia and I are back at Clarke's Diner, and I am recapping the breakup.

"Hey, look. You dated. That's dating. You went on dates. You kissed the frog. He stayed a frog. There are other frogs," she responds when I finish.

"There are so many fucking frogs, Liv."

"Well, you don't have to kiss them *all*." Her eyes widen before sipping her coffee. "We gotta narrow down your type and start there. Who's a celebrity you would date? Ryan Gosling?"

"Nah. I probably wouldn't even like Ryan Gosling. I mean, sure, he's really cute and all, but I'd probably find something wrong with him or my failing heart wouldn't start beating."

I genuinely think as I take a bite of my omelet. It's a real omelet with actual eggs and some bacon and cheese, unlike Olivia's egg white water looking thing. She's so much healthier than I am.

"OK, pick one then. Who seems like someone you'd really get along with?"

"Why?"

"I'm psychoanalyzing you."

"Hmm, OK. Trevor Noah."

"What do you like about Trevor Noah more than, say, Ryan Gosling?"

"He's darker."

"That's shallow. And you've liked tons of light-skinned and hairy guys before. Scott was light, and he was beautiful, and you were attracted to him."

"No, I don't mean his skin color! I don't have any preferences with that. I mean, his general disposition. He's so analytical. Thoughtful. He's intriguing, but also so witty. He seems like someone you could really talk to about so many things. Plus, he's inspirational."

"What if you found out he thinks about nachos all day long?"

"Nachos? What the fuck?" I laugh through a mouthful.

"Nachos. With cheese. That's it. All he wants to talk about."

"Well, I'd be really disheartened." I shake my head at her and eat a home fry.

"Interesting."

"So, what's the prognosis, doc?"

"Not done yet. What do all the guys you've liked have in common?"

"Hmm, smart. I've never in my life liked someone stupid. I prefer smarter than me really, but in different ways most of the time so they still respect my intelligence. I want someone who makes me want to be smarter. Better."

"OK, that's a start, but you've rejected a lot of really smart guys, too, so there's more to it."

"Oh, there's definitely more to it. I'm saying one thing I don't like is stupidity. Can't handle it. No matter how great a man someone is, if they can't have intelligent conversation, they're out."

"OK, so what else? Tall?"

"I mean, that's a quality I prefer, but not necessary. Jason wasn't tall. Eminem isn't tall."

"Oh for god's sake!" She puts her fork down and leans back in feigned drama.

"What? I'm just being honest!" I defend, sipping my iced coffee.

"Well, if that's your taste, you're really just totally fucked."

"Yeah, that's probably true. He's so sexy, though. All dark and intense and sarcastic and so good at English . . . "

"OK. Enough of that. I'm not even entertaining that one. Hair?"

"Indifferent."

"Job?"

"Preferably has one . . . "

"But what kind?"

"Doesn't matter as long as he's passionate about something. Like it doesn't have to be work. I'd sure be a huge hypocrite for that one. But you know, have something they are really into. Ideally not just sports."

"OK, well, what else do the people you've actually really liked have in common besides intelligence?"

"OK, honestly?" I realize one thing about each man I've liked all the way back to high school, and it's probably why I'm so closed. "They all intimidate me when I meet them, and I'm inspired by them in some way or another. I think what I'm really looking for is inspiration. A muse. Fuck a boyfriend. I want someone to bring me back to life."

"OK, you're officially impossible to set up. I quit."

I laugh. "That's what I keep trying to tell everyone who is always trying to set me up! I'm weird! I don't like things other people like! Mr. Perfect is never Mr. Perfect to me. Ever. I don't know why. I want to be adored by someone with incredible intensity who can handle mine . . . and you know what? I want to go back to being my intense self again. That's why I can't date. I'm not me."

"You're gonna be single forever."

"That's fine as long as I have good friends and a vibrator."

"And the occasional sex friend." She lovingly rolls her eyes.

"Those are nice. Ugh, it's not even just the guy stuff. Do you think I'm a bad friend?"

"Why would I think you are a bad friend?"

"Gail thinks I'm a bad friend."

"Lyren, you are a great friend. You're always there when I need to talk to you, or to take me out when Chris and I fight. You're fun. You're thoughtful. You made a whole empowerment CD for me when my high school best friends were being bitches to me. Other than your PDA issues, you are one of the best friends I could ever imagine. What happened with Gail?"

I debrief her on the argument while she picks at her side salad and steals some of my potatoes.

"We haven't spoken since," I say.

"How long ago was that?"

"Two weeks."

"So maybe you really just needed to have that blowout. You really don't have anything in common these days."

"It's just, she's so ready to be settled, and that's all she wants, and it just bores me to tears. And she can't relate to my life at all either. She has a good job. And she has always been incredibly straight-laced. Maybe that's why we were good friends in college. We'd cook together. But she never partied with me or anything. But I mean, I was in a serious relationship then too, and I guess I liked being boring then. I'm the one who changed."

"Do you feel bad about it?"

"On some level, I feel bad that she thinks I'm a bad friend and that I haven't been there for her when she needs me. On the other hand, I think she's wrong for being so damn needy. Like who wants to listen to someone whine about their lack of engagement ring every time you have a conversation?" I pretend to bang my head into the table.

"I mean, you're there for me. You're there for Sarah."

"You guys aren't needy. Maybe Gail is right. I'm a really self-centered person. I wasn't like this when I was younger. I was actually really altruistic. It's just, you get to a point where you're always helping people and always putting other people's needs before your own and suddenly you wake up and feel lonely and like people are walking all over you. Maybe I'm a shitty person. I'm happier this way. I think."

"I see what you're saying."

"Well, you're a really altruistic person."

"Yes, yes, I am. But I've been walked all over a lot. I've had a lot of friendships not work out because of how badly people have taken advantage of my kindness, and I never want to be the bad guy and be an asshole to them. I had friends who always expected me to be the one to cave on what I wanted. Where I was always the person making the concessions and sacrifices. As you well know, since you were there to help me pick up the pieces when I finally stood up for myself a little."

"Well, being a kind person is one thing, but you do need a ball sack here. Can't let people say they are your friend and then

they constantly take advantage of you and not be there in return."
I almost start another one of my empowerment lectures. It
reminds me that I used to feel powerful. "And if you ever start to
feel like I'm taking advantage of you, tell me to shut the fuck up,
OK? Because I might not realize I'm doing it. I'm a bulldozer
sometimes. Don't let me be. Just put me back in my place. I
never want to take advantage of your kindness. But I can see
how it's really easy to do."

"Yeah, I guess. I'm getting better about it. I never let Chris
walk all over me, at least."

"Thank god! But I wonder if that's why I am never happy in
relationships. Too much compromise goes into them. I like
feeling I have a hold on my life, and when I fall in love, I just
totally lose that."

"It's not always a bad thing, though. When you're in a
healthy relationship."

"Obviously, I know that. I know enough people in good relationships, that I believe they can be good. I'm not sitting here
saying I hate men or dating as a whole or that. I just don't know
if it's ever going to be for me."

"You know I agree that you don't need a man to be happy. I
stumbled upon my own relationship and wasn't looking for it."

"Isn't that how it always is, though? The rare interests I do
have come out of nowhere."

"Yes, but what I'm saying is, I'm all about the independent
woman, but what will make you truly happy in life?"

"How do you mean?"

"Like, I don't think that having a man will make you happy.
But I also don't think you're fully happy now. You're kind of
weird and complicated and all that, which is why I love you. You
think about shit. There are a lot of people in the world who are
truly satisfied with having a significant other and starting a
family. That is what they know will fulfill them. Like Gail,

maybe. She wants a husband to complete her, and that's really normal and true for a lot of people. But like, as much as I love Chris, if I don't volunteer or help people in some way, I will never be fulfilled and happy. I feel like I'm not doing what I'm supposed to be doing. I'm wasting time and energy. I should have done Peace Corps or something, and instead I fell in love, and I judge myself for that. And if we get married and have kids before I do some real volunteering, I won't ever do it. But I am also not making moves. I don't have it all figured out either just because I have a nice boyfriend."

"OK, I get you now. I fully have that sense. I am wasting time drinking and partying and screwing your brother when it's not what is ever going to make me really happy. And dating someone great isn't the answer to that either. I don't know. Some people seem to get lost in relationships and feel like they'd die without someone else. I don't think I'll ever be that person. I'd like someone to balance me out and complement the crazy. The other day, I read through all of my college papers. I miss the academic I used to be. I used to care about the world, and I used to be a good student and a good writer. I used to bake all the time. I'd come up with new recipes and try things and just sort of put all of my mental energy into that. And now, I dunno. I feel vapid. I stare at blank paper sometimes, but there is no heart in it. The words I write are, I dunno, void." I sigh.

"You're still really talented, though."

"I've never been really talented, but at least I had some level of creativity and some manifest form of self-expression."

"You use 'manifest form of self-expression' in general conversation. I don't think you've quite lost your touch just yet," she laughs.

"Well, I want to do more than copyedit other people's lame technical work. I want to start something that is just, I don't know. Me. Something that belongs to me. Something I can be proud of. And maybe when I have that, I'll stop being such a horrible person."

"Stop saying you're a horrible person. You're a good person. You're just having a little fun and thinking about your own needs right now."

"Which makes me kind of a heathen."

"I dunno. It sort of happens sometimes. You get a dead-end job because it pays the bills, and it takes away your energy. Then you don't do the things you said you were gonna do," she agrees. "A lot of the nonsense they tell us when we're young is bullshit. That you can have it all. That you can be anything. That if you go to college and get good grades and don't fuck shit up that you'll get a great career and be satisfied. It's a lot of nonsense. Even good jobs still suck."

"My job has been so mundane that I let it stifle my creativity. You start to focus on paying those bills, and you're stressed, so you go drinking. Then you're bored, so you look for attention and start screwing a friend and liking random people and suddenly, you just aren't you anymore. It's so weird how it just happens like that."

"Exactly. I've killed so many brain cells this year it's ridiculous. I was supposed to go abroad and volunteer, and I hate admitting that part of why I haven't is Chris, but I'm comfortable. I mean, you act like I have my shit together because I have a fulfilling job and a boyfriend, but I'm also generally as drunk as you. It's fun. It's something to do when you're stressed out over life."

"Right. I've done the same thing. I don't want to be an empty party girl. It's not me. It's been fun. I have no regrets. I like that I sort of stepped out of myself and saw the world from another side, but I'm really realizing I need to release my energy in a positive way. I'm trying to write again. And maybe have some concept of what's going on in the world again outside of my little world and social life."

"Well, isn't acceptance the first step to recovery?"

"Something like that."

"Then you're already on your way to recovery from the black hole you lost yourself to."

"Damn straight."

"It's time to make your comeback."

"I was never anyone to begin with."

"You will be. Maybe you'll be the next winner of Cupcake Wars."

"Not a bad idea. Maybe I can get my own Food Network show."

"I'd watch it."

"Maybe that is where I should start."

"The Food Network? That's sort of a huge start . . . "

I laugh. "With cupcake baking. Just baking cupcakes for people. Maybe selling them. A little business online or something." I'm throwing ideas out there, but thinking about starting a business awakens something small in me. My nerves fizz up.

"Do it."

"And I should start watching the news and reading again. In college, you get all these assignments, so you have to do it, and you have to focus, and I just felt better about my life when I was doing homework. With no one to say, 'Hey, read this article and write an analysis', I just don't even know what I think about things or what's going on in the world anymore!"

"That's a really good point, actually. I feel the same way. I used to care so much, and I want to believe that I still do."

"First, I have to get that intensity back in the first place and stop spending my Sundays with my head in the toilet."

"That could be a good start."

"I feel more alive after this conversation."

"Good! April is your new beginning!"

"Yes! Spring Awakening!"

We toast our now-empty coffee cups.

"OK, now you're just freakin' weird."

"You already knew that."

I get back home feeling motivated. I blast Eminem's *Recovery* album to inspire me while I figure out how to get my shit together. If Eminem could almost die of an overdose and come back with this banger album, I can improve my attitude at work enough not to get fired and maybe bake some damn cupcakes for people or whatever.

But for now, I'm organizing and cleaning my apartment. Clearing spaces, going through drawers. I leave my college papers out on top of my desk as a reminder of the person I was and maybe still am somewhere. Reading them again helped me remember me.

While cleaning my junk closet and filling a whole trash bag with old CDs and VHS tapes, I come across some reading games I got from an education center I interviewed for a paper in college. They are simple. Just tricks to help with reading comprehension that are maybe a little more engaging than basic worksheets. Looking at them ignites a new idea. I'm not going to let Jarron fail English and not get to stay on the football team.

I have been such a shitty tutor for the last couple of months. Completely phoning it in. Jarron doesn't deserve that. I need to do better by him.

I abandon the closet project to write out a strategy of how we are going to improve his writing and reading before the end of the school year. We have about a month left, but he is doing OK on his own. We can make enough progress for his final paper and test.

I am going to help him make Facebook pages for the characters in *Animal Farm,* which his class is reading, to help him better understand their motives and relationships. We'll create dialogues with them. Maybe his teacher will let him turn them in or even present them to the class for some extra credit. This is going to be fun. I suddenly feel more invested in Jarron's English grade than he is as I draw out the Facebook page templates at my kitchen counter. He's staying on that damn team.

Chapter Fourteen

Alec can't stop checking his damn phone, and I know it's a girl. I already had it in my head that we'd be going home together based on the fact that we seemed normal and cool in the beginning of the night and have since consumed that lovely substance that uninhibited various desires. I've been making the mistake of looking forward to it.

I spent the week excited about my work with Jarron, and think I got him a little excited too. That was my win this week. And I have put enough effort in at work to at least be noticed for my improvements. Clare begrudgingly complimented me on Thursday. Now it's the weekend, and I find myself again at a bar. I don't even know if it's fun anymore. It's just what I do. And now I'm disappointed about Alec not paying attention to me.

Emma comes up and buys me yet another shot. She doesn't come out all that often, but her man is out of town. This shot is probably the last thing I need.

"So who's going to be your date at Sarah's wedding?"

"Oh jeez, Emma. That's four months away!"

"Just wondering."

"God knows who I'll be dating then." I hate thinking about wedding dates. I always RSVP last minute, hoping I'll have magically fallen in love or lust before the due date. It has never happened.

"Are you gonna end up taking Alec?"

"Maybe. Who cares? At least he's fun, and I can get some after. No worries, no commitments. Weddings are intimidating dates with new people."

"You need to stop overthinking every single thing and go with the flow now and then. If you ever want one of these"— she holds up her glittering left hand—"you need to give guys a chance and not dump them at the first thing you don't like."

I roll my eyes. "Look, I never fall. I don't know why. I am closed and guarded and weird about boys. Keeping Alec around is comfortable and convenient in a world where I can say that about very little. It's nice to have the attention and arms of a person you can count on to be there for you and whose heart you know you never have to break and who doesn't have yours to break."

"He's not the only thing. Your job is comfortable and convenient, although passionless. I just feel like it's not like you in either case."

"My job pays for my life." *And god knows I'm still on thin ice with that.* "What's so exciting about being a dental hygienist?"

"I didn't say it was that exciting. Just that yours makes you miserable. And I have a guy I love to go home to. Don't you think if you keep fucking Alec, that you'll pass on opportunities to meet guys because of that comfort? Like what Mom said when all of this started?"

"No."

"If dating sucks so much and Alec is there and comfortable

and makes you happy, you'll never go on a date with someone new instead."

"Not true. I dated Steve! I just didn't like him."

"It is mostly true. But Alec wouldn't do the same for you. You're his default, Ly. I'm not saying that to hurt you, but you need to be honest with yourself about what is happening here. Alec goes out with girls; he goes out and can't wait to meet girls to try to bring home. If there is no one new around, he'll fuck you."

"That's not fair, Emma. Alec is never anything but respectful to me."

"So stop watching him from across the room while he texts someone else."

She's right, and I hate it. I want to slap her. I *am* watching him text. He does go out on dates way more often than I do. I've only slept with one other person since Alec and I started hooking up (well, and had a close encounter with floor shitter). I have no clue who Alec's been with in that time. I don't want to be the default, but I don't want to give up what I have going with him either. I just need to stop being a psycho girl about it and enjoy it for what it is. Maybe I do need to date more . . . prove to myself that this is casual. I can do that.

"He's a guy. I don't want to go around sleeping with strangers, and he does. What's the big deal?"

"I didn't say you should go off and hook up with everyone. Just that you need to give good guys a better chance, and not pass up on them for Alec when he doesn't do the same for you."

"How do you even know someone is a good guy? Guys who are good in theory can be the most possessive." I flashback to Steve's arms feeling like a straitjacket.

"OK, sure, sometimes. But sometimes you find someone who really cares about you for you and will prioritize you. Do you want a guy who never listens to you, doesn't pay attention to you, and shows no interest in getting to know the people who matter to you?"

"Of course not!" Maybe I'm overly defensive, but what can someone expect when they corner me to talk about my personal life over my ten millionth shot? "I want a guy who does those things out of love for me, not because they were told somewhere that it's the right way to be or because they saw it in a movie once. When I was with Jason, I did things I never thought I would. I started cooking, I dressed up, I couldn't wait to kiss him and love him and show him affection that I had never known I had in me. Remember how cynical I used to be? Loving him changed that . . . for that particular time period. I want to be that for a guy, or I just don't think it's genuine. I don't trust guys whose first impulse is to be sweet and romantic just because. I want a guy to be sweet and romantic because I'm special. I would never go balls out like that over someone I barely knew. So when a guy does it, not only is it proof he likes me too much without enough information, but it's quite honestly not hot."

"You're gonna end up with a huge asshole."

"I'm gonna end up with a guy who is interesting, has a life, a sense of sarcasm, who can't be walked all over because he is strong. Someone who adores and respects me for the person I am without suffocating me. And you know what? If I don't, I'll end up with a great place, a few awesome dogs, and maybe go adopt a baby if that's something I one day decide I want. There is more to life than a perfect relationship."

"You guys look way too serious up here." Alec barges in as if on cue. "It's Friday." Of course, he buys me another drink. The world is spinning, and by the glazed look in his eyes, it is for him too.

"What's up, Alec?" Emma asks.

"I have no idea what's going on right now." He laughs and puts his arm around me.

Emma shakes her head, but smiles at me and lovingly rolls

her eyes. "Alright, I need to get going. My hubby-to-be is probably calling me off the hook. I left my cell at home."

"Night, Seester." We hug goodbye.

"Hey, you know I mean well, right? You mean the entire world to me."

"I know." Emma squeezes me and walks out of the bar, leaving me alone with Alec.

I look back at him. Even all glazy-eyed drunk, he is still so cute in his white button-down with the sleeves rolled up over fitted jeans.

"Tomorrow's gonna be a disaster," he says, taking another sip of his drink.

"What are you doing?"

"Supposed to go out with the family later."

"Good luck with that. I'm not leaving my couch all day."

His phone buzzes and he pulls away. I don't know how not to show my irritation, and I can't help thinking about what Emma said. I know what I should do. What my sober self would want me to do. Walk away and find someone else to talk to. Go home alone. Get a burrito. Like I did in the days when we'd make out in the bar before we started having sex. But instead, when he looks back up at me, I roll my eyes.

"What?" he asks.

Shit, I should have just let it go.

"Nothing."

"What?"

I shrug. *What do I say? How do I say it without sounding pathetic?*

"You. You're just . . . texting. Constantly. Like, obviously, it's some booty call by this point in the night, and I just don't get why being out with your friends isn't enough."

"It is! That's not why I'm texting at all! But being out with friends is gonna end soon, so I'm just working on a little something for later. What difference does it make?"

"You spend half the time you're out texting. It's just rude to be out with friends and thinking about what you'd rather be doing or who you'd rather be doing." My tone is cutting; I can't hide it.

"If I'd have rather been hanging out with her, I'd have been out with her. What? Do I have to be here all night to prove I'm a good friend?" He's focused intently on me.

"I'm sorry. I guess I'm just used to friends who don't need to fuck a stranger at the end of the night to have a good time. Nevermind. Go check your phone again. I'm sure she's waiting religiously by it to hear from you and can't wait to suck your dick tonight."

"What the fuck is this really about?"

I didn't mean to start a fight. I've totally fucked up, and I can't think clearly enough to get myself out of the mess I've created.

"I don't know, Alec." I can barely look at him.

"What the hell is your problem?"

"OK, whatever. I don't ever ask what you're doing or who you're doing, and I really don't care. But I don't understand how you can be out, supposedly having a good time with good people, and be, well, what about her makes her better than me?"

I regret it the minute I say it, but of course it's the most honest thing I've said all night. I hate that Alec is texting a stranger because he wants to go home with her instead of me. I always knew this would end poorly, but I am not ready for it to end right now. Luckily, no one else is paying any attention to us. I don't even know where any of our other friends are.

"I don't know . . . She's just . . . new. It's something different, so it's exciting." He actually seems sincere and not defensive now. "Look, Ly, it has nothing to do with you or with anyone else being in any way better than you. We always have fun. But this is casual. It was always supposed to be friends with benefits. I think maybe we should cool it for a while."

This makes me want to scream and slap him and storm out, but I've caused enough drama for one night. Now I need to patch shit up. It shouldn't be him that gets to call us off. I should be moving on with some nice guy, like everyone says. But here I am, ready to hide in the bathroom and cry.

"Why, Alec? Because I'm not shiny and new anymore? I'm old fucking news? Do you know what most of the guys in my life would fucking give to be in your fucking place?" I start to shake. I'm trying not to cry. Why do I always do this? Get attached to people who aren't attachable?

"Lyren, it's not that! You're amazing. You're stunning. Seriously. And you are fucking amazing in bed. You're fun. I love hanging out with you. My god, if it were just about getting to fuck you, I'd be calling you on random Tuesday nights just to come over."

There is a part of me that wishes he would do just that. And I love that he called me stunning and said I was amazing in bed, so I want to ignore the rest of his intentions.

"But you and I have gotten to a point where we go home together every time we hang out for several months now."

"So?"

"So, it's awesome in many ways, but it's just that if we keep doing this, that's when people start to get jealous. I've been there before. Quite a few times."

Great, Alec. Keep reminding me how unspecial I am.

"I just don't want things to get out of hand. I don't want to lose your friendship."

"Alec, making me feel like a secondary piece of shit doesn't really make me psyched to stay friends with you."

"Lyren, I NEVER meant to make you feel like shit or secondary. You mean so much to me. But my friendship with you comes first. Sex with anyone, including you, comes second. I feel like sex is starting to jeopardize our friendship."

"Quit comparing me to your stupid hook ups. I'm not in love

with you, alright? My favorite thing about my friendship with you is that I have a lot of fun with you, and it's comfortable, and I don't have to worry about the bigger picture. I've had other flirty friendships with guys where we end up making out once or twice, then they are into me for real and I lose a friend. I get it. It works both ways. But like, you're here with me and you claim you love having sex with me and yet you're texting a stranger you don't even like."

"Because the difference is, I don't want something comfortable. The fact that I don't know her that well does make it interesting. And like you just said, I'm not worried about the bigger picture with her. Like, what about you and Evan? You guys were friends. I see how upset you get over him, and I worry. I don't ever want to do that to you. I care about you."

"Don't you dare flatter yourself. You are not Evan. Nothing about my feelings for you can be compared to my feelings for Evan. I loved Evan. I never even pretended to be casual with him."

"I didn't mean that you're in love with me."

"Then what the fuck did you mean?" I'm annoyed at his audacity even if I am the one being jealous. Alec has been supportive of me seeing other people, and I'm the one seething, watching him do it.

"Just that you act jealous sometimes, and I want you in my life, but I need to know that when I have a girl out, you're not going to treat her like shit."

"Fuck you. I've never treated any girl you've ever brought around like shit. I always leave you alone whenever you're interested in hitting on someone."

"That's part of my point. I don't want you to ignore me or go away. I want you to be friendly."

"Oh for god's sake, that's just ridiculous. You want something impossible. You think any of the girls you are looking at are going to want to be friends with me? Are you kidding me?

Are you going to lie to them when they ask? Because they will always ask. Say you've never been with me or been attracted to me? Even the dimwads you bring around aren't that stupid."

"So what then? This is why I just need to move." Of course that's his immediate reaction. Don't take anything seriously or be attached or care.

"Sure, run away from it. That's going to help. You're over-complicating this."

"How am I the one overcomplicating this when you're the one who is getting all crazy? I want to have one of my best friends get along with other people in my life?"

"All of your friends like me except those who are jealous, and you know that. Alec, if you meet a girl who you really like and really want to date, I will be awesome to her. But why should I go out of my way for someone you're gonna toss aside in a week? I'm nice to people when I want to be. My jealousy is nothing more than not liking to feel second best, as I stated before. If you bring around a girl who is cool, I have no reason not to like her. The fact that most of the girls you like are children without brain cells is not my problem. I'm jealous because I like the way you flirt with me, not because I want to be with you, for god's sake."

I have no idea whether this is true anymore. If it is, would I be this upset about him texting a booty call instead of going home with me?

"I'm not saying that."

"You are. Hate to tell you, Alec, you aren't all that great. You're not even my type. Here's the truth you so badly want to ignore. Friendships like ours don't work in the long run. Good friends don't stay good friends. Not because we're having sex, but because our entire friendship is based on partying, flirting, and the fact that we're attracted to each other. It's the things that lead to us having sex in the first place that are why we won't be long-term friends. That's not gonna change. Without it, we have never even been friends."

"Why does it have to be like that?"

"Because no one we ever date seriously will accept the other person in their lives. You act like your girls are the only ones who ask about my relationship with you and doubt you over it. Before we even acted on anything, every guy I brought around questioned things with you. Guys sense jealousy in you, too. Stop acting like this is all on me and I'm the clingy one."

"I didn't mean that."

"You did. And whatever, it's fine. Act like you don't care. But stop worrying about our friendship because it was doomed from the beginning. Don't regret the sex, and don't think that if we stop right now that anything will be saved. The damage is done. You want things to be different, you shouldn't have flirted with me. And you shouldn't have been hot. We both knew we were gonna cross the boundary lines long before we did. Sorry. That's just how it is. If you want to stop screwing, or you've got all these girls that are more interesting, fine. Whatever. I'll move on. But you're going to miss me."

I lean against the bar, staring at the wall. I can't look at him. I'm mad and sad and hurt and just want to go back to when this was fun and easy.

"Lyren!" He grabs my arm to make me look at him, and I stare back angrily.

"Hey, you two! Closing! Get out!" the bartender yells at us.

I didn't even notice when they turned the lights on, or that they had been trying to kick us out. I'm not ready to end this conversation just yet. I hate that I messed things up, but I said things I needed to say. He needed to know.

"Whatever. Go text your booty call. I'm going home." I pull away from him and grab my coat, walking toward the door.

"Lyren, don't. This is ridiculous." He chases after me, and

the bartender literally starts shoving us out the door. "I don't want things to change."

"Neither do I!" I stop and turn around again, close to the door but not leaving. "But in the beginning, you weren't blatantly texting booty calls in front of me. You flirted with me. You made me feel wanted. And we had fun. And you're pushing me away."

"Get OUT! Leave!" the bartender shouts.

We finally walk out the door. I scan the streets for a potential cab. I just want to be alone.

"I don't know what to do, Lyren."

"You want to stop what we have, and you are concerned that I'm not nice enough to the other girls who are fucking you. So fine, we're done with this. I'm not gonna beg you to remain my sex friend. And I am too good to be part of your stupid little harem. I can replace you tomorrow. With someone who actually wants me and doesn't take me for granted. You're telling me we have too much sex. I didn't think that. I thought we had a great time. I thought things were awesome. I loved having someone in my bed at the end of a fun night and being comfortable with him. I loved that more than some awkward stranger who doesn't know how to please me. Sorry. I like fucking you. I don't want to stop fucking you. Fucking you is my favorite pastime involving you. Well, and the flirting and attention that make me want to fuck you."

Alec just stands and smiles at me. That stupid, beautiful smile of his. Those perfect lips. That thick dark hair. We're way too drunk to be having this conversation, although god knows we'd never say any of it sober. I hate him for his attitude, but I also want him. I don't know what is wrong with me. He shakes his head and looks down, but he's kind of laughing. I laugh too when I realize how ridiculous what I just said was.

"Hey you." He comes up and pulls me closer to him, putting his arm around my waist. "Let's keep talking."

I hesitate. His glossy vodka eyes are undressing me, and I'm melting into it. Should I stay mad at him? I hate how much I don't want to lose him. Default again.

"Alright."

"We can walk to my place."

Somehow, I convince myself I am winning because I'm getting what I wanted after all. To keep him. Even if I went about it the childish, psychotic way.

"Look, I'm sorry, Alec. I don't mean to be dramatic."

"You're right, though. I didn't mean to change things. I just, I don't know. I don't want to believe that things will end badly. I guess I thought they didn't have to."

"I don't know that they have to. I just don't see our friendship ever being totally cool. We're worse than exes who are friends. Even though we don't see each other as a threat to a relationship, anyone we like will. Even if we lie about our history. We have the kind of friendship where you show up at my door on Sundays and we make breakfast and screw and then go to the bar and get drunk and screw some more. No one is ever going to be cool with that, Alec. When this ends, it ends for good. Completely."

"I know," he says sadly. "So now what? We're still single . . . " He smiles that mischievous smile.

"I'm cool with crossing that bridge when we get there." I smile back, and he pulls me to him and kisses me. I sigh in relief the minute his lips are against mine. I'm not losing Alec. Not yet. *Fuck you, Text Girl.*

"So much for trying to push you away." He laughs and keeps kissing me.

"You just can't. You'd miss me too much." I look at him and, somewhere in my messed-up head, I know it's true.

"I know. I adore you, you crazy, crazy woman."

We're against a random apartment building making out hard now. His hand slides up my skirt. I have half a mind to screw him right in the alley. I need him this minute. I'm not sure if my thrill is greater for approaching sex or just out of relief that Alec isn't bored with me. I'm holding onto this with all that I am.

"Get a room!" someone calls out as they stumble by.

"Jealous!" Alec shouts back, laughing, but takes my hand, walking us to the sidewalk.

"True. Have fun!" the stranger calls back. We laugh, stop, and start kissing again.

"Fuck this," Alec says and hails a cab.

We're those obnoxious people making out at 3 a.m. in a cab, dying for it to get to his place faster, and I don't care. The world has fallen back into place.

Chapter Fifteen

"I'm so glad you told me about this and that you decided to do it with me!"

"Yeah, cause taking a cake decorating class was really the smartest thing for me to do three months before my wedding. I'm not going to fit into my dress." Sarah laughs.

Michaels, the arts and craft store, is hosting a Wednesday night cake decorating class throughout May, and Sarah saw an ad for it online. She sent it to me, thinking it might be up my alley and a fun way to spend some more time together. I leaped at the chance. Between my conversation with Olivia about focusing on things that bring me creative outlets and new energy, and my renewed mission to be good at tutoring, I'm finding myself open to more opportunities. I'm excited about the possibility of doing something new, even if I don't know what it is yet. But saying yes to non-alcohol-related friend time and trying to improve skills I already have feel like good steps.

"You will be fine and look gorgeous. I'm excited. I've never learned real decorating techniques. Just always have tried to mimic things I've seen here or there. Truth be told, I haven't really baked anything since Christmas."

We find our places at a table for 12 and start to organize our supplies. To prep for the class, we were asked to purchase food coloring, frosting tips, a basic kit with some techniques, and of course we had to come with a baked cake (undecorated) and a tub of buttercream icing. Just buying the supplies had me feeling like a kid excited to start a new year at school.

"Well, that's why this will be good. You need to do something new and fun. Your job is seriously deteriorating your life, Ly. I'm gonna be honest, I'm taking this class with you because I think it will be really fun, and we totally need one-on-one time, but I'm also worried about you."

"Why do you say that?" I ask, although I know what she means. Sarah has known me since I was 12. We went through a wannabe pop stars phase, a depressed high school phase, and a jealousy of popular people phase. We've been through everything. She knows me better than anyone else in my life, even when I've been pulling away and spending all of my time killing brain cells.

"It's just, you're not you. You are always down. I know you hate your job, and that totally sucks, but you've let it consume you."

"I don't think I let my job consume me. I hate it, yes. And I hate Claire, but I leave it at the door."

"You don't. You have so much resentment for Claire, and I'm not saying she isn't horrible. It sounds like she really is. But you let her get to you. You let her make you feel like shit. You let her make you angry. And because you feel your job is so dead end, you drink so much to combat it. And I know you say your thing with Alec is fun, and it's been a good distraction in a lot of ways, but I think he's also part of why you're feeling so unmoored and insecure. I'm not saying I think you have a drinking problem; you don't. You have a life problem."

I let out a sad laugh. "You're so right. I know. I'm sorry. I really haven't been myself lately. To be honest, I think I forgot who I even am."

I'm not offended. Maybe because I know she's right and there isn't much to defend. I got defensive with Gail because she needed me to relate to something I just couldn't, but Sarah's concern isn't that I'm not there for her. It's that I'm not there for *me*.

"She's really good at writing and baking cupcakes."

"That's a start. Thanks for looking out. I'm sorry I've been so wretched. I actually spent the last two weekends in and not drinking. I am trying to focus on some stuff. Not sure I'm getting anywhere. And maybe it's just cause Alec was on another trip. But I know I haven't been the most positive person. Which reminds me, I probably owe Gail a phone call."

I don't want to keep fighting with Gail. We are too good of friends for that kind of nonsense. The thing is, Gail isn't like Sarah. Gail doesn't know me and get me like Sarah, but that doesn't mean our relationship isn't worth saving. Maybe she's done some thinking, too.

The instructor calls the class to begin and discusses how we'll be learning basic designs like florals, color mixing, and cursive writing with piping bags. I already find myself daydreaming about the beautiful little cupcakes I might create. How I can make them speak to an occasion and double as decor but also be delicious. Who am I baking all of these future fictional cupcakes for? That's not the point. I need to get back into the kitchen.

I smile and pick up my little smoothing knife, ready to be a good student and make this the most beautiful damn cake Michaels has ever seen.

"Lyren, look!" Jarron holds up his latest English paper for me, and my heart leaps.

"An A? Are you serious?! Jarron, I'm so happy for you!"

"Yeah, Mom's gonna be so excited! She's really been on my case."

"What did Ms. Shannon say?"

"She was really excited for me too. She said good job!"

"You'll have to make sure you put that on your refrigerator when you get home."

He stares down at the paper and smiles, almost like he doesn't believe it. My personal life may be a total disaster, but at least I've helped someone out in this world. Over the past four weeks, I really stepped it up with him. It wasn't even all for him. I actually found that I liked doing it. Once I started looking up reading and writing supplements for middle school students, my left brain finally kicked back in, and I was staying up late, coming up with engaging projects that I couldn't wait to do with him. It's like I was tapping into new parts of myself. It didn't fix everything. It didn't fix most things, even. But it felt like something.

"Yeah, I will."

"Jarron, I'm really proud of you. You have worked so hard this year, and you've really brought your grade up."

"Thanks for all of your help." He is beaming, and I have so much pride I could burst.

"You did it on your own. I just sort of guided you there."

"Are you going to be my tutor again next year?"

"Maybe. I'm not sure how it works, but I'll put in a special request if you like. If you get a B in English at the end of the year though, you won't be in tutoring at all."

"That would be awesome because if I make Varsity football and have to miss practice because I have a tutor, that would be a travesty."

"Where on earth did you learn the word 'travesty'?"

"English class!"

I laugh. "Wow, I'm impressed. So when will you know if you made Varsity?"

"Hopefully today. I'm really nervous."

"Well, I'll tell you what. We'll run some skills practice, because we have to make sure that your English grade *stays* up since you still have a final big test, but we'll try to cut out of here a little early so you can get to practice. How does that sound?"

"Sounds good."

I drop Jarron off at football practice a little early as promised before I go to dinner with Olivia.

"Hey, how's it going?" Jarron's football coach approaches me. Olivia was right. He is cute. He's got that tall, rugged thing going for him.

"Oh, hi!" I feel stupid for a minute. I don't know why he's talking to me.

"Just wanted to check with you when tutoring ends."

"Oh, we only have a couple weeks left." *Duh. He has a question about tutoring.* "They get the last two weeks of the school year off."

"Awesome. I haven't actually told Jarron this yet, but he made Varsity for next year."

"Oh my god! That's great! I'm so excited for him!" It's nice to feel genuine joy for someone else's success. *Good job, Lyren. You're not jealous of a 12-year-old.*

"Yeah, I plan to tell him today. We have a lot of training to do over the summer, but if you're still working here next year, you'll have to check out the team."

"I will definitely do that," I say, probably taking more pride than I actually deserve given how checked out I spent most of the winter.

"Hey there!" Olivia comes to the field. Tutoring must officially be over for today.

"Oh hey!" I say to Liv, then turn back to the football coach.

"Alright, I have to go. Have a good practice!" I say and walk away with Liv.

"So what were you talking to hottie football coach about?"

"About Jarron, fool!"

"Hmm." She smirks, and I shove her lightly.

"Don't you give me that. We weren't even flirting at all. He told me Jarron made the team. He's going to be so excited! I'm actually going to miss him next year."

"Will he not be in tutoring?"

"I don't think so. He really worked hard this year and brought his grade up."

"That's awesome!"

"Yeah, I honestly feel kind of awesome about it."

After my first cake decorating class, I kept thinking about how Sarah said I am good at writing and baking cupcakes. People always said they loved my baking. My family wondered why I hadn't done anything with it. I always said it was because it's so hard to make it in that business, but isn't it hard to make it in any business if you really care? If you're trying to do something you love. Maybe this is it. A start. A new thing to be excited about. I used to love baking cupcakes for everyone's events. Maybe someone somewhere would pay me to do it for real. Especially now that I am getting some updated decorating skills.

So I am now the owner of LylacBakery.com. I don't know exactly what to do with it yet. It seemed worth the $7 investment. But since I have zero HTML skills, I am staring at a blank page. Maybe I should have started with a MySpace page? Facebook for cupcakes? I email my friend Peter, remembering he works in computer stuff, offering him free cupcakes in exchange for his tech support.

Fortunately, he replies quickly that he's more than willing to help, excited about cupcakes, and that while he can put together the basic backend stuff for orders and UX, I need the content. Which means I need to get busy making, testing, and photographing cupcakes.

"The best part of your new website is that I get to be a judge," Olivia says, licking her fingers of the buttercream frosting coating them.

She and Sarah are over a few weeks before I plan to launch to help me finalize some recipes and take photographs to use on the site.

"Any recommendations or changes you think?" I ask, handing them a yellow cupcake frosted with basic chocolate fudge buttercream.

I need some staple cupcakes, some unique cupcakes, and some really prettily decorated ones. This will be the most difficult part if people actually start buying them in any sort of quantity. I haven't put much thought into transportation. I figure in the beginning I can just hand deliver. I don't exactly expect my site to reach outside of Chicago. Or maybe people can pick up. I'll figure it out if anything ever actually goes anywhere. I can't say I've put a ton of thought or effort into this new business. Planning too much may scare me away from it. It's better to just dive right in and work out the kinks as they approach.

"This is absolutely delicious," Sarah says. "I'm really excited for you to get started! I want to see the site."

"I still have to change a bunch. It won't be up until I've got the pictures, but I have a slow week at work, so I plan to mess around with it a little bit there. Just don't tell anyone." I laugh.

"I think you should keep the basic cupcakes simple. Like the chocolate and vanilla ones. And then make some of the more unique ones really fancy on the site to attract people's attention," Liv suggests.

"Thanks. That's a good idea. Obviously, if anyone wants to start ordering them, I will design them however they want them.

I just want them to know the different kinds of options they will have available. I certainly don't expect this to totally take off or to quit my job or anything, but it's just fun to be out there sort of doing something I am actually proud of and that's more me. Maybe a couple of people will enjoy it, you know?"

I've managed to hold on to my job by the skin of my teeth. Claire still hates me, but my numbers went up so much that she has no legitimate grounds to fire me.

"I think it's so awesome that you are doing this. I mean, we all need to take jobs just because we need one and stuff, but it gets really easy to get caught up in just living life and not really doing what we originally wanted to do," Sarah says. "You sound more like yourself than you have in a really long time, and it's really great."

"Thanks. If it weren't for you signing us up for that class, I might never have remembered how good at this I am or how much I really love it. So thanks. Seriously." I smile at her. "Anyway, I'm launching in a couple weeks or so since it's the beginning of summer, and I figure I can really tap into some fruity summery flavors for things like barbecues and gradua- tion parties and such. Maybe even wedding showers or something."

"Perfect!" Sarah replies.

I don't have actual reason to believe I'll attract all of these graduations and barbecues yet, but I have to at least be prepared. I'm glad my friends are supportive and excited instead of keeping me grounded. I need something to daydream about. Besides, it's a pretty low opportunity cost.

"So my business model basically centers around the fact that you really can't be sad if you are eating a cupcake. They are so little, cute, and tasty. They are truly the happiest food in the world."

"It's nice to hear you sounding so happy yourself," Olivia chimes in.

"I'm just excited about doing something for once. I've wasted a lot of time lately, you know?"

"I know the feeling. I'm obviously loving that I am getting married and all, and the planning has definitely had its moments of fun, but I can't wait until it all dies down. It's funny. You dream of getting married when you're a little girl, but it's so much stress and chaos. All I really want is to be settled down and living with Nick comfortably," Sarah says.

"Just between helping you and Emma plan your weddings, I think I want to elope if I ever do get married," I laugh. It boggles my mind how much time and energy and money people spend on one celebration that will be over in the blink of an eye.

"Well, if you go to Vegas, I will be there," Olivia laughs.

"So how are you actually figuring out the logistics of the site? I wouldn't know where to begin actually creating one," Sarah asks.

"Peter works in computers, so he has been helping me set some of the stuff up. Making sure the links are working and all of that. Designing and uploading pics and that is really easy. I figure if anyone actually becomes interested in the site, I'll have to register it as a business, and the computer end of things might get more complicated, but I want to take things one step at a time and just get it going. In any case, I'm happy to be working toward something besides being hungover all day. I plan to use Pinterest to try to direct traffic to my site. Actually, maybe that's something you girls can help me with!"

"Oh, good call. As soon as you get started, I will definitely start advertising for you!" Sarah says.

"I was also thinking I might try, if this starts going anywhere, to print my website on the cupcake wrappers themselves. That way, if people are at a party and grab one, they have the information right there."

"Great idea!" Olivia says.

"I should have had you do my damn wedding cake. The thing

costs more than my dress, and people are going to eat it in ten seconds. And let's be honest, does anyone really even care about wedding cake?"

"I'm sure your cake will be incredible. Your whole wedding is going to be beautiful. Besides, I haven't the slightest clue how to make a wedding cake. This is a cupcake site. Any idiot can make cupcakes."

"Yeah, whatever. I want it to be fun and simple. And I think it will be. You've been great about helping me plan and stay calm," she replies.

I think she's just being nice. I have been a C- at best. Definitely not great. But I am grateful that Sarah isn't the kind of friend who holds that against me. I am her maid of honor because I am her lifelong best friend. Not because I am good at planning weddings. I'm trying to be more enthusiastic with both her and Emma. Having something of my own to look forward to helps.

"So, hey, I have an idea."

"What's that?" I reply.

"Well, obviously my wedding itself is totally planned and ready to go. But you said you want to launch this site at the beginning of July?"

"Yeah, that's the goal if I can get all these pictures and recipes down by then."

"Then you'll already be launched by my wedding."

"Yeah. Don't worry. While your wedding is going on, you are the sole focus. I'm all yours." I nod and salute like military personnel reporting for duty.

"Oh god, dork, I'm not worried about that. You're the best friend ever, and you've been fabulous. Even if your cupcake company takes off massively, which it should because these are delicious, I know you'll be fine. Anyway, what if you make the cupcakes for my shower? We were just going to have a little cake, and it's not the most exciting thing ever, but there will be a decent amount of people there. It could be great advertising for your new site, plus a little business to get you started."

"Oh my god, that would be so awesome, Sarah! I would be honored!"

"Only if you aren't too busy or anything."

"Are you kidding me?! I'd absolutely love to! That would be great! You'll have to tell me exactly what you are looking for and what flavors and kind of theme and all that so I can start thinking about it. I know your mom is doing most of the planning, so I don't want to step on her toes, but I'll connect with her," I start talking faster as I think about how fun this will be. "Maybe I could do something new just for your wedding! Just let me know, so I can start testing and perfecting recipes for the event. We could do mini cupcakes so people can try a few different kinds if they feel like it!"

"Oooh! Mini cupcakes are so dainty and pretty," Olivia adds.

"Will do. 'Everyone, this is my amazing maid of honor slash pastry chef. She's also available if you have eligible sons'." She laughs and puts her arm around me.

"You lost me at the end of that introduction." I laugh.

"So, no new men? Only cupcakes?" Olivia asks.

"Just cupcakes for now. Honestly, I've had enough less-than-perfect man situations for a while. I need to figure some shit out. Gotta grow up sometime."

"Yeah, it's not even necessarily growing up, though. Part of it is just realizing what you really enjoy," Sarah says. "You sort of hit a point where all the partying just isn't fun. Don't equate getting married with being a grown-up either. None of us really have our shit together. You do know that, right?"

"I do feel like you guys have your shit together. You have stable relationships and jobs that are actual careers."

"Yeah, I'm getting married, but that is scary too! I love Nick, but I'm not ready to start a family. I'm scared of our finances. We're not ready to buy a house. Work is fine, but not some massive enlightening thing either. Don't put too much pressure on yourself. No one is really doing anything that amazing, Lyren."

I absolutely love Sarah for saying this. For reminding me of this.

"And adults also can party. You don't die just because you grow up. You can still have fun."

"OK, let's be honest, I'm not totally done partying or anything," I assure. "And it's not like I have anything going on to really replace Alec in my life, so I don't feel the need to, although I feel that sort of ending. Whatever, I am really just realizing that I need to focus on doing things for me and not for any external reasons."

"Well said," Liv says and raises her Diet Coke to toast. "Men are overrated."

"Yeah, well, can you just wait at least a few months to get engaged?" I ask her. "I might need a little break after being in two weddings at the same time."

"With all the cupcakes I'm eating and planning to eat, I bet Chris isn't going to want to marry me anytime soon. So don't worry."

"Oh, shut up. And you know it's coming."

"Yeah, probably eventually. But I don't want to talk about it or plan ahead. If and when he asks, he'll ask. But you'll have some time to relax. I don't see it happening too soon. We're just getting settled with living together, which, by the way, is a huge adjustment. Like Sarah said, having a partner doesn't mean you're a grown-up. Half of what Chris and I do is argue about what to eat for dinner. And besides, I think I'm going to Africa in the fall."

"What??" I almost choke on a bite of cupcake I just took. "Why do you always do this?"

"Do what?" she asks, all innocent-like.

"Let me babble about unimportant shit in my life and put me

as the center of attention when you have something huge going on! Last time, you just casually mentioned you and Chris were moving in together, and now you just throw in, an hour after we've been hanging out, that you'll be going to Africa in the fall? For what? For how long? With what organization? I'm so proud of you!"

She laughs, "Calm down."

"Well, seriously . . . are you pregnant too?"

"No, definitely not." She pauses. "Well, at least I hope not. But it's through an organization I found that looks really legitimate. You know, I was telling you how I felt like I wouldn't be fulfilled in life unless I really went out and did some volunteering. It's something that has always meant so much to me, and with Chris asking me to move in with him, it just made me realize that I might be settling down soon. I'm 25. It's not like I'm going to be getting any younger. And I'm really cool with my job and comfortable in my relationship. I just don't want to get married and have kids and suddenly it's too late to do the things I really wanted to accomplish before all that. So, I just applied for this program. I'm trying to get a grant. It hasn't all gone through yet. It would just be for a month. I can't leave work or Chris for more than that, but it's a start, you know? And my work doesn't care that much because it actually looks good for them to say one of their social workers did something like this."

"I can't even believe you're really doing it! I mean, I can. You've always wanted to. But you're really doing it! Where in Africa are you going?"

"Ghana. It should be really good. I don't even know for sure what I'll be doing, but I'll probably be working with children. They were really impressed with my background."

"I'm so excited for you! I can't even explain how excited I am for you!" Finally, I am excited for another person who isn't a 12-year-old.

"That's really incredible!" Sarah adds.

"Whatever. I tutor a junior high kid once a week and think I deserve a medal for it. You guys are just way too good of people."

"I'm really excited about it. And a little nervous, to be honest. It was always all talk, but it's different when it's real. I've done a lot of volunteering around here, but it's a lot scarier when it's actually over in Africa. I'll have to do a lot of research and all, but yeah. I'm so excited to finally be doing it."

"You better be careful. I don't want you getting malaria while you're out there."

"Yeah, I don't want that either."

"At least it's only for a month. I'm proud of you for fulfilling your dreams. And I'm glad I don't have to help plan yet another wedding immediately. But if you were going away for more than a month, I might freak out. Especially since Sarah will be married then."

"Oh, don't worry. You won't lose me as a friend just because I'm married," Sarah replies.

"Psh!" I laugh and wave my hand. "At least I have my cupcakes to keep me busy. You guys have weddings and Africa, and I have cupcakes."

"Yours is the tastiest," Sarah laughs.

"So what's going on with you and Gail, anyway?" Olivia asks.

"Oh, we're talking, but sort of reservedly, I guess. I think it might just be better for us to let things cool off. She's got to figure out what she wants to do in her relationship without my advice or guidance, and I need to learn how to not be so selfish, but we need space."

"Sometimes that distance is the best thing," Sarah says.

"It's just weird because I'm not used to fighting with friends. Ever really. I was never one of those girls who got into it with my friends or name-called or anything. The only time I came close was with you, Sarah, sophomore year of high school."

"Well, and that wasn't even a fight. We just had gotten new friends and some different interests. We never actually fought."

"But we made a valiant attempt to get our friendship back to normal. I suppose I should do that with Gail, too."

"You will when the time is right. You're right. She can't expect you to have the answers to her relationship problems. You have already given her all of the advice she can handle. And maybe that's why you've been selfish toward her. Because she needs the space. I don't think you've been selfish to anyone else."

"Thanks for that. I do feel bad about it, but sometimes I think things just run their course. I think we'll be friends, but not like we were in college."

"It happens to everyone."

Chapter Sixteen

"Thanks so much for these tickets! I'm so excited. It's my first Cubs-Sox game!" I say as Sarah and I sit down. She was going with coworkers on the company dime, and someone backed out last minute, so I got the invite.

"I'm so excited you could come! They are really the most fun. I can't believe you've never gone to one! Lyren, this is Greg and Angela."

I say hello and settle down with my beer.

"Great seats, too!" We're sitting near first base in the one-hundred level. It's a beautiful early June day. I'm thrilled to spend the day outside at Wrigley Field.

"I know! We can thank WestCorp for that." She laughs.

"So what do you do?" Angela asks me.

I explain my job and that I still don't know what I want to do for sure, except be a Food Network host.

"Oh my god, I LOVE the Food Network!" Angela exclaims.

"Lyren is a really good cook," Sarah throws in.

"Really? I wish I were a better cook."

"I'm not that good. It's a hobby. I taught myself in college just because I needed a means of procrastination."

"Most of us drank for that," Greg adds.

"Well, I did that, too. But on weekdays I pretty much tried to keep it to cooking as a nice break in my day."

"What do you like to cook?"

"Everything. I try anything that interests me. I love baking the most, but I try not to keep baked goods around the house, so that's reserved mostly for people's birthdays or barbecues."

"Well, I'm having a barbecue next weekend. Thanks in advance for the cupcakes. I like buttercream," Greg replies.

"Good to know," I laugh. "I'm actually in the process of starting a cupcake website. I'm pretty keyed up about it." It's fun to have something to talk about that actually brings me joy. I'm remembering what it is to have vibrancy. To light up. Even if it's small.

"Oh wow!" Angela looks genuinely interested.

"Lyren is making the cupcakes for my shower," Sarah adds. "Get excited."

"I am!"

"Goddamnit!" Greg shouts.

I turn my head to see the Cubs error, allowing the Sox to score.

"What were you expecting? A W?" Angela laughs.

"It would certainly be nice for once," I add. "I really just want the Cubs to win because I am so damn sick of Sox fans getting in my face. I could not care less what the Sox are doing."

"I know, me too," Sarah adds. "My fiancé is a Sox fan."

"I always knew there was something wrong with Nicky," Angela replies.

I, of course, receive a text message mocking the Cubs. *Shocking.*

ALEC

You ready to convert yet?

LYREN

Not on your life. This game isn't over.

ALEC

May as well be. If you're in the area after the game, we should meet up.

LYREN

I'm at the game.

ALEC

So am I!

There's a part of me that doesn't want to meet up with Alec. It's time to move on from him, but at the same time I want to prove that things are still the same. I hate how badly I still want him in my life, even after all the stupidity. We have barely seen each other over the past two months. Some quick outings here and there. I haven't been going out much. I don't know where he's been or who he's been doing, but it hasn't been me. I'm not sure how much of it is intentional on his part. Or maybe it's mine?

"Well, at least you're a fan of the right team. The Sux may win more often, but why anyone would really be a fan of them is beyond me," Greg says.

"I always say I'm a fan of sports because they are fun. Someone is throwing a ball at someone else. This is not a life or death situation. Cubs are by far the more fun team. I don't care if people say we're a bunch of drunks, or that it's about the field and the obnoxiousness or whatever. It's all a part of it. I do love the field. I do love pretending to be 21 and hanging around all day in Wrigleyville. I don't need every stat to appreciate a great day out in the sun with friends."

Taking a sip of my beer, I can't help but smile. I'm genuinely happy, and it's nice to talk about the Cubs instead of work or disappointing dates or weddings.

"Sox fans are just jealous that the only place they have to hang out is their parking lot!" Angela interjects.

"Oh, come on!" Sarah yells as the Cubs let another Sox player on base.

A few beers and hot dogs later, no amount of cheering is going to save the Cubs.

"That was brutal." Greg shakes his head.

"Well, where are we going to drown our sorrows?" Angela asks.

"I hate when we play the Sox because all the bars are going to be full of assholes," Sarah adds. "But what do you guys think?"

"I know a bartender at the Stretch. Want to just head there?" Greg asks.

Sounds just fine to me. I decide to wait and see if Alec bothers to text me instead of texting him first. I hate to admit that I'm really hoping he does, but for all I know he's probably at the game with some girl. And he probably paid over a hundred dollars for her ticket. Just another reminder that I am not that girl to him.

"At least it didn't rain like it was supposed to," Angela says as we walk to the bar through a sea of blue and black falling all over the place. I'm not even sure I can handle the Wrigleyville scene right now. I feel my purse buzz.

ALEC
Hey fool. Where you headed?

Of course I couldn't avoid it, but I'm sort of relieved he is still interested in meeting up.

"I think Alec might meet up with us," I say to Sarah before responding to him.

"Cool. How is that going?" she asks, but looks at me with hesitation.

"Oh, I don't know. The same. We're still screwing, I guess. I think?" I pause. "We sort of got in a weird talk about it back in April, and we haven't spent much time together since. I guess it was a fight. But we made up and were fine afterward. But since then, it has just been a few quick outings before doing other things. I haven't really felt like going out without a specific reason if I'm being honest."

"Sounds like maybe you're both over it."

"I know. This thing with Alec is still cool and fun. We talked about things, and I told him I was upset that it felt like he was changing toward me and was trying to push me away for some reason, and by the end, we were totally fine, and I stayed at his place."

"Who started the argument?"

"Me. He was texting some other girl, and I asked why I wasn't enough. Or something needy and jealous like that."

"That's not needy or jealous, Lyren. That's honest," Sarah replies.

"Yeah, I guess. I think the conversation needed to happen. He said it wasn't about me, but he doesn't want things to get messy, and he wants us to stay friends no matter who we are seeing. I guess the problem has always been that I'm not really seeing anyone else."

"Because you're monogamous to a fault. I mean, I get that you want some good sex. We all do. And I know you've gone on some dates that weren't great. Just don't sell yourself short. You guys have been boning for a while. Maybe it's time for a break."

"Yeah, I know. I mean, it can end at any time, and it will be fine. I'll miss him as a friend, and I can't get rid of him, obviously, because of Olivia. The problem is, we go out not intending to end up together, and it always just sort of happens."

We're trailing behind Angela and Greg as they make their way to the bar.

"OK, but be honest. He has some part of your heart."

"No, he really doesn't."

"Some little part."

"OK, yeah, I *care* about him. I get a little jealous and all. But it's not enough to hurt me."

"You're gonna be surprised at how much that little piece of your heart hurts in the end."

"You don't know that."

"No. I don't. And I want you to keep having fun, if that's what you're doing. But you're fighting. And that's not something friends do when there are no complications. You guys have really been more of an open relationship situation than true friends with benefits. You cuddle. You hang out. You see each other all the time. You fight."

"I know." I wonder how much of what Sarah is saying is true. If that little tiny piece of my heart will hurt like hell when this thing with Alec is over. I knew when I was into Evan that he had a huge chunk of my heart. Maybe all of it. This can't be like that. It won't be. I'm just not ready to let it go yet.

I look back at my phone to tell Alec we're headed to The Stretch.

"Are you even sure you want to meet up with him?" Sarah sees me wait a second before pressing send.

"Yes, and no?" I think about it. "If he's going to be fun and flirty and make me feel pretty and wanted, I want to see him. I guess I want to test the waters to see how much has changed since we aired those concerns."

"It's up to you." She shrugs.

I text him back, telling him where we are. Greg and Angela

found a table, then left to get beers. I keep looking over my
shoulder to see if Alec is already here, and if he is with a girl, in
which case, I hope he doesn't find us.

Eventually, I hear his voice behind me.

"Heeeey!" He gives me a big hug, and sure as shit, there's a
girl next to him. "This is Anne. She's friends with some of my
work people, so I thought I'd show her a pretty accurate compar-
ison of baseball here in Chicago. She lives in Boston and is here
for a week for work. I didn't want her to get bored."

"How nice of you. I'm Lyren," I say, extending a hand and
studying the girl. She's mediocre-looking. Skinny and mousy
with a short brown bob haircut and an awkward smile. But that
doesn't mean Alec isn't trying to sleep with her. Or that he didn't
buy her ticket. Every time Alec has some girl around, he buys
her tickets to awesome places. Every time he gets a ticket to
anywhere, he invites some girl he is trying to sleep with. Never
just a friend. Or a casual hookup.

"Hey Sarah, how have you been?" He gives Sarah a big hug
as if they have known each other forever instead of only meeting
a couple times through me. He's being his normal charming,
friendly self. It's just so easy for him to win people over.

"Hi Alec," she says, getting out of her chair to hug him as
though she wasn't just warning me that I should stay away from
him. "Here, we'll make room. My colleagues got up to get our
beers from the bar, but I think you can order from the waitress.
She's around."

"Thanks!"

"So what exciting travels have you been up to?" Sarah makes
pleasant conversation with him as he finds a seat between us.

"Just LA a few weeks ago to see some old friends. It was a
busy weekend."

It always is when he goes back home, and I know damn well
what he means when he says "busy".

"Before that, it was Italy." He smiles. His life is ridiculous.

Greg and Angela come back with beers, and the conversation is good. It doesn't take long for me to realize that Alec isn't into Anne. He's not paying her attention in the way he does when he is trying to get in a girl's pants. He's fidgety and texts someone new every few minutes. Of course I don't know who he is texting, but I assume it's girls, and I'm dying to know who they are.

"Greg, let's take a lap, man." Alec gets up with Greg. They bonded quickly. Alec never has much trouble making friends, especially when they realize what an expert pickup duo he can create. When they return, Alec is texting again.

"Who are you texting all this time, for god's sake?" I ask it semi-kiddingly. "You really aren't that popular, you know."

"Evidently I am." He smirks, then straightens his face. "Ryan. I think he's meeting us."

"Need your wingman?" I laugh.

"You know it." He smiles. I hate admitting how thrilled I am that he was texting a dude. Alec once tried to set me up with Ryan. Alec can go out and meet whomever he wants, however he wants, when I'm not around, but I'm sure as hell never going to start introducing him to my friends hoping they hit it off. It obviously says something for how little he must actually care about me that he'd want to set me up with his friend. Or maybe it means he wants me in his life and wants all of his friends to be genuinely happy? Either way, I am not into Ryan.

When Ryan arrives, Alec introduces us for the fiftieth time.

"I know who Ryan is, Alec!" I am almost rude about it as I hug Ryan hello.

"I'm sorry! I don't know when you met."

"We've met so many times," I joke. "But it's OK since everyone was probably drunk every time." I'm pretty drunk now, I realize. Things are a little hazy. I go back over to Sarah. I need to get away from their boy talk conversation, and Alec only wanted Ryan here to help him meet girls. I want to flirt with someone, but I can't see anyone worth flirting with at all.

"Lyren, I think I'm gonna head out. I'm getting tired," Sarah says after an hour.

"OK. It was so good seeing you!" I hug her. "Thanks so much for the tickets. I seriously had a great time."

"You staying here?"

"Yeah, I think I'm going to stay here a while." I glance over to where Alec is talking to two girls at a nearby table as I say it.

"OK," she says and goes over to the table to start saying goodbye to everyone.

I stay where I am and start texting. I scroll through my contacts, thinking of anyone to text that would make me feel wanted. I can't stay here alone with Alec and those girls. Greg and Angela left. But why don't I want to go home? Why do I so desperately need attention?

"Who are you texting?" Sarah asks when she gets back to me.

"No one."

"Seriously," she demands.

"I'm booty calling," I laugh, trying to play it off casually instead of sheer desperation.

She looks over at my phone. "Floor shitter? Oh my god, Lyren, I am not letting you booty call Floor Shitter."

Yes, I am texting Sean. Or, was about to. I know that's insane. He shat on my floor. Why would I want to ever see him? But I don't really have a Rolodex of sure things. It might be wrong, but doesn't everyone win? Isn't that what you do in your 20s? Booty call each other and use each other for sex when someone you really want to go home with is busy talking to a bunch of people who aren't you?

"Lyren, put the phone down. You don't need a booty call. What are you gonna do?"

I glance at the table. If I stay, I'll end up going home with

Alec. He's only talking to these girls. He's not really trying to get them home with him. I can tell by the look on his face and the way he is moving his body. Definitely not really into them.

"I think I'm gonna stay and see if . . . "

"You're not staying. Come here." She grabs my arm and drags me out of the bar.

"What?" I ask as she hails a cab.

"You're not staying there watching Alec put you at the bottom of his list, hoping for his attention, that's what."

God, this girl knows me so well.

"What do you want to do?" she asks as we get in the cab.

"I just want to go home." I look past her, afraid to really let her look at me. I'm lonely, desperate, and angry. And really, really, pathetic.

"If you go home, are you going to sit there and be sad?"

"Yes." *What's the point in lying now?*

"No way. I'm kidnapping you." She puts her arm around me.

Damn her. I really wanted to go home. I feel a good cry coming on. I don't even know over what.

"Justin's bar, please."

When we get into the bar, I'm glad we stayed out. Alec doesn't deserve me being sad about him at home. Remembering the rules, and that he and I are only friends, I have no right to be upset with him, anyway. We sit at the bar, and Sarah gets us one more round of Bud Lites. And waters. She gives me the water first.

"OK, Lyren. Be honest with yourself. Why are you texting booty calls right now?"

"I don't want to go to bed alone."

"Right, because Alec wasn't paying attention to you."

"When did he stop?" I hear my own voice sounding so meager as I ask this. When did I become the girl so needy of a man's attention that I'll wait around, hoping to be his tenth choice?

"I don't know, Ly. I don't know what things used to be like. But you're lying to yourself. You're not OK with things anymore. It isn't healthy anymore. I think in the long run, he's going to miss the shit out of you. I really do. But right now, he's taking you for granted, and you're letting him. You deserve so much more than what you're settling for. Lyren, you are stunningly gorgeous, OK? If you want a freakin' booty call, have one. But you are starving for that dumbass's attention, and I can't deal with it anymore. He doesn't deserve your tears, or your heart, or your vagina."

She's right. I used to sleep with Alec because we had a great time all night, and it led me to desire him. Now, it is just what I hope will happen at the end of the night, regardless of our actions together before it. I just need the assurance that things aren't ending. I've become desperate for his attention.

"Oh, I know. I promise I'm not falling for him. It's not like that. I'm just . . . lonely. I spend so much time trying to be strong and acting like I don't want a guy, and I'm secretly terrified that I'm not really OK. I just want something real, and Alec fills a void." I move from the water to the beer.

"I know. But it's not in a good way anymore."

"You're right. I know you're right. I got so used to it. It's much nicer than dating because I have so much space with him. He was just sort of always there when I was lonely and when I wanted someone. And he made me feel so sexy and all. I don't know when it turned into me feeling like I was pleading with him to want me."

My phone buzzes almost on cue.

ALEC
You didn't say bye.

I show the text to Sarah.
"Don't respond."

"Is that petty?"

"No. You're out having fun. You're just not paying attention to your phone."

"Is it bad that I'm happy he texted me?"

"No. He notices you're gone. That counts for something. But it could also just be because he realized those lame girls he was talking to weren't going to sleep with him and he's wondering where his booty call went."

"Ugh. When did I get so pathetic?"

"You're not pathetic. You're drunk and missing the way things used to be with Alec. You'll be fine. Just don't let that asshole walk all over you. You're supposed to be good friends. Remember that. Friends don't abuse each other or take each other's company for granted, whether you're getting naked or not."

"Thank you for making me leave. I wouldn't have on my own. I'd have gone home with him."

"I know."

"I just wish I didn't feel so lonely at night. I mean, most of the time I'm fine. I used to feel strong and powerful, and I didn't feel like I needed a man for anything. And then something happens when I drink where I just need someone's attention and I just want that space in my bed filled."

"I get that. And you'll find someone who is worth filling that space in your bed."

"I'm not some girl that needs a guy to validate her." I'm not sure if I'm saying it more to convince her or myself.

"Of course you're not. You get lonely. That's pretty damn normal. But don't lose sight of who you are and what you really want over a guy. I think all this partying and casual sex stuff you've been doing is great. I really do. You were so straight-laced in college and about relationships, and you never ever screwed up. You always did everything according to the rule-book, and I think it's really good for you that you're stepping out of that box. You'd have regretted it your whole life, I think, if you never got a little crazy and did some things just because they were fun. But don't lose sight of your values. You are still a strong and powerful woman who is in control of your situation."

"I am. I know this thing with Alec is going to end. I just really am not ready for that yet. I am not ready for the fun to end. I just think we need some space for now. He's got some new girl coming to visit him from Vegas or something. I don't even know if she's of legal drinking age. He doesn't have that many friends around here, so he thinks somehow that I'm going to hang out with her. I don't want to be here for that. I don't want to be near him. He thinks somehow that our being just friends means I want to spend time with girls he's into. Like I'm supposed to switch from flirting with him to playing all nicey nice with the girl he's adoring. He's so excited about her coming in. I have no right to wish him anything bad. I just know I need to stay away."

"When is she coming?"

"I dunno. A week or two."

"OK. Keep yourself busy. Don't think about him while she's here."

"I won't."

"And seriously? Isn't this like the third girl he's had come to fuck him from some vacation he's been on?"

"Something like that."

"Next time you are sad about this boy ignoring you, please remember that he's ridiculously immature and probably the least impressive guy you've ever had a thing for. He's having a child come visit him from Las Vegas. He's almost 30. That's just wrong."

"God, I know. It's so disgusting. I hate men."

"Well, that's a new low for guys you've liked. I mean, I know Evan liked insecure girls, but at least they had made their First Communion." I laugh. "You will be single until you actually find a *man*. And it will be grand."

My phone rings. I hold it up to show Sarah that it's Alec.

"Ignore it. Let him wonder what you're doing."

"Isn't that trivial and stupid?"

"So is ignoring the hottest girl in the room while he talks to random boring strangers and then calling her to see where she is and pouting that she didn't say goodbye. One day, maybe this dumbass will realize that you've been the best thing in his life."

"I love you, Sarah." She puts her arm around me. "I'm ready to go home without crying now." And I mean it.

Chapter Seventeen

I'm running around like a crazy person before Sarah's shower. It's at a little bistro in Lincoln Park, and I have made three different kinds of cupcakes. It's my first time making mass quantities, and everything that could have gone wrong has seemed to.

I ran out of butter and had to drive over to Jewel in the middle of baking the first batch. Then, the lemon frosting I made was runny, and I needed more confectioner's sugar, so I had to run back yet again. The whipped cream frosting on the cherry sundae cupcakes kept on wanting to melt, so I had to create more storage in my refrigerator to keep them there, and I just pray they don't melt before the shower itself. This is my cupcake-making debut, and it's a huge undertaking. I really should have started with a small birthday party or something. You know, thirty cupcakes rather than two-hundred minis.

Because of all the chaos actually finishing the cupcakes, and it taking significantly longer to package and prepare them for the car ride, I have absolutely no time to get ready. I stare at my closet. *Damn it! I really should have figured out an outfit in advance.*

I grab one of my sundresses I haven't worn in a while. It's peach and lacy and perfect for a daytime wedding shower as long as my fat ass can fit in it. *I really need to stop eating my own frosting.* I make a mental note for the umpteenth consecutive week to start a diet and exercise program on Monday. I've just been crazy busy between my actual, hated job, and my new, exciting job.

I look at my hair in the mirror. It's flat, but it's going to have to do. I don't have time to mess with it. I throw on some mascara and a pair of wedges and start bringing the cupcake boxes to the car. If I'm going to be a business owner, I have to get better at being prepared and organized.

I put the cupcakes in the trunk, and all I can do is cross my fingers that they are going to be OK there. I don't want to make an ass of myself as a baker in front of all of Sarah's friends and family. Why do I put myself in these situations? It's been a while since I've been so nervous about something, and I can't help but think, maybe it's a good thing. I actually care.

"Hi!" I run up and give Sarah a big hug.

We have a half hour to set up the cupcakes and the rest of the room before the guests arrive. Sara is wearing a simple white lacy sundress. She looks completely classy and serene. Classic Sarah. "You look seriously stunning, Sarah!"

"Thank you so much! I love your dress!"

"God, Sarah! This is your wedding shower!" I almost cry as I say it. I look at her in amazement, thinking how far we've come since junior high, when we had a crush on the same boy and used to fight over him at recess. As if he ever paid attention.

"I know. It's crazy. It's really happening!"

"Seriously, just think for a second about all the times we never believed this could happen. All the stupid boys you'd cried over, thinking it was the end of the world and thinking you'd never be happy."

"God, remember David?" She rolls her eyes.

"I'm pretty sure David is gay," I say, laughing.

"No kidding. And when Tara and I got into that huge fight over Thomas?"

"I seriously have never wanted to punch a girl more. Thomas always liked you the whole time."

"Well, our two-year relationship would prove that to be true. What if I had married him?"

"You'd probably be divorced by now. What if I had married Jason?"

"You'd probably be divorced by now." We laugh.

"God, it's just so crazy to think about how all the things we once thought we wanted so badly just work out in the long run."

"I couldn't be happier for you or more confident that you are with a person that is perfect for you." I blink back tears and hug her again.

"Lyren, you've been such an amazing friend. Even through the shit that Nick and I went through in the beginning. You've always been such an incredible voice of reason. You will seriously get yours one day. Just keep being the person you are, and the most amazing man is going to love you."

"I know." We're both crying now. "Damn it! We need to stop all this stupid slobbering! Pictures are going to be taken, you know!" I wipe under my eyes in case there is loose mascara falling.

She laughs. "I know. Oh, and by the way?"

"Yeah?"

"These cupcakes are unbelievably stunning. I seriously could not have asked for a better shower dessert. I can't wait to show them to everyone, and I really can't wait to eat them."

"Aww, thanks."

"I'm serious. You've even exceeded my expectations. This is so perfect. Thank you. Thank you for everything."

I add the cupcakes to a tiered display stand near the gift table and look around the room as guests start to come in. Everyone is beaming over Sarah, and it's nice to see her get this attention and fuss. I still think weddings are stupid, but Sarah deserves all the attention and recognition in the world, so if she gets it because she found a man who loves her and whom she loves back, I can be OK with it.

Her mom looks so proud. There were years I spent so much time over at their house, I got her mom an extra Mother's Day card. It's nice to see everyone so happy.

"So, Lyren, are you dating anyone these days?" As the shower nears its end, one of Sarah's bridesmaids, who I was never a big fan of, asks me.

"No, just focusing on a lot of other things in my life. No time for a relationship."

"Oh, don't be silly. Pretty girl like you? I'm sure you'll find someone right away."

I want to punch every person who does this. Who acts like because I am not dating someone that there is something significantly wrong with me. Or that being pretty is the only prerequisite to having a boyfriend. As if plenty of unattractive people don't find love every single day. And what makes it OK for people to come up and just bombard me with questions about my personal life, anyway? Do I go up to people and ask if their relationship is boring and horrible yet? *Hey, do you still like to bang that caveman who plays video games five hours a day? Wow, you've been dating the same guy since high school? Sounds like you should get out more! I'm so sorry you've only slept with one person.* I'm almost laughing at my own inner train of thought and realize I haven't responded.

"Not really my priority right now." Maybe they only ask so they can validate their own choices. Maybe their relationship sucks, but at least they aren't, *gasp, single!* Sarah picks up on my irritation and saves the moment by standing up.

"I just want to say thank you so much to everyone who has made this shower and the whole wedding planning process so great. I seriously couldn't have done it without all of you. I am so excited to be planning my life with the most amazing man in the world, and all of your guidance and support throughout everything in my life has honestly put me in the place I am today, and I couldn't be happier. Thank you so much to my amazing mom, who not only planned this shower, but who has been a rock throughout my life. I don't know what I would do without her."

She looks over at her mom, who is crying. And then she turns back to me. "And I especially want to thank my maid of honor, my best friend since junior high, and one of the most sincere, awesome people I have ever known. Lyren, thanks for being such a place of guidance for me throughout everything in my life that has led me to where I am. Not just with my recent relationship, but for literally everything you have done from helping defend me to Bailey when Dan wanted to go out with me instead of her in the eighth grade, and from crying over Thomas in high school, and liking David, and everything that followed. Also, you should all know that these absolutely gorgeous cupcakes are compliments of Lylac Bakery, Lyren's new online bakery. They are so amazing, and I'm so thankful to her for bringing them. If you ever need cupcakes, seriously look up her website. All of her information is up here. Thank you again so much!"

We get all teary again and hug while everyone applauds.

Sarah's mom gets up to say a few words. After the shower, I walk around and mingle a while before people get ready to go.

"Lyren, these cupcakes really are to die for. And so gorgeous! Do you run your cupcake shop out of your house?" A girl I don't know approaches me.

"Yeah, I literally just started. This is my first real event. I always baked for people, and it's such a strong hobby of mine that I decided to try it out for real. Maybe one day it'll pick up and I can get a storefront or something, but we'll see what happens. I'm just glad I was able to safely get all of these here." *One step at a time.*

"Well, they really are awesome. I'm not just saying that. I know there are a million little bakeries and cupcake specialty shops now, so it's a really tough business, but it's awesome that you're doing something you care about and love."

"Thanks. I feel the same way. It's scary because there are so many. But I kind of feel like I have to just go with what feels right right now, and that's cupcakes."

"I was that way, too. I was working as a recruiter out of college just because I needed a job, but I hated it. I did it for a few years and felt so cranky all the time. I was a jerk to my family and to my boyfriend. I wanted to be a food writer, so finally I just started writing articles and sending them places."

"Really? That's actually the other thing I've always wanted to do. Write about education issues for papers and stuff. I was a journalism major in college."

"Well, that's a bit harder and more intense than writing about restaurants, but that's awesome. Seriously, just do it. I assume you're busy with the cupcake stuff, but just start writing. It feels amazing. Anyway, I got a job at the *Red Eye* now, and it's seriously insane to think about how much my life has changed for the better since pursuing what I actually wanted to and am proud of."

"Wow, good for you!" It's inspiring to hear about someone

else who wasn't feeling happy and took a leap of faith. Maybe not everyone around me has it all figured out all the time.

"Thanks. Anyway, I was thinking that I really do love to showcase start-ups and self-made places. It feels like what America is about. Would you be interested in having me write a little article on your cupcake shop?"

"Are you serious?"

"Yeah, I really am. It's small. I don't have a big column. What I do is just a cross between reviews, advertising, and really tiny articles. But it might help you get noticed and get some business coming your way."

"I can't even believe you're willing to do that." My heart wants to leap out of my chest. I don't want to jump and scream and hug her . . . but I want to jump and scream and hug her.

"I really love your work."

"Wow! Yes, I would absolutely love for you to do that. If I can start getting enough business, I can't even imagine how happy it would make me to quit my job and just do the cupcake thing full time."

"Well, I'd be glad to help. Give me your information, and I'll set up a time to interview you and take some pictures."

I write my information down and feel my heart pounding. A write-up in the *Red Eye*. This could seriously be my big break! Or at least A break.

As I help Sarah clean up and haul presents to the car, I notice most of my cupcakes are gone. She tells me how huge of a hit they were.

For the first time in a while, I feel like things are finally going right.

Chapter Eighteen

I haven't seen Alec in over a month. The last time we hung out was at the Cubs game. I haven't wanted to admit anything is changing or different, but everything in my gut knows it is. We've had the occasional brief Facebook interaction or whatever, but nothing of any substance. Not that we ever really had conversations of substance, but comparatively, our relationship is empty. Our friendship is slipping through my fingers, and I am powerless to stop it and too stubborn to make it clear that I care.

He has been dating a lot. Pretty much constantly. How he manages to meet all of these girls, I have no idea. I don't need to hear the details. I can't fully admit we aren't friends anymore, so I look for excuses. When I've made a comment about him not being around, he'd say he isn't going out much or just not in the city or whatever. I don't know what it will be like when we actually hang out. As much as I want to believe it'll be OK, I know it won't be.

Olivia's boyfriend's birthday, I figured I'd see him. Actually,

I am sure I will. In one of our few conversations the previous week, he'd said he'd be there, *"Saturday, for sure."* Hopefully, we'll be sort of normal.

I texted him earlier in the day to see his plans, and he said he wasn't sure. He was "still recovering".

I know what that means, and I shouldn't be surprised. Why would hanging out with Olivia's friends be important enough not to get shit-wasted the night before? The only thing that matters in life is seducing random chicks, and that's not going to happen in a dive karaoke bar with mostly testosterone, your little sister, and your no-longer-exciting fuck buddy.

Sarah is coming with me. We went to dinner and are now getting ready at my place.

"Is Alec coming?" she asks as she curls her long, dark hair.

"Probably not. He's gotten so annoying, but whatever. We'll see."

"Are you upset that he might not?"

"I suppose it's a stupid thing to be upset about. It's pretty clear proof how little he cares to see me again. I want to see if we're OK or if we're still even friends."

"Why wouldn't you be? Last I saw you, he was calling wondering why you left."

"He used to call me regularly. He used to want to meet up and hang out or even stay in and watch movies. We used to make plans or just assume we'd be at each other's events. Doesn't happen anymore," I explain as I shoot him a text message.

"Well, maybe it's just time to move on, Ly."

"Yeah, probably overdue really. I just wish I had a replacement."

ALEC
I'm gonna be lame tonight.

My heart sinks. So he really doesn't care about ever seeing me again.

"Seriously, Ly. Move on."

I pick up my phone again. It is a bad idea; it always is, but I have to test this; see how bad this really is. Push my own buttons on this issue.

LYREN
Guess it's time for me to find a new partner in crime.
You're getting old or something.

"You'll have fun without him."

"Oh, I know. I knew this would suck. I just have to deal with it. I have no one to flirt with."

ALEC
Yes, I have taught you well. On to the next one! ;)

It is single-handedly the worst response he could have had. My stomach drops again. This is it. This is more or less a break up. As much of one as you get from a friend who doesn't want to be your friend anymore. He really did move on, and is telling me I have to, too.

"What?" Sarah asks, no doubt noticing my facial expression.

"Nothing really. This thing with Alec just really is officially done, I guess."

"I'm sorry, Ly."

"Yeah, oh well. I knew it would happen. I knew I wouldn't like it. Maybe I was foolish enough to believe I'd move on first. I always thought he'd at least miss me."

"He will. More than he knows. He's an idiot. But you didn't want him, anyway."

"No, I know I didn't. I just have a hollowness or something

where I want him to be, you know. I wish I had someone to fill it."

"You'll get someone better. For now, you look hot. We're going karaoking, and you can flirt with your friends freely. Don't think about that stupid slut." She toasts her pregame vodka soda against mine, and we take a final look in the mirror. We do look hot.

I give her a half-hearted smile, check to make sure I have my ID and cash, and follow her out the door, locking it behind me.

"We're going to Circle Street," Sarah says as we get in the cab. I check my phone.

PETER

Where are you? We're missing your baked goods!

This night won't be so bad. Dive bar karaoke with friends is really all I need at this point, and after my stint with Steve, I actually have the balls to go up there. What do I need Alec for? And then I check my phone again.

"Oh my god," I say aloud.

"What?" I show Sarah Olivia's text.

OLIVIA

Evan is here. With a date. Thought you'd need a
heads up.

I start shaking uncontrollably. I am holding in the need to regurgitate my dinner all over the backseat of the cab.

"I've . . . We've . . . I've never had to deal with this before. I've not seen him out with someone. I know it's nothing, but . . . oh god." I don't know why I feel so sick. I am not supposed to care about Evan anymore. I don't even think about Evan. I no longer stalk Evan; I no longer write about Evan or fantasize about Evan or text Evan. What difference does it make if he is there with a girl?

"Oh, you'll be fine. He sucks."

"I know. I know he sucks. I just hate that he's got someone and I don't. He doesn't deserve someone. He's a selfish piece of shit. I'm a better person than him. I want to love someone. Why does everyone have someone except me? Goddamn, do I wish Alec was going, and we were still normal."

I remember when Alec made a point to flirt with me so I'd feel better about Dickface. This is what I am going to miss about having Alec in my life.

"You don't need Alec. You'll have a great time singing and being fabulous and not worrying about boys who aren't worth your time." I take out my phone again. "Don't text him."

"Why?" I ask as I push "send" on a text chiding Alec for not being there when I need him. It's like I have to touch the cauldron to know it's hot . . . again. I am not even drunk and already need someone to take away my phone.

"Lyren, seriously. You're freaking out for nothing. You don't like that Alec and Evan have moved on, but think about all the guys you've upset by moving on or never letting them be a part of your life. This timing sucks, but you have way too much going for you to be upset about these douchebags. Think about it. This is just more advertising for your cupcakery! You're too good for this. Remember that."

"Ugh, I know! I know I am! Somewhere inside I know I am. But it's like, my job is so fucking pointless, and I can barely pay my goddamn bills, and I'm drinking myself stupid on a regular basis, and I just don't feel like I have anything of substance. Evan was the last person I really opened up to, and that was years ago. I just pick and choose people to fill stupid voids. I don't know when this is going to end or when I'm going to have something real in my life. I'm sorry. I know this is stupid. It's just . . . why both of these things in one night?"

"To prove that you can handle anything."

I know why I texted Alec. I wanted him to tell me that I am going to be OK. But I need to learn to move on without approval from Alec. To be OK around Evan without having someone else to flirt with. I am terrified. And Alec isn't even responding.

"If I were alone in this cab, I'd probably have asked him to turn around after I read that text message."

"And that is exactly what you don't want to do. Don't let Evan's arrogant, irritating ass affect you in any way."

"Why does he?" My stomach is turning inside out. I keep picturing walking in, wondering how I'll say hello . . . wondering how I can possibly act "normal" in this situation. "I mean, seriously, it's been over a year. Almost two YEARS! How the fuck does he still have any power over me? I don't even want to be with him. I'm never letting my guard down or liking someone again. This has been the worst fucking thing my head has ever had to deal with. I think I'd rather get shot in the gut than fall in love again."

"Lyren, you're just upset that he moved on before you got someone else, but that's just silly. It's a date. She might not mean anything."

"I think part of it is that I know everyone is going to be watching me for my reaction. And I don't know how to control it. Do I say hi? Do I avoid him? What do I do?"

"You just don't worry about it. You smile. You be confident. You karaoke. You laugh. If you come home and want to bawl your goddamn eyes out about hating your job or feeling empty or never wanting to love again, you can absolutely do that. But you wait until you're home. Got it?" She makes me look at her. I take a deep breath. I can do this.

"Got it. I can do this." I try to sound confident.

"You can do this."

"I've got it together. At least Liv texted me. I'm good. My stomach is getting better."

"Of course Liv texted you a warning. Now let's go. Your adoring fans are waiting for cupcakes, and no one gives a fuck about Evan. You're the star of this show. Well, you and Chris." I hug her as we pay the cab driver.

I take another deep breath and step out. I can hear Peter rapping as I show the doorman my ID.

I can do this.

Peter looks at me from the stage, and I run up and hug him just in time to chime in, "I've got 99 problems but a bitch ain't one . . . HIT ME!"

Nothing wrong with making a grand entrance. I laugh and go around hugging those friends who cheered upon my arrival. I may not have a great career or be in love, but I have fucking awesome friends.

"Ly!" Olivia comes up and squeezes me, and I thank her in her ear. "Well, duh. I just had to make sure to wait a second to text you after he walked in or it might have been obvious." She laughs.

"Ooooh, what are these?" Chris comes up and asks, putting his arm around me, eyeing the coconut key lime cupcakes in my hand.

"Happy birthday!" I hug him with my free hand and go to set the cupcakes down on a table.

"Thanks. Let me at one of those. It's my birthday!"

"I haven't even finished saying hi to everyone yet!"

"Well, fuck saying hi to people. Feeding me is more important." Chris grabs a cupcake and stuffs it in his mouth. "Goddamn, these are good!" he mumbles.

"You're too sweet."

"Shot?" Sarah asks.

"Oh, fuck yes. Vodka, now!"

Liv joins in the shot. There are enough people blocking me from Evan that I don't have to make a point to say hello yet.

More ways to avoid having to meet the cute little thing on his arm. Fuck Evan.

"Peter and Lyren!" the KJ calls, and I glare at Peter.

"What are we singing?? You did NOT consult me in this matter!" I laugh as we get up and I am handed a mic. The music starts, and my heart sinks. "Separate Ways" comes on. *Stop it!*

It is weird singing this song that I always thought of as my song with Alec and having the lyrics almost make sense in some silly 80s rock kind of way. But I let go and try to focus on not making an ass of myself. We get way too into it, and I let loose, attempting to headbang and risking losing my voice for the rest of the night as I scream out, "Noooooooo!!!!!" Our performance is met with roaring applause as I high five friends and get back to the regular part of the bar.

"What's up, rock star?!" Evan comes up and hugs me, too close, and kisses me somewhere meant for the cheek but is really a lot more like my neck. *Ugh.* I really don't have feelings for him anymore. I no longer care what he smells like or what his arms feel like around my body. I just want him to go away. This was about winning, and with Evan, I lost. I lost really badly. Truthfully, I don't know if I'm even capable of real love or if it's always about some stupid sort of challenge to get someone smarter and more confident than me to reciprocate some sense of feelings that I don't even understand myself.

"Hey," I say, then start talking to Olivia and Sarah. I don't have any desire to meet the tiny brunette on his arm, and I figure he probably has little desire to introduce her to me. She stands awkwardly behind him as she has been there the entire time. I find it strange he is with a brunette. She is not at all his usual type.

Someone calls him, and he walks away. I did it. I was fine.

"She's cute," I say when they are out of earshot.

"Cute, yes. Gorgeous, no," Sarah responds.

"Little," I say.

"Yes," Sarah acknowledges.

"Whatever. You're prettier than her," Liv states.

I sort of always wondered why we girls need to know this. As if it makes any difference at all. For some reason, whatever it may be, the guy likes her more than you, so why does it matter if she's absolutely fugly? Technically, shouldn't we feel better if she's absolutely stunning? So you have some tangible reason why she's better? I mean, wouldn't that be better than "Well, you're cute, but her personality is better"? I mean, if she's ugly, then you must really suck. Nevertheless, I like feeling that I am prettier than this brunette. Even if she is all skinny and small and stuff.

———

When I get home, I don't cry. I had a fun night with my friends. I didn't freak out over Evan. I didn't make an ass of myself. But there is one thing that keeps on creeping into the back of my head as I try to fall asleep. Alec never responded to my last text.

———

"Lyren, I need you," is all Gail's voicemail says.

I get home from work, change into sweats, and call her back. We haven't really spoken except for a couple Facebook Messenger exchanges about nonsense for three months. We haven't discussed our fight, but this voicemail makes it clear we could skip that part for an emergency.

"Gail, what's going on?"

"Hey," she manages, and it's obvious she has been crying.

I sit cross-legged on the couch. "What happened? Are you OK?"

"I will be. I think I did the right thing."

"Did you leave Brad?" I hold my breath. I know it is hard for her to get the words out.

"Yeah."

"Wow. Do you want to talk about it?" Should I feel guilty that my first reaction is relief? Brad was bringing her down.

"I just, I don't know. You were right. I was letting him control my life by deciding he just didn't feel like getting married. I want to be married. I want to have kids. And I've been holding on to him because I'm afraid that by letting him go I'm setting myself even farther back. But we're just not on the same page. He doesn't want what I want."

"What'd he say?" I am glad Gail felt she could call me about this despite our fight. It makes me feel like I must not be such a horrible person. We just really weren't on the same page before.

"He's really sad. We are trying not to talk for a few days just to let it settle, but I want to talk to him so badly. I miss him so much. What if I'm making a mistake?"

"Well, something in your gut obviously told you to do this, right?"

"Yes."

"So, one way or another, it has to be a good thing. Maybe you'll get back together, but a break is probably something you both need. Maybe he'll realize how much you mean to him and that he doesn't want to lose you, and that he is ready for marriage. Or maybe you'll realize how many other people there are out there who can make you happy and be what you need."

"I know. I am just so sad. Would I be this sad if I were doing the right thing?"

"Of course you're sad. You didn't end things because you are totally sick of him as a person. You love him. There will be things you will always love about him. That's what relationships do. They get in your head, and they change you, and you don't just get over them because they end. It takes time and process-ing. You'll stop being sad, eventually. You will get married, Gail.

You will meet someone who makes you unbelievably happy. I assure you. Maybe it just isn't Brad. And I'm really proud of you. This isn't an easy thing for you to do. Just give it time and see how things go."

"I'm trying to. Thanks for talking to me. I feel a little better now, actually. I know we haven't really been getting along amazingly, but you've always been the friend I can count on to be real and give me honest advice—even if I admit that sometimes I don't want real advice."

"I know that I'm very to blame for all of it, too, Gail. And I'm really glad you called me. I don't want our friendship to end just because I've been a really selfish person, and we have different things going on. We have too much history for that."

"I agree. It's sad this is the circumstance that finally got me to get over my pride, but at least maybe some good will come of all this. How have you been lately? Anything new?"

"Good will come of it for sure outside of just you and I, anyway. You'll know you made the right decision because it might not be the end, and if it's not, your relationship will be strengthened. And if it is the end, well then, you don't want to spend one more day wasting your time."

"You're right. You tend to be."

"I don't know about that. I certainly can't seem to control my own life."

"How is Alec?"

"Over," I say wistfully. It's weird to think it's really over. Not that there's been a conversation about it.

"I'm sorry."

"I'm certainly at no place where I should care. I knew this was coming. It's just, now that it's really here . . . I don't know. It sucks."

"Of course you care, and of course it sucks. How could it not? How could you not care?"

"Because it's not a big deal. We are sex friends. That's it."

"Lyren, I'm sorry. You're a girl. We aren't fully capable of having emotionless intimacy."

"I wanted to be."

"It's not possible."

"I did pretty good."

"How long has it been?"

"Oh, December, so almost eight months. Over a year since we've been hanging out."

"That's a really long run for friends with benefits."

"Yeah. I mean, like I said, I always knew this would end badly. There was no alternative. Now I really need to let it go."

"Why are you so sure it's ending or that it has to?"

"What do you mean?"

"I don't know . . . I guess I sort of thought you'd work it out."

"Like as in be together? No way!"

"Why though?"

"We have nothing in common. We have nothing real. Our whole friendship is based on flirting and getting drunk. I think the major difference is that is what his whole life seems to be based on."

"Seems that way."

"He's a good friend and family member and all that, but the person I am is not made to be with someone like the person he is. No one is wrong or anything. In any case, I never thought that would be the result, nor did I want it to be. I just feel that it's ending prematurely."

"Why is it ending? How do you know?"

I recap the events of the karaoke party, where Alec never texted me back.

"Just because he didn't respond doesn't mean you guys aren't friends anymore," Gail says.

"Whatever. You know what I need to do? I need to focus on myself. Maybe I needed him to move on so I could remind myself of what I love and what I want without some stupid boy getting in my way."

"That's awesome. What are you gonna do?"

"I'm starting a cupcake business. Sarah's shower was sort of my debut. Fuck Evan, fuck Alec. I need to stop trying to fill what's really missing with people that don't mean what I need them to. Evan fucked me up and Alec was a lot of fun, but it's just not me."

Gail laughs. "You're pretty angry, aren't you?"

"You know what? It's not worth getting angry about. It's not even worth thinking about. When I really think about it, yes, I'm angry. I hate feeling thrown away. I hate wondering why I'm not sexy or interesting enough anymore. But realistically, I'm being a huge hypocrite. I always said I knew him and accepted him for what he was. So, a part of me thought he was better than I knew in my head or just different. A part of me hoped that some of his shallow shell was a façade. But it's not. He's shallow. He needs constant stimulation in the form of getting laid by random people. He's transient. He doesn't look for things that require thought or real effort. He brought out a party person in me. It was fun, but it's not who I want to be. I already feel like I lost years of my life by just doing a mindless job, crushing on assholes, and drinking myself stupid. I'm not wasting another minute on this guy. I'm just focusing on me."

"You'll find a great guy when you really want one. You're way too deep and awesome for a guy like Alec."

"That's just it, Gail. I don't want to even think about a guy. I'm done filling voids with pointless shit. I'm not looking for a guy. I don't need that shit."

"Well, I'm sort of hoping for the opposite for myself."

I don't know how to tell Gail that her dependency on Brad was the complete downfall of her own creativity. She is the epitome of what I never want in my relationships. Sometimes I think about being alone while everyone else has someone, and I have no one to hang out with, and I wonder if I'll be OK. But it's gotta be better than spending my life completely understimulated.

"Well, I've come to the great realization that I will never be understood when it comes to dating or my mind or whatever. But hey, Emerson thought that was pretty cool."

"Huh?"

"To be great is to be misunderstood."

"You're really weird, Lyren."

"Yeah, but that's part of why you're friends with me."

"Go change the world or something."

"Well, I'm probably not going to do that, but I can at least produce something I am proud of in my life."

"That sounds good."

"I know everyone thinks that at almost 27, I should spend all of my free time husband hunting or some crap, but you people really need to understand it's seriously last on my list right now."

"Yeah, well, I hope you figure it out, but either way, when you decide you want a man, you'll have no trouble finding a good one." She's clearly not getting my message, but I'm sort of thrilled at the moment. It's like I sort of had an epiphany and just woke up, thanks to Alec's douchebaggery.

"Alright, Gail, thanks for being my sounding board for all this chaos."

"Anytime, Lyren."

"And I know you're going through a tough time now with a lot of adjustments. Just stay strong and know I am here for you. I may be focusing on myself and my needs, but I am also going to consciously try to be at least a little less selfish," I say jokingly and let out a little laugh. "Seriously though, if you need to talk, I will always listen."

"Thank you."

"Glad we talked."

"Me too."

Chapter Nineteen

TWO WEEKS LATER

I put the lid on my cupcake container and then frantically run around, touching up my mascara and fixing my hair one last time. I'm running late for Olivia's birthday because cupcakes took longer than anticipated (mostly because I felt the need to fancy them up with extra decorations and multiple special frosting flavors). I don't feel that I'm looking my absolute best, but it will have to do because showing up too late is not acceptable.

I slide into one stiletto, take another sip of the vodka soda I've been consuming while doing ten things at once, and then put on the other heel, almost stumbling over because I'm doing it while walking. One day . . . one day, I will be prepared for my life and not run around like a crazy person. I almost laugh at the thought. I've been running late my entire life.

I throw my purse on my arm, close the shades, grab the cupcakes and my keys, and step out, locking my door with my barely free hand. I know I'll never get a cab on my quiet side street, so I'm trying to walk as fast as possible in my brand new four-inch heels while carrying two trays.

I see a cab and try my best to balance the cupcakes on one hand while I hail it. *Success!* I breathe a sigh of relief while carefully getting in. I managed not to mess up the cupcakes at all. *I'm getting good at this*!

"Aw, how nice! You brought me a little cake!" my driver says as I arrange myself comfortably in the back.

I laugh. "You can have one if you like. There are about a hundred of them. I'm going to Armitage and Sheffield, by the way."

"Ah, no problem. And I was only joking. You don't need to share your cakes with me. Pretty though. Going to a party?"

"Yes, one of my best friends' birthdays. I'm sort of always expected to bring desserts now. Especially since I started my own little online bakery."

"Is that so?"

I like making small talk with cab drivers. It makes me smile to see people who are pleasant while working, and I love taking any plug I can to get this new cupcake business thing working. Business is definitely starting out rather slowly, but the shower absolutely helped. I've had a few people email me with questions at least and did one birthday for a stranger, which was a great success.

"Yeah. It's called Lylac Bakery, and actually, I will give you one of the cupcakes because my business information is on the wrapper. You know. In case you ever need cupcakes. I do kids' birthdays, wedding parties, showers, etc. It's a really new business, but feel free to tell your friends!"

I hand the cab driver the mini banana split cupcake I invented for this occasion. Banana cake with strawberry ice cream flavored frosting, whipped cream frosting, chocolate ganache drizzle, sprinkles, and a cherry on top. I'm proud of my own idea to print my information on the wrappers. Maybe I'll actually get some business this way.

"Oh, this looks very nice! Thank you! It's no poison, right?"

I laugh. "Don't worry. I'm just starting a business and am pretty excited about this party. Going to jail for murder is not on my interest list today."

He laughs and eats the cupcake as we pull up to my destination, and I fish for money.

"This is delicious! I very much enjoy this! I will keep your information!"

"Aww, thank you so much!" I say. "Keep the change."

"Thank you and have a good night!"

I smile and carefully get out of the cab feeling confident.

I fix my dress as much as I can while holding the trays, and the bouncer opens the door for me and laughs while I try to find a place to put them down to show my ID.

"Do I need to take it out?" I say, holding open the clear panel of my wallet.

"No, you're fine. I might have to grab one of those later, though . . . " He observes the cupcakes through the clear plastic lid.

"You are more than welcome to. Where is the party for Olivia?"

"Back room."

"Thanks."

"Ahhhhh, hello my love!" Olivia runs up and gives me a huge hug while one of her friends takes the trays and sets them on the table we have reserved.

"Happy birthday!"

"Thank you so much! And thank you for bringing cupcakes! These look amazing!"

"Hopefully, they will get eaten. They took long enough, but I figure it's good practice."

"How's the website going?" Chris comes up and asks, giving

me a casual hug. "And this was a brilliant idea putting all of your information on the wrappers, but now what? I can't throw away my wrapper?"

"Well, not if you want to remember. I have business cards too for people that really want to be careful about not losing the information. But Peter has been a great help with the website. It's obviously starting out pretty slowly and all, but I'm really excited about it. My interview with Gina from the *Red Eye* is next week, and I'm nervous about that because it could sort of make or break me. I'm making a few kinds so I can put them up on my site."

"Awesome. Good luck with it. I mean, it's about time you actually do something with it. We've all been telling you to for years," he replies.

"Yeah, no kidding."

"Baby steps," Peter jumps into the conversation, throwing his arm around me while eating one of the cupcakes. "Sorry, I couldn't wait. I think being your website guru extraordinaire gets me endless cupcakes for life."

"I can put a clause somewhere in your contract," I laugh.

Alec is across the room talking to a girl I don't know. *Shocking.* I don't want to go up to him. I have too much going on in my life to focus on him not caring about me. At least I'm trying to convince myself of that.

I walk up to the bar to get a drink and strike up a conversation with one of Olivia's friends from high school whom I haven't seen in a while.

"Love your dress!" she says to me, and we make girly small talk while waiting for our drinks.

I keep peering out of the corner of my eye to see what Alec is doing, trying to look nonchalant but inside, hating that he doesn't pay me attention anymore. Hating the way this is going. *God, what if I really do like Alec?* If I don't like Alec, then why does it bother me so much that we are done sleeping together and that he doesn't hit on me anymore? I used to be one of the first people he came up to. He used to barely take his eyes off of me. *Stop thinking about it!* I yell at myself. I need to let it go and just enjoy myself at this party. I started a business; I'm focusing on me, remember?

"So, is it true that you made these ridiculously amazing cupcakes?" I turn around and recognize the person, but I can't place from where. They seem to know me, which is embarrassing.

"Um, why yes, yes it is. Glad you're enjoying them."

"So aside from tutoring the needy children of the world, you also create delectable treats. What else are you capable of?"

Aha! He's Jarron's football coach. What is he doing here?

"Oh, I am capable of plenty of things. You can just call me Ms. Fantastic." I laugh.

"Well, you can call me Eric." He puts his hand out for me.

"Lyren."

"Interesting name."

"Yeah, my parents are interesting people like that."

"What are you drinking, Lyren?"

"Vodka soda," I say, finishing my current drink more quickly in order to accept his.

I'm thrilled to be talking to an attractive man at this bar. Not only might it make Alec jealous, but more importantly, it might make me forget that Alec is even here at all. He's moved on to talking to yet another ditsy-looking girl at the bar.

"That's boring."

"What? And what are you drinking that is so fancy?" I ask as the bartender hands him a Bud Light. I crack up.

"Drink of only the classiest men on the planet." He laughs. "I don't often drink Bud Light, but when I do, it's because I'm poor and want to get shit-faced," he says, imitating the Dos Equis commercials.

I hold up my vodka soda and toast his Bud Light. "To being poor and getting shit-faced!"

"You got it!"

"So, what are you doing at Olivia's birthday party, anyway? Didn't realize you guys had gotten so tight. You hanging out after hours?" I ask.

"I had no idea that this was a South Side tutors type of party, or I'd have definitely tried to make myself look more presentable."

I observe his worn-out jeans and faded t-shirt. I can barely make out what the advertisement on said shirt originally was.

"No, really, my buddy is friends with one of Olivia's friends evidently. I asked what he was up to, and he told me that I should come to this with him. He said there'd be attractive women, but I'm not impressed." He smirks as he says it, eyeing me.

"Ouch!" I playfully shove him and hold my mouth open as though in shock.

"Yep. No good-looking women. None anywhere to be found."

"So, Eric. You obviously coach football. What else do you do?"

Something about him makes me want to keep the conversation going. Probably the fact that he chose to playfully insult me as opposed to saying something about how pretty my eyes looked or other cheesy pickup lines. He must be at least slightly interested in me, since he came up out of nowhere and bought me a drink.

"What do I do for money or what do I do that actually interests me?"

"Hmm, both. Unless it's top secret or something."

"Well, I don't usually like to tell this to women I just met but . . . well . . . I'm a model. I know you probably already guessed it by my devastatingly good looks and impeccable abs. You know you can just sense them through the shirt."

I laugh. While I certainly cannot see any abs through his shirt, he does have a rather nice stature. Tall and lean without being skinny or overly built. Actually, just sort of perfect. I'm impressed despite his lack of fashion sense. Then again, I have never really fallen for anyone with a fashion sense.

"Well, that much is obvious. It's your unbelievable charm, though, that keeps me guessing. You really know how to be so modest and lure women."

"Yes. That is actually one of my many talents. I'm also a male escort."

"Excellent."

He shakes his head and laughs, then turns to me a bit more seriously. "I work in sales for an IT company. But that's really just something I do to pay the bills. I got my degree in business and got a job but never really felt like I was doing something very fulfilling. You ever hit a point and feel like you aren't doing what you are supposed to be doing?"

"You have no idea." It's so refreshing hearing him say exactly what I am feeling.

"Well, I realized I had a good, stable job, so it would be pretty stupid to just quit it, and besides that, I didn't know what I really was all that passionate about. But that's where the football thing came in. Football really changed my life when I was a kid. For a lot of reasons. I just want to be that influence on someone else. So I was able to work my schedule out to do both, and it has really made a lot of difference in my general disposition. I'm doing something important, and something I love, all while getting fresh air."

"That's awesome. I get what you're saying, though. I graduated college with all these ideas about changing the world and doing something productive and impressing people or something, but I took the first decent-sounding job I could get. I don't even know if it connects to anything I'm passionate about. I started it thinking it could be a stepping stone, but have done nothing about moving forward or finding another company."

"Yeah. I mean, I love football and getting exercise. I enjoy drinking. I enjoy my friends. It was important to me to have a job where I felt successful, but it didn't take away from the rest of my life. I never want to be one of those people whose entire life's value is their job, or who are so stressed because of their job that they can't do anything they enjoy."

"I'm totally with you there. I thought I wanted to go into reporting and journalism, but those jobs are impossible to come by, so I do the tutoring thing to make myself feel better about being lazy, I guess. The cupcake thing is totally new, but I'm really excited about it."

"Yeah, tell me about that. I think it's fascinating. I saw your name on the little wrappers."

I laugh. "Yeah. Brilliant marketing scheme."

"It is actually. Too bad I can't bring that to IT. Actually . . . maybe I can . . . have a cupcake! Buy software!"

"I like it!" I find myself smiling. His humor mixed with serious anecdotes have me intrigued, for now. "Nah, it was just one of those things that struck me. I taught myself to bake in college and did it for fun. Gave baked goods to people for their birthdays and such. I sort of missed the 'starting a real storefront' bandwagon. I didn't really think about it until way later when I was already sort of stuck. I let my job and the dullness of it consume me and stopped baking as much and started partying a lot, and I dunno, it was time for a change. My friends and family are always telling me how much they like my baking . . . so, we'll see what happens. I figure I'm not getting any younger. It's time to be a bit more proactive about my career."

"Isn't that a weird feeling? When you start to realize you're just not that young anymore?" he asks sincerely.

"Well, we're still young."

"Yes, but I'm 28. So it's like, you have to at least start

figuring it out now because if you keep floating for another five years, then it will actually be too late to do anything about it. Things are always subject to change, but you can't sit around waiting for the answers to come to you anymore."

"Exactly. When I was 22 and 23, I felt like it was OK that I wasn't doing much because I had so much time to figure it all out. And I did then, but instead of figuring any of it out, I coasted. I moved out when I could afford it, but I dated half-assedly, I worked half-assedly, and all of a sudden I realized that everything was just sort of passing me by. I don't know. I feel like I'm at the start of something right now. Maybe it's a cupcake empire, maybe this falls through. But either way, I'm ready to start acting and doing rather than thinking, you know?"

I find it weird how open I am being with a total stranger. It's not like me to have real conversations with guys I meet in bars. Maybe I'm a bit more comfortable because I technically know who he is and what he does, and we have mutual friends.

"Exactly. I think I'm finally OK with where I am in my career. I work hard, I'm good at it, and I've already been promoted twice. It's a fine job and I'll stick with it and all that, but I like that I have a lot of passions outside of it, too. It's amazing how much more fulfilled your life feels when you are proactive about it. Everyone always says that they would love to just win the lottery and sit on their ass all day, but you'd never be very happy doing that. At least I wouldn't be."

"I'm realizing the same thing. Having too much time on your hands and no focus or passion or purpose is a dangerous thing. It's an easy rut to get stuck in and you just don't feel all that good about yourself. I don't know that cupcake making counts as doing something all that productive with my life or anything, but having some sort of focus and goal that I am actively working toward has made a huge difference in my general disposition. Sorry, I feel like it's weird that I'm telling you all of this. It's an odd first conversation to have."

"It is, but I like it. I like how effusive you are, not just about making cupcakes but about making a difference in your life. It's something I can totally relate to. And we obviously have a shared interest."

"What's that?"

"Well, we have a few. For one, you like baking and I like eating. So, that right there is quite a beautiful coincidence." I laugh. "But beyond that, we obviously both volunteer our time on the South Side. While you are helping them academically, I'm helping with team building. Not everyone has that."

"Very true. You should talk to Olivia. She's the one who is really a great person and all about volunteering. That's actually how I met her. She's incredibly passionate about it, and she's just so deep and worldly. She's a great person to know, actually. Heading to Africa in the fall. So it's a good thing you stumbled upon her party tonight."

"I can think of a few reasons I'm glad I stumbled upon her party tonight." Eric smiles at me as he says it. Although I usually find guys cheesy when they flirt with me, there is a touching sincerity in his approach. He seems genuine, and it catches me off guard how much I want to share details of my life with him. I could talk to him all night. I remember how Olivia said I should have flirted with him back when I first met him and how I didn't even consider it. Timing is everything.

"Hey! You're that football coach guy!" Olivia comes up as if on cue, spilling some of her drink. She's clearly enjoying her party.

"Hey! Something like that!" Eric laughs. "Happy Birthday! I'm Eric." He holds his hand out for her to shake, but she awkwardly misses the cue and goes to hug him instead, surprising him. His reaction amuses me. "Oh, I didn't realize we were hugging friends."

"It's my birthday, and I love everyone today! Also, I'm an awkward person, so I apologize."

"Excellent. Awkward is my specialty in life. I'm quite good at making other people uncomfortable."

"What an amazing quality to have!" Olivia cheers and lifts her drink for an unsolicited toast.

"Hey there, stranger." Alec approaches finally, giving me a possessive hug and looking Eric up and down.

"Hey. This is Eric. He works at the school where Liv and I tutor. Eric, this is Olivia's brother, Alec."

"Hey man, nice to meet you." They quickly shake hands.

"Congrats on the cupcake business. Do I get a special friend discount?" Alec's suddenly reignited interest in me irks me. It's like he's intentionally trying to get in the way of my flirting.

"I think you've gotten plenty of special-friend discounts. You can pay for the cupcakes and support my business," I snark back.

"Psh! After all of the drinks and delivery food I've provided for you!"

"Yeah yeah." I wave him off. He's trying to show Eric that we've been close. I like that he seems jealous. It's nice for once to give Alec a taste of his own medicine. I turn my focus back to Eric, and eventually, Alec wanders off.

Throughout the night, we joke around, talking about our favorite bands, books, foods, everything. We disagree on The Rolling Stones but agree on Eminem and The National; he loves ethnic food as much as I do; he knows more about beer and wine than I ever could. He's sarcastic and intense and interesting, and I can't believe how much I think so after one night of conversing. When the bar lights go on, I'm truly disappointed the conversation is ending.

"How are you getting home?" he asks.

"I'm gonna hail a cab."

"I thought you said you lived a few blocks from here."

"Yeah, city blocks!"

"It's gorgeous out. Are you kidding me? You're not taking a cab. We're walking. I'm going to walk you home." His adamancy is kind of cute, but I start to wonder what it means that he wants to walk me home.

Of course I'm interested in him and would like to see him again, but is it stupid to let him walk me home? A goodnight kiss at the door I could handle, but surely not anything more than that. I have no intention of inviting him in. Is it stupid to trust him? But a voice inside my head tells me to go with it.

"Late night?" Alec approaches as I'm ready to walk out the door. "Big Shitty?"

"No Big Shitty for me tonight, Alec. Have fun."

He pouts. Evidently, the many girls he tried talking to all evening aren't feeling it, which is weird for Alec. I think he doesn't like that I'm leaving the bar with a guy. He keeps looking at me funny. I wonder if Eric notices it, but it can't hurt if Eric thinks I'm desired.

"When did you get old and lame?" Alec asks.

"Right now," I say. I turn back to Eric. "See? I told you I've been partying too much. My friends can't even fathom that I'm not going to a 5 a.m. bar."

"I can see that." Eric shakes his head at me. "I don't think I have Big City in me tonight."

"You cannot trust someone who calls Big Shitty by its proper name." Alec smirks.

Big City Tap has well earned its nickname by being the consistent late-night shitstorm in the area.

"Don't worry. I don't have it in me either. Whatever you want to call it."

A part of me wants to go to Big Shitty with Alec. A part of me wants Eric to take my number and leave so I can go home with Alec. But the old magic has somehow faded to a passing dust. Yes, Alec is still looking at me like he wants to take my clothes off. But without all the flirting and buildup, it's just not the same.

Alec walks away, looking for other people. He needs to stay

out so he can meet some new girl drunk enough to go home with him. So he can boost his ego. So he can feel the night was a success. I have never been special to Alec. And the fact that I was a sure thing was when everything went wrong. Sure, we could both feel casually about the whole situation, but it still didn't put us on the same page.

"Ready?" Eric distracts my train of thought, and I realize I've been watching Alec.

"Let me say good night to Olivia, and I'll meet you outside."

I walk up to hug Olivia and wish her a happy birthday one more time. Chris is helping her find all of her things and get organized. She can barely stand up.

"So what's the deal with the football coach?"

I laugh. "I don't know . . . he's cute."

"Definitely. You guys have been talking all night. Did you get his number?"

"Not yet. He's walking me home . . . "

"Oooh . . . I like it."

"Don't give me that look. I'm not going to hook up with him."

"Sure. That's what they all say," she adorably slurs.

"I'm not! I might actually like this one!"

"Well, have fun and keep me posted immediately!" Olivia makes a lewd gesture, and I laugh.

"Let's go home, babe. Have fun tonight, Lyren!" Chris smirks at me.

I'm a little drunk but feel in control enough to not let Eric in. He seems like a stand-up guy. He'll take no for an answer if it comes to that.

"Hey, so we're walking?"

"Yes, we're walking."

Even though it's August, the air is a little crisp. It's nice because it's not humid, and I don't think I'll start sweating because that would be really gross.

"How long have you lived here?" he asks.

"I've lived in my current apartment for a little over a year, but I moved out three years ago. They raised the rent on my first apartment like 45% the second year, so rather than re-sign the lease, I found something else. Hoping to save up and buy something but not there yet."

"Sounds intense. I haven't taken that step yet. I've thought about it, but honestly, I'm not sure where I want to be and all that. This is a great area, though. I live over in the West Loop with some friends, but that's starting to get old. When does it become unacceptable to have roommates?"

"When you're rich enough not to need them."

"Do you have a roommate?"

"Nope. I do better on my own. I like the space."

"Must be nice."

"It is."

"Do you get lonely?"

"No, not really. I have so many friends nearby that there's always someone available when I want, and then I get to come home and be alone when I want. It's really a perfect deal. Living alone causes me some stress knowing that I have to stay financially stable to keep it, which means I can't just up and quit my lame job to look for a new one. But other than that, it has been a great decision. I knew for sure what area I wanted to be in, so that was a no-brainer. I found my place and just fell in love with it. I guess I'm the kind of person that when I know something, I just know. I'm only indecisive when nothing is quite right."

"I think that's a good way to be. I'll race you."

"Huh?" He points to the empty schoolyard track we are walking next to.

"Around the track. One time."

"You've got to be kidding. I'm in four-inch heels!"

"I'll run backward."

"Not the same." I laugh.

This really should sound like the least fun thing in the entire world, but I'm caught up by the spontaneity and I love the idea. We walk over to the track.

"I'm going to kick your ass."

"Don't be so sure about that, Mr. Big Talker."

"Go!" I run, trying to be as fast as I can while not losing or breaking the heels. Out of breath and laughing hysterically, he zigzags around backward, unable to keep in a straight line. He destroys me.

"OK, that was so totally unfair!" I can barely get the words out.

"I so defeated you. I can't wait to post on Facebook how badly I destroyed this girl in a simple race around a track while I ran backward. I have every intention of leaving out the details of it being 3 a.m. and those eight-inch heels you are wearing so you look like a fool."

"Well, that's really nice of you."

I'm desperately out of breath, but trying to pull it together. It's hard when I'm still laughing. I've never met a guy like him. So casual and at ease with himself. Something about it completely disarms me, and I'm disappointed when we arrive at my door.

"So, this is my place." I wonder if he'll make a move. If he's expecting an invite. Will there be a struggle? Will it be awkward? My heart is pounding in anticipation.

"I had a really great time talking to you and kicking your ass in a race tonight."

"Despite the ass-kicking, I actually had a really great night, too."

"Well, ball's in your court," he says, handing me a slip of paper with his name and phone number on it. Then he turns and walks away. Doesn't kiss me, doesn't try anything, and it leaves me wanting more.

Suddenly, I have an overwhelming desire to kiss him as I

watch him walk down the street. He makes it about thirty feet, turns back to check that I'm looking, smiles, then keeps walking.

I stand dazed for a second, then walk into my apartment feeling even more so. Something about the way he left as a total gentleman while still being fun and sarcastic and not making a move but still letting me know he is interested . . . it's the hottest thing a guy I just met has ever done. He makes my head spin.

Wow. This is what it's like to like someone.

I can't help but dance around my couch. I want to tell the entire world.

Chapter Twenty

E ric and I set a simple date for a Friday night. We had both agreed we didn't feel like drinking and we preferred to do something low-key. He is meeting me at my apartment, and we're going to walk to an ice cream place nearby. I love how casual and low-pressure it is. No formal dinner or set amount of time. And no alcohol. Just a sweet date getting to know someone new. I don't know if I've gone on a first date without alcohol, well, ever. Unless you count some silly high school outings. I'm a little nervous that I won't have my personality crutch.

"You look okay," Eric jokes when I answer the door.

I'm wearing a sundress and flat sandals, which is rare for me, but we're just getting ice cream. Eric looks even taller when I'm not wearing my usual heels, and I love it.

"You look sort of all right yourself," I respond, closing the door behind me and locking it. He's wearing casual jeans and a t-shirt, although a nicer one than what he had on before. Style is definitely not Eric's thing.

"So where are we going for this ice cream?"

"There's a little place down the street I've been wanting to try. It's walking distance."

"That sounds excellent. So how was your week?"

"It's actually been really cool. I was interviewed about my cupcakes for the *Red Eye* the other day, and it's supposed to be in one of next week's issues." In many ways, I am still beaming from that. Gina was so nice and made me feel very at ease after a morning of frantically trying to overdo it.

"That's so awesome! Congratulations!"

"Thanks."

"Hey dog!" Eric goes up to a boxer walking in front of us with its owner and stops to pet it. "Aren't you just an awesome little beast. What's his name?"

"Ralph," the owner says. He looks like he wants to get on with his walk, but is obviously proud of his dog.

"Wow, what an awesome name. Great dog. Love boxers."

"Thanks," the owner says, and Eric gets up and keeps walking with me.

"So, I take it you like dogs?"

"Obviously. If you say you don't, then this date is officially over. I don't trust people who don't like dogs."

"Damn. I think they are disgusting."

"What?" He looks horrified.

"Kidding. I just wanted to see your reaction. I absolutely love dogs and completely agree that I don't like or trust people who don't. Do you have your own?"

"Not yet. So busy, and I live with roommates and all. I grew up with labs, and they were just the greatest. I really do miss having one. You?"

"Same. I'd love one, but I'm so busy and I'm not home enough. Plus, they can be expensive. But my mom has a bulldog, and he's so funny."

"Bulldogs are great. What's his name?"

"Meatloaf."

"That is the greatest thing I have ever heard." He laughs. "I love it. I want to name my dog Awesome. And go around telling people how jealous they should be of my awesome dog, Awesome."

"That's . . . um . . . awesome?" I laugh.

We approach the ice cream shop, and I realize it's closed.

"Way to go, Lyren. Way to go." His sarcasm somehow makes me feel even more comfortable with him. Like we can kid around the way I do with family.

"I'm so sorry! I looked it up online, and the online hours are different from the store hours, apparently. I feel like an idiot!" I do feel embarrassed, but he doesn't seem to actually care.

"Don't be silly. It's a gorgeous night. We'll think of something else to do."

"What would you like to do? I can look something up."

What do people even do when they aren't drinking? It's sad I don't know. *Have I already managed to sabotage this date?*

"We're in your neck of the woods. I'm trusting you to lead the way."

"Well, we can walk until we find something to do. How about that?" I don't have a better idea, but just walking with him seems like a good way to get to know him.

"Cool with me. So, you bake cupcakes, you are good at grammar, you like dogs, and you suck at planning dates. Any other pertinent information?"

"I am terrible at sports."

"Ugh. Deal-breaker." I shrug. "Just kidding.. Obviously, I know you are terrible at sports. I've already beaten you in a race."

"Won't be able to practice football with you."

"Well, shit then. Why am I even bothering getting to know you?"

"I have no idea." I laugh.

"What are your deal breakers for real?"

"Hmm, smoking."

"Sick."

Conversation flows so easily, and he manages to keep me guessing without being a jerk about it.

"Glad you think so. Total douchebaggery would be another dealbreaker, I suppose."

"What makes someone a total douchebag?"

"I guess I should say that I'm not into the clubby kind of guys. Or those who do a lot of drugs. I mean, I don't have a problem with some recreational pot smoking or something, but if you're popping pills, that's gonna be a problem."

It's always scary when a guy you are kind of into asks about deal breakers, because you're gonna find out really fast if he has them. But it's also really good to get them out of the way.

"Damn, I just popped seven Vicodin before arriving." But he smirks when he says it.

"Sweet. What about you? Deal breakers?"

"I don't like fake girls. I don't necessarily mean fake-looking, although it often goes hand in hand. But I don't like when girls have to impress people and change who they are to do it. I've been out with a few girls who I think would like something just because I like it or who would do something just because it's cool or because they don't want to say no as if they are still in high school. Not into it. And I need someone who is passionate."

"That's something we seem to share."

We end up aimlessly wandering the city for two hours. Just walking and getting to know each other. He's from the East Coast and is one of four siblings. His last girlfriend cheated on him. He loves fishing and convertibles. He's a really good cook. His dad isn't a part of his life. He's completely fascinating to me.

At the same time, I'm comfortable telling him about my past insecurities, about problems I've had at work, about my parents nagging me, about how my friends are all in different places in life than me. Everything about our evening flows. It's funny I was finally coming to terms with not wanting a relationship to define me, and here I am on a date with a guy who not only my mom and sister would love, but I'm liking more by the minute.

We realize we're hungry at 11 p.m. and grab a sandwich at one of the few places open before walking back to my place. I'm tired and not used to doing so much walking, but I feel rejuvenated. And I'm still completely sober.

"Well, what now?" he asks. "I have some friends who are out if you'd like to meet them."

"You know, I would love to meet your friends, but I'm kind of tired and really did mean it when I said I didn't feel like drinking. I've been drinking too much lately, and I have a lot going on that I'd rather be focused on. I completely understand if you want to go out and meet them, though. I promise I won't take offense."

"Don't be silly. I scheduled this particular Friday to be lame with you. So, what lame thing would you like to do now? Or does you're tired really mean: 'I'm so sick of you. Go away before I unleash Meatloaf on you. The singer, not the dog'."

I laugh. "Definitely not. Although unleashing Meatloaf on someone would be really interesting. Both versions, actually. I don't know what we can really do. I mean, if you want to come over and watch a movie or something, you are welcome to do that."

"That sounds nice."

I'm kind of nervous about inviting Eric over. I like him, and this date has been perfect so far. If he tries to make a move, I'm not ready to go beyond kissing, and I don't want things to be awkward.

But my fears are unwarranted. Eric sits respectfully on the other end of the couch, eventually putting his arm around me, but not trying to make out with me or do anything assuming. It's clear he's an old-fashioned gentleman who will respectfully wait for me to give an indication on such things. I'm sitting on the couch with him, trying not to move. I don't want to adjust my body in any way that will make him uncomfortable.

"OK, well it's after 2. I need to hop on the bus and head home," he says when the movie ends.

A part of me doesn't want him to go. I want to ask him to stay and cuddle or something, but I can't do that because it's ridiculous. No man wants to just stay and cuddle without the other stuff.

When I walk him to the door, we stand awkwardly for a moment, just gazing at each other. He's so masculine. It's sexy. We're clearly both thinking the same thing, but neither wants to make the first move. The moment becomes so tense I can't stand it. I reach my hands up, grab his face, and kiss him passionately.

"Thanks for breaking the ice there," he says.

We stop and smile a second before kissing again. It's perfect. I don't want to let him go. I watch him as he walks out the door. I can't stop smiling.

I go to sleep with a level of warm fuzzies that I'm far from accustomed to.

Chapter Twenty-One

LYLAC BAKERY BRINGS CREATIVITY, COMFORT, AND A LOT OF SWEETNESS TO NEW ONLINE CUPCAKERY

When Gina shared an advanced copy of the article, I broke down in tears. *I can't believe this is really happening.*

The article was brief, but thoughtful. It shared some of my funny anecdotes about family and friends expecting me to provide dessert for all of our functions. It discussed how I drew inspiration from the seasons and the themes of the event. How for years I'd been saving clips and Pinterest images of different cupcakes and ideas. Gina chose to highlight how my staples were everything you want in a basic chocolate or vanilla cupcake, but how my flair really came through when inventing something new for a cause, calling out my newly perfected Summer Bomb Pop cupcakes. The pictures came out great too, and I have to say, I look pretty cute in my little apron. The article and advertisement gave me some kind of new lease on life.

I know I can't suddenly expect to get so many cupcake orders I could up and quit my job or buy a storefront. And I don't have the bandwidth or capacity to take them on yet, anyway. But it definitely gives me room to dream. Once the excitement sets in and settles a little, I spam pretty much all of my contacts with the article. My mom texts back right away.

MOM

So very proud of you! Come over for dinner tomorrow? I want to celebrate you!

I smile. Maybe now my mom is less worried about me. Plus, now that I offered to provide cupcakes for Emma's bachelorette party, I think I have found my best value. I'm still not leading arts and crafts. But I can show my support and enthusiasm through what I'm actually good at. I can't wait to do some fantastic fall cupcakes for her "Pumpkins and Prosecco" event. Having my own thing has made me a lot more engaged. Maybe that's selfish, but at least I'm being a better sister/maid of honor, even if I have to admit, I still hate her chosen bridesmaid dress.

I did not text Eric the article. To be honest, I have been freaking out a little since our first date. I thought it went so well, but he hasn't made a point of planning another date. We've texted a few times. He said he had a wonderful time. But it has been five days now. Is he already over it? Is he not feeling it as much as I am? Is he playing it cool? Or maybe he's just cool and not the clingy kind of guy I can't stand? But if I can't stand clingy guys, why am I panicking that this one is giving me a little space? Sarah's wedding is in two weeks, and I want to ask him to be my date, but is that way too intense of a second or third date?

I am sitting on my couch, spiraling a little and debating whether to text him, when a text comes through as if on cue.

ERIC

Well, hey there, Martha Stewart.

Seeing Eric's name on my phone sends my already excited heart jolting through the roof. I want to run around in circles. I love that he texted. I love that he saw the article. I love that he wants to share the moment with me. Before I can stop smiling long enough to respond, he texts again.

ERIC

Still have time for the little people?

LYREN

It depends. Only if there is something in it for me.

ERIC

How about dinner Thursday night?

I am jittery with excitement. I have a new business, a positive article advertising said business, and a cute guy asking me to dinner. Everything in the world is joyful.

LYREN

I'd love to!

ERIC

OK, so I was thinking about Indian because I know you said you love it, but I have to be honest, my stomach is not ready for a second date Indian food. I have to make sure you are madly in love with me before we risk that or you might run away. So how about something safer and we go with sushi?

I laugh at his honesty. I love that he actually thought about what I said I liked and that he has a very valid reason for not going for it on a second date. And honestly, probably also relieved for the very same reasons he just admitted.

LYREN
Sushi sounds fantastic. Rise is one of my favorites. On Southport.

ERIC
Already have a reservation for 7. Was counting on your saying yes.

Incredible. Here I was freaking out that he hadn't texted for five days, and he was already making dinner reservations. Confident. Cool. And funny.
Please don't fuck this one up, Lyren!!

LYREN
Presumptuous. I am very important now. Did you already forget how famous I am?

ERIC
Well, I made the reservation before I saw the article, like ten minutes ago, so I do understand if my people need to work it out with your people.

LYREN
I'll see you at Rise at 7 on Thursday. :)

My smile is still spread ear to ear. I can't make it stop. It kind of hurts.

TWO WEEKS LATER

When I walk into the reception—well, dance into the reception —to the tune of Backstreet Boys' "Backstreet's Back" per the determined bridal party entrance sequence, I scan the room and smile at Eric. The room is spacious, with airy bright windows. The vibrant sunflowers I helped Sarah pick are standing tall above the tables as if watching the event themselves. Her red and orange colors signal that this event is exciting and full of joy. And instead of being the dark, wedding-hating curmudgeon I felt through most of this planning process, I am thrilled to be here.

Over sushi with Eric ten days prior, I sheepishly got the guts to ask him to be my date. I felt like a teenager asking a boy to the Sadie Hawkins dance. Which I've actually never done. I was too nervous. I almost asked this guy my sophomore year. I was talking to him about math homework. We were friendly but not good friends. He was cute. I never got the words out. I was too scared. And someone else asked him like two periods later. Anyway, over lychee martinis and spicy salmon rolls, I said something along the lines of, *"OK, so I know this is only our second date, and this might be way too much to ask because it's kind of a long day and night and I will be busy with maid of honor duties for a lot of it so you'd be alone with people you don't know so it's fully OK if it's not your thing . . . "*

"Yes, I will be your date to Sarah's wedding. Give me the details," he had cut me off.

We had another great night together. Dinner and drinks, and he walked me home, and we made out. Part of me is now concerned it's moving too slow. Is his hesitation intentional or just respectful? We've now gone out four times and not done more than make out. I'm OK with the pace so long as it isn't a sign he's not all that into me. I'm not accustomed to men taking this much time.

But he beams back up at me as I awkwardly twirl with the

best man and make my way to the head table. I wish I could vacate my place up there and sit with Eric. He has kindly been positioned with the other wedding party dates, and I know he'll be personable enough to be fine, but I'm a lot less interested in conversing with Sarah and Nick's friends, perfectly nice as they all may be.

I am not usually nervous giving speeches. But with Eric's eyes on me, I want to come off as poised, funny, pretty, fun, sweet . . . Oh, and I also want Sarah to like it.

"I would like to start by reading a letter of disappointment and objection I received this morning from Brian Litrell, second-best member of the Backstreet Boys for those of you less cultured. 'Dear Lyren, it has come to my attention that Sarah Caldwell, the great love my life, whom I was supposed to have picked out of the audience at our 1999 All State Arena performance of the Millenium Tour based on her sparkling spaghetti strap, perfectly twisted butterfly clips, and braces, is getting married to some guy named Nick. I have to object' . . . "

I go on to share how Sarah and I bonded over our dreams to become famous and marry one of the Backstreet Boys, how we carried each other through high school friend drama, stayed close despite different colleges, and how truly happy I am knowing that Nick loves her and sees her for her. I get some laughs. I choke up. And then I sit down and let Nick's best friend take over with a ridiculous speech about beer bongs. I win.

When they finally open up the dance floor, Eric suavely walks up to the table to take my hand. "Great speech," he says as we start dancing.

"Thank you. It was actually really easy to write. Sarah and I go so far back. She's the best, despite my not loving having to wear bright orange."

Despite being in a much better headspace about all the weddings, I still don't love having to wear orange. Though I will say the overall vibe and pictures are great. I can handle it not being my favorite dress.

"Well, I think it makes you look like a very sexy felon." He smiles. "I personally think I'm more of a spring, though."

"Oh yeah? You learn that in Cosmopolitan magazine?"

"I think it was a quiz in Teen People, thank you very much."

By the end of the night, I have been dancing so much my entire updo has fallen, and I'm hoping my sweat isn't showing through the dress. I am barefoot and just the right amount of tipsy. Having Eric as a date made me understand for the first time why people have fun at weddings. It *is* fun when you have someone you can't wait to dance with and be close to. And show off. Eric has been attentive but not possessive. He has danced with Sarah and some of the other bridesmaids. He's been easygoing, but sexy. As the final song ends, I barely notice anyone else in the room. He stares at me with complete intensity, like he is seeing me. *Really* seeing me. I'm about to break from how badly I want him to kiss me when he instead pulls me in for a side hug.

Did he break the moment because he isn't feeling it the way I've interpreted? Or does he just not want PDA? We've kissed several times throughout the night. Not the gross, over-the-top kind of making out Alec and I always did. But that's obviously good. I don't want to be that girl at Sarah's wedding.

We start packing up our things and say goodbye to everyone.

"Now, did your mom prepare you for what happens on the wedding night?" I joke to Sarah.

"Honestly, what I think is going to happen on this wedding night is that I'm going to have Nick help me out of this dress, then I will stuff myself with the cake I never got to actually eat." She laughs.

"Whatever you do, make it the best night ever."

"It already is. Thank you so much for everything. I loved your speech so much. And, uh, you make it the best night ever too . . . " she says, nodding at Eric, who is shaking hands with the groomsmen. I sure hope we do.

Eric and I barely talk in the cab back to my apartment. I had given only my address and smiled at Eric, hoping he realized that was my invitation for him to stay over.

I'm still trying to read him. We keep looking over at each other and smiling. Staring at each other. Are we going to have another night of just kissing? I am so ready for more.

But my concerns are unwarranted. Eric and I get out of the cab, he pays, and we barely make it through my door. Unlike his previous respectful kisses, we are aggressive. We are kissing so hard I have to use my foot to kick the door closed. I want his clothes off faster than they want to get there. I'm trying with the buttons when he just pulls it up and over his head, taking the undershirt with it. I am so excited to be close to his body, I'm ignoring how much he is struggling with the zipper on my own dress.

"I literally will never wear this dress again, Eric," I say between kisses, giving him permission to just rip it, and he does.

When we are free from our wedding clothes, I don't even want to bother stumbling to the bedroom. He lays me down on the floor with intention and then pauses to look me in the eyes.

"Are you sure?" he asks with clear sincerity.

"I need you right now, Eric. Right. Now."

I pull his face back to me and reach for his boxers, and we laugh as we both struggle to wriggle out of our various underwear. And then it's just us. The weight of his body over me fully engulfs me, and suddenly there is no way to be close enough to him. He's so intense as he pushes into me, and the only thing I can feel is desire for as much of him as he can give me. My mind is otherwise blank.

"You are so beautiful," he whispers into my ear before biting it.

"I cannot get enough of you," I reply between heavy breaths.

I have never orgasmed with someone the first time having sex with them, but it comes without expectation or effort. As does the scream I let out in passion, which triggers him to come with me. I feel like he could drill so hard into my body I would break, and honestly, I would be OK with it.

When we're both finished, he stares at me in disbelief, and I kiss him but barely have the energy for it.

"Wow," I say as he rolls over.

"Yeah," he replies.

We don't say anything else for a moment. My head is dizzy, which I'm accustomed to, but this time, I'm intoxicated with Eric.

"So, I've never orgasmed on a first go with someone," I decide to tell him, rolling up on my side to look at him.

"Promise you weren't faking it?"

"God no. And honestly, that scream? I really thought people faked that shit too. Like I've always thought they were putting on a show and that it wasn't natural. But I can now confirm it's natural."

"You're not just saying that to inflate my ego?"

"No way. That was incredible." I shake my head, still trying to get a handle on how truly incredible it was.

"We are so good at sex together," he says, pushing up on his side to face me. "High five." He holds up his hand, and I meet it with mine, then he turns the high five into a hand hold.

"I guess we should get off the floor?" I look around and smile.

"Probably better for our backs."

We leave our clothes in scattered heaps. I lock the door and turn off the lights and meet him under the covers.

Chapter Twenty-Two

TWO WEEKS LATER

"So how are things with Eric?" Olivia asks me at the bar.

We are having an early going-away party for her. It's Labor Day weekend, and she will be in Ghana the entire month of November. I can't even imagine what it's going to be like without her.

"Really good. Really, really good."

"Ooh, details?"

"I mean, we have only gone out once since the wedding. We've both been busy the past two weeks. But we have such a great connection. Best sex with someone new I've ever experienced. I think even with like Jason, Evan, and Alec, as much as I enjoyed sex, I still was kind of putting on a show. You know, like I was into it, but also was worried about whether I looked good or smelled good, or whether what I was doing was good for them instead of focusing on what was good for me. Not that it wasn't good. But when Eric and I have sex, I like the actual sex more than I am used to. It's not about the buildup and the "are we going there?" thing because I just know we are going there. And sex aside, I actually like hanging out with him. He makes me feel comfortable in my own shoes, if that makes sense."

"You guys are really cute together."

"And he's the best cuddler, too. Honestly, I haven't woken up feeling that happy and at peace with things in a really long time. It terrifies me."

"Why? This is awesome! You really like a guy! He really likes you!"

"Yeah, it just makes me nervous. We haven't talked about where it's going or anything. I don't want to get too attached and then have him leave me. It's really nice to have someone that I'm into. And I guess I like that he keeps me guessing."

"Right, you never like a guy that is too all over you. So this is probably a good thing. Where is he tonight?"

"He's out-of-town visiting his family. I haven't heard from him, actually. I guess that's why I'm nervous."

"Don't be nervous. Things are fine. And anyway, you're out with me now!"

"Yeah, celebrating you going on the most incredible trip! I can't even believe it!"

"Me either!"

"Hey girls, let's do a shot." Alec approaches us. "I'm going to miss having my baby sister around so much. What am I gonna do?"

"You'll survive somehow. It's only a month," she says.

"Yeah, at least Lyren's not leaving, too. I don't know what I'd do then."

I laugh, but it's weird he says this. I guess Alec is hoping we can stay friends. We are, of course. He's Olivia's brother. We didn't have an actual breakup. But we haven't seen much of each other either. He's been traveling again. Now that Alec and I have distanced, I've realized how much of a placeholder I was in

Alec's life. While he was new here and I was the only person he knew, we hung out all the time. But now that he has a lot of other friends, I'm old boring news. But it makes me smile that he says this, anyway. Maybe he's bothered that although he pushed me away, I could actually be gone?

"Yeah, don't worry. I'm not a do-gooder. I won't be leaving the country to go help refugee children anytime soon."

"That makes two of us." We do the shot, and someone calls Olivia away.

"So how have you been, Ly?" Alec asks me.

"I've been really awesome. Really excited about a lot of things in my life. It's been a productive summer. Looking forward to maybe easing into things in the fall. What about you?"

"I'm pretty good too. Busy as well. I was offered a job in New York."

Woah.

"What? With your same agency?" My heart sinks.

"Yeah. Not a promotion so much as a change of scenery. Could be cool. I haven't really decided anything yet. I love my life here a lot, and it really is nice being near my family."

I shudder as I think about Alec actually leaving. But maybe he won't go. I don't know why it matters; I just don't want him to go. Things are going well, but my sexual-emotional crutch leaving is still scary. I don't actually trust things with Eric.

"Yeah, it would be hard for them to have to lose you again so soon."

"They are used to it. But I don't know if I'm a New York guy. I kind of like the idea of establishing roots here. Not getting any younger. Anyway, you look gorgeous tonight." He takes my hand and leads me to the dance floor. It's been a while since we've done this.

He swirls me around and swoops me into his arms. I hate that I can't help but think about how sexy he looks. It's just obnoxious how good-looking Alec really is. He's being respectful, though, and we're just dancing. There is nothing wrong with a little dancing with a friend. Maybe Alec and I *can* have a normal friendship after all.

Olivia and Alec's parents come up and talk to us for a while, and I make small talk with their cousin. I'm being friendly, but deep down, I'm sad Olivia is leaving, and I'm nervous for her safety while she is out there. She comes up and joins the conversation for a while. Alec keeps looking over at me. The way he used to. I give him a sly smile. He's so good at making me feel sexy and wanted when he wants to.

"I'm going to get going," Olivia says. "Don't worry, I'm still here for a few weeks."

"I know. Thank god. I need you to help me sort out my life." I squeeze her and say goodbye to Chris and their parents and try to decide if maybe it's time for me to go home, too.

"Vodka soda?" Alec puts a fresh one in my hand without my having to ask.

"You know me so well," I say.

He takes a seat at the bar next to me. "I've missed you, lady," he says sweetly.

"I've missed you, too. "

We're being sort of awkward. He congratulates me on the cupcakes and tells me about some of his recent travels. When he looks at me, it's with a comfortable desire. He leans in closer, so his chair is almost on top of mine, and puts his hand on my leg.

"What are you doing?" I whisper. I shouldn't like this, but I don't push it away.

"Thinking that as good as you look in this dress, I know how much better you look without it."

"Who said I was going to let you take my dress off?"

"A man can dream," he charms into my ear, gently running his hand up and down my thigh, sneaking it up my skirt when he's sure no one's looking, but pulling it back out immediately just in case. He bites my ear softly, pretending to be saying something to me.

If I were watching a movie, and the main character was doing exactly what I'm doing, I'd be mad. I'd want the main character of the movie to tell Alec to go to hell for all the shit he made me feel all summer. For putting me on the back burner and making me feel used and worthless. I'm supposed to turn him down and make him go to bed thinking about me. Let him know I've been seeing an amazing guy. A guy who is bigger than him where it counts. Who I don't need to drink with. And who won't text stupid other girls in front of me. But the spell is already cast. All I want to do is let him take off my dress. It's comfortable. It's easy. It's familiar. I want him naked.

I still want him.

"I think if your parents catch us, they're going to start planning our wedding, so you better be careful."

"I think I have no desire to get married, but wouldn't mind doing a little consummation." He kisses my neck.

I'm yearning for him with everything in my body. How can he still have this effect on me after all this shit? And what about Eric? Do I let go of that this fast? But Eric and I are new. We haven't talked about monogamy. We're moving slowly. It's not cheating if we're not really in a relationship.

I picture the way Alec touches me, and a chill runs through me. It's like I'm on fire. After so many months of having regular sex together, you learn each other's bodies. You learn where to touch them, what is going to make them moan. You learn just how to turn them on and keep them satisfied. Alec plays the home-court advantage. He knows everything about my body. I am defenseless.

"Let's get out of here," he says, standing up and taking my hand to pull me away.

We don't even say bye to anyone. I'm sure the whole party

watches us leave together, and I don't really care. I can't wait for him to ravage my body. He is winning yet again.

He still wants me. Isn't that all I ever really wanted?

Eric calls when he gets home the next day. I left Alec's house around 10 a.m., wondering what the hell I was doing, but not quite feeling bad about it either. Nothing with Eric is official, and it's good to know Alec is still there and things aren't that different after all. I'm not the first person to have two things going at once. If things with Eric fall through, maybe I can still have Alec to fulfill my needs. Isn't that what Alec has been doing all along? Isn't that exactly what so many guys in my life have done to me so many times? Flirted with me, hooked up with me, but actually had someone else on the side the entire time? Or was I the one on the side? How are you ever sure which way that actually goes?

"How was your family?" I ask Eric, truly happy to be hearing from him.

I really hope he's as into me as I am into him, so I don't wind up getting my heart broken. Within moments, I forget Alec and I even had sex again. *Who the hell is Alec?*

"Great! We played some touch football. Mom made my favorite recipe. Her specialty pot roast. It was seriously awesome. So I have to coach Tuesday. Do you tutor afterward?"

"I do."

"That's perfect, then. Do you want to have dinner after I'm done coaching? You can stay and watch Jarron practice. It would mean a lot to him."

I have a new student I'm tutoring this year named Raven. She's sweet, but I miss crazy little Jarron.

"That would be great. We can catch up."

"I'd love to cook for you."

"Wow. Sounds like a date."

We go to Whole Foods together, and it feels nice. Being in the grocery store with a guy I'm seeing, about to cook dinner. It's what people my age are supposed to be doing. I look around at the shoppers. If they look at us, they'll assume we are married or in a serious relationship, and the thought actually makes me smile. *Weird.*

Eric makes bacon-wrapped dates and scallops over risotto at my apartment. He is a fantastic cook. I am amazed by the way he moves in the kitchen so effortlessly. Like he's been cooking his whole life.

"My mom taught me," he says, almost like he's reading my mind. "She has always been a great cook, and I stayed in the kitchen a lot and learned from her. My brothers, of course, thought I was a momma's boy, but now they are jealous that I can cook and they can't. It's obviously how I get all the ladies."

"You're really good."

"What can I do to help?"

"Just pour us another glass of wine, please."

"Consider it done."

We sit at my counter and enjoy our wine and dinner over real conversation. There is no topic I feel he won't get into with me. By the time we are doing the dishes together, I'm melting into his eyes.

"So how's tutoring going this year?"

"It's good. I'm finally looking into the education issues more. And I'm writing about them. Not publicly or anything. I'm not ready for that yet. But for myself to know I am still capable of putting thoughts into words in some fashion."

"What are you finding?"

"I stepped away from all of it for so long. It's just, I was reading this stupid teaching manual the other day. And I guess it has some good points, but if a school like ours uses things like that alone to teach kids, it is going to take away all the creativity and passion of the teachers. So where are the students supposed to learn to be creative individuals when the teachers can't be?"

"Interesting point."

"The answer to raising our nation's test scores isn't about rotely understanding basic skills, the way Raven's homework is asking her to do. We need to teach kids how to think outside the box. How to problem solve. How to figure things out. And we're not doing that."

"I love how you say 'we'."

"Well, we're a part of it, aren't we? We're tutoring and coaching and we're affecting kids' lives. I don't think any recent legislation has been the answer, and they aren't coming up with anything new."

"Any legislation that is cleverly named but doesn't actually bring support to the schools in need is worse than if it didn't exist at all. It takes away money from the schools that need it most by focusing everything on a few exams that aren't really evaluating student growth or learning."

"Exactly!" I love that Eric is up for engaging with me. It turns me on. "If we keep focusing so much on all these stupid skills and ACT points in the classroom, our kids in the inner city will never catch up to the kids in the suburbs because they aren't being asked to see the bigger picture. They could look at a super zoomed-in picture of a piece of hair on a dog and tell you what that piece of hair looks like and what it is, but couldn't tell you that it's on a dog."

"Interesting analogy."

"I just get so frustrated when I think about it."

He grabs my hand and looks at my eyes, stopping me mid-conversation.

"I love your passion," he says, not breaking his gaze.

I lean forward, grab his face, and start making out with him. He is kissing me as though he wants to devour me. It's evident both of us have wanted to jump each other for a while, but the conversation only made that desire grow. He runs his hand up my shirt and then takes it off. The sink is still running. I start fumbling with his pants, without even worrying about his shirt. I need to have him right now. He reaches up my skirt and slides my panties off, lifting me up and putting me on the counter. *Oh my god, this is so hot.* He drops his boxers and starts pushing against me until he is inside of me, engulfing me right there on the counter. I can barely breathe.

Chapter Twenty-Three

I wake up in Eric's toned arms the following Sunday, feeling safe and skinny and sexy even though I can tell my hair is a disaster and I ate dessert last night. He's completely out still, and it's sweet. He's usually so abuzz with energy talking about world issues or coming up with new drills to motivate his kids or how to go above and beyond with one of them if they need that attention.

God, there is nothing wrong with this man. I debate getting up and starting the coffee, but his body is too tempting as he half-wakes, readjusts, and pulls me closer to him. I've all but completely forgotten that the morning after can be sweet, and it almost catches me off guard the way he enjoys cuddling and looking me in the eyes, and other things I've become accustomed to pretending are cheesy and unnecessary.

"Mmm . . . hi," he whispers, smiling at me and closing his eyes again.

Even though I'm wide awake, curling against him is a natural reflex. "Hi." I smile back.

As much as I love morning sex, just feeling adored is something I can truly get used to. After a while, his hand starts to slide down my back, slowly but purposefully, and I immediately melt into him, touching his chest. His ridiculously perfect chest. Everything about him is masculine and strong. He kisses my neck and runs his hand along my stomach, the most sensitive part of my body, as if following my perfect "what to do in bed" script. Things no guy has ever figured out on his own, he does instinctively. I'm still getting used to being with someone so strong, and I'm nervous about wanting to impress him. He's not afraid to kiss me on the mouth, in spite of our morning breath. He almost sneaks inside me, carefully, but it startles me. Everything he does is hot. Everything about him feels right.

I get out of bed and look for something to wear. It's 10 a.m., and I'm wondering if he'll stick around or find a reason to run out now that our day is starting, though he has never actually done that before. I still don't know how to trust something this good.

"Aww . . . it's clothes time already?" He pouts and puts his boxers on, standing up and putting his arms around me from behind, kissing my back.

I pause after sliding into jeans and appreciate the moment before reaching for a t-shirt. I wonder if I should be putting effort into wearing something cuter since this thing with Eric is new and all, but he doesn't seem to care.

"Want coffee?" I ask, not wanting to push my luck, but hoping he accepts.

"I'd love some."

I start a pot, put my messy hair up, and scope out my refrigerator situation.

"Want me to make some eggs or something?"

"Wow, celebrity treatment? This is the best B and B ever."

"Yeah, but here you can call it BBB. Bed, Breakfast, and Benefits—all encompassing." I laugh, pulling eggs, ham, peppers, and cheese from the fridge. For the first time in my life, I am nervous about cooking eggs. I want them to be the absolute best eggs he has ever had.

"You're kind of cute in the kitchen." He smiles. "Not in a misogynist way."

"Oh, sure. You just think all women belong in the kitchen. Don't push your luck. These may be the last eggs you ever get from me!"

"Interesting double entendre."

"Look at that! I'm an amazing wordsmith."

"Sure thing, sweetheart. Just don't burn my breakfast." He rolls his eyes. It's almost like he studied a manual on winning me over.

"I'm gonna drop them on the floor and not even tell you." I laugh as I pour him a cup of coffee. "Cream?"

"Cream is for sissies," he says, reaching for the sugar and adding way too much.

"Nicely done. Sugar is hardcore."

"Fuck yeah! Nobody messes with sugar."

I add cream to my coffee but leave the sugar on the side.

"So you don't have a million things you need to do for work today?"

"I'm already way ahead of the game. All planned for the week."

"Of course you are, Mr. Organization."

"What about you?"

"Mreh. I have to be honest, I've been so busy making cupcakes and running my site and organizing all of that, my real job's taking a huge back seat. I won't be surprised if they fire me, and I don't even know that I care. I guess that's terrible, but things have really been picking up since the shower."

"So the article has brought you a decent amount of business."

"Pretty cool, huh?"

"I feel like I'm screwing a celebrity. Maybe you should just quit your job and focus on this baking thing full time. You're really good at it, and I think it could go somewhere for you. Your job isn't."

"That's true. I've been thinking about it. I'll give it some more time and see how things go."

"I thought when you know, you know . . . "

"Nice job remembering, but that doesn't mean that I want to risk losing my home just yet."

"Well, that's probably wise."

"I'm a wise woman."

The eggs come out pretty good, and I hope for the best as I serve them to him. I generally think I'm a pretty good cook, but eggs are a generic food and probably not going to impress anyone. Especially now that I know what a phenomenal mastermind he is in the kitchen.

"These are delicious!" he exclaims.

"You have to say that."

"Fuck no, I don't. I could have just said, 'These eggs taste like balls. Throw them away'." He's laughing, clearly enjoying the scramble, and I feel victorious.

Little things. It's weird actually sitting at my counter with him. Sharing my space. Sharing my food. I've grown so used to being very much on my own with these things. We converse about work and about life. We tease each other. He helps me with the dishes, even though there aren't many. It's comfortable. It's what a morning is supposed to be with a guy you are really into. It's just right.

We sit down on the couch and turn on the TV. We channel surf, then settle on an old episode of Anthony Bourdain. There is no reason for Eric to be here; he's choosing to stay. We're not drinking or partying. We're spending a Sunday together like mature adults who are dating. It's nice.

"God, Anthony Bourdain has the best job in the world," I say. "I mean, the guy gets paid to try interesting things across the world and see everything and party."

"That's very true. I guess I never thought about it. I figure the best job in the entire world would be a food critic. Get paid to go to the best restaurants and have them serve you their top entrees. Not to mention, you'd get the absolute best of everything because they want to impress you so badly."

"Yeah. I'd probably just get huge. I wouldn't be a very good food critic. I'm not critical. Whatever they served, I'd probably just be like, 'Oh, this is delicious!'" I pretend my mouth is stuffed when I say it, and he laughs.

"Yeah, that's a really good point. I can't say I have the most discerning palate myself."

"See? I knew you were just humoring me about the eggs! You'd have liked anything!"

"Yeah, probably. You could have put stale leftovers on my plate and I'd probably have been like, 'You're the best cook ever!'"

The doorbell rings. *Who the hell is at my place at 1 p.m. on a Sunday?* I buzz downstairs and open my door to see Alec.

"Hey Alec, what do you need?" It's not like Alec to be making a house call. At least not lately. Eric is surely going to wonder what the hell he's doing coming over.

"I was driving by and figured I'd drop this off. You left it at my place last weekend."

Goddamnit!

He hands me my jacket, wearing an obvious smirk on his face. I'd completely forgotten I had left it at his place. As he steps forward, he notices I have company. We look at each other awkwardly before it dawns on him that he may have completely screwed something up for me. He looks sorry, but it's too late.

"Uh, thanks, Alec."

"Hey, Eric!" Alec says, trying to pretend like this is a totally normal occurrence. They've only met once, briefly, but Eric knows exactly who Alec is.

"Hey," Eric says from the couch, looking confused.

"OK, well, I've got to get going. Have a good Sunday guys," Alec says and leaves.

Now let's see what damage has been done.

"What was that about?" Eric asks, although he heard every word.

"I left this jacket at his place. We were all hanging out last weekend, and I forgot it."

Eric glances away as if he's collecting his thoughts. I'm terrified.

Fuck, what have I done? Please don't leave me over this.

"So, Lyren," he says after a moment, then hesitates. I have a split second left to hope he didn't pick up exactly what just happened. I hope I'm not visibly trembling. "I guess this is awkward to say, but what is the deal with you and Alec? Honestly. Just tell me the truth so we can figure out what is next."

"Honestly, Eric, there is no 'deal' with Alec and me. We're good friends and all, but it's nothing. I'm not into him."

"You're sleeping with him."

I don't know how to respond. Obviously, I am sleeping with Alec and have been sleeping with Alec. God, do I want to say that I've never touched Alec, and that everything is going to be fine.

"I'm not trying to be that blunt and rude, but I really just need to know."

"I mean, I've slept with him, yes. If you must know. But I don't see how that affects you and me. I've been drunk and single, and Alec was, I dunno, there."

"OK, but Lyren, we're not talking about this as something that happened once or twice in the past. This is something that happened last weekend. The one weekend I wasn't hanging out with you."

I can't lie to him. He'd know. He could read it on mine and Alec's faces. It was too obvious. I want to curl into a ball and hide.

"I didn't mean for it to happen last weekend."

"But that's almost worse."

"How is that worse? We were out drinking with Olivia and some other people, and you weren't there, and I was lonely, and at the end of the night it just happened. We were used to it, I guess. You and I never said anything about being monogamous. I know that doesn't make you feel any better, but to be fair, I haven't asked who you've been sleeping with since you met me."

"But you're the only person I've been sleeping with since I met you."

"I didn't have to be."

"No, but I'm into you, and when I'm into someone, I'm not out looking for a cheap piece of ass in a bar. I thought you and I were headed somewhere better than that, Lyren. I really did. I didn't think I was just the guy you liked to keep around for the time being and the second I'm away, you were the type of girl to fill your bed with someone else."

"OK, now you aren't being fair. I'm not just some whore that needed a space in my bed filled. You and I are new. I still haven't been sure of where we were going or what we were doing. This morning? This has been one of the best mornings I have ever had. I want this to be real. I want to believe this is going somewhere with you. But I don't know that. And I didn't know that. And I'm sorry that this happened. I really am. Alec is nothing. We're nothing. We don't have what you and I have. I'll be honest with you. I'll tell you anything and everything you want to know. Seriously. And if you want to say anything else, you do that, but I'm not letting you walk away right now just because I happened to sleep with a friend last weekend when nothing has ever been official with you, and we've never talked about what we are or where this is going."

"What? Is this high school? I need to officially ask you out? Make it Facebook official?"

"Yes! Yes, Eric! You do!" There's desperation in my voice. The look of disappointment on his face hurts worse than if he had just called me a slut and run out. "Because without that, without you saying that this is official and you want to be with me exclusively, I have to be guarded. I have to protect myself. And maybe part of that means pretending you don't mean that much to me and that I'm OK without you. I don't know if that's even true anymore, and we've only been seeing each other for one month!"

"OK, I get it. But the thing is, it's Alec."

"What difference does it make who it is?"

"Alec is just . . . he's such a player and a party guy. It's just, is that the kind of guy you want?"

"God no! If he were the kind of guy I wanted, I'd be dating him or someone like him. I wouldn't be dating you. A guy who works like crazy and has ambitions and likes to sit and watch Anthony Bourdain with me sober on a Sunday. Don't act like you've never slept with a girl, who by all accounts, was shallow and meaningless. You're telling me you've never had a brief fling with some girl who was really hot just because it was fun?"

"No, I have. It's just been a while, and I'm just over that."

"Well, good for you. I had a really serious boyfriend when I was younger, and maybe I needed to experience some of the partying that I missed out on. I don't know. I was single and sick of people hurting me. Alec filled a void in my life for a while, and I do not regret that. We were never dating; I never counted on him. It was casual and fun, and it's over."

"But Lyren, it's not over. You're right. I have no place judging anyone you've slept with in the past. And Alec is actually a nice guy from what I can tell. But the thing is, it's not over. If it was still happening last weekend, then it's not over."

"Just say the word, and it's over now! It should have been over then. I thought it was! It just happened. But that's it. It was the last time. We're done."

"It's not that simple. You have something with him that you need to work out. I don't care that you're saying you're just friends and it was casual and now, just like that, it's over. He's a person you care deeply about. And I could tell by the look on his face when he saw me that he felt guilty. He came over planning to stay and hang out. Lyren, look, I'm not trying to be difficult or judge you at all. But, however casual that was, I really don't think it's over. I don't think whatever feelings you have there are over, and I don't think his are over for you."

"We never had feelings for each other!"

"You're full of shit. You wouldn't have been sleeping together if you didn't. I wondered the minute I met him what your deal was. If you were sleeping together or if it was just that obvious that you wanted to be. You were so intentionally avoiding him, and he so obviously wanted you. Lyren, I ignored it then because we had just met, but it's no longer OK for me to ignore it. You need to settle whatever it is you have going on with him."

"OK, Eric, seriously. What is it you want me to do? Walk over to his house right now and say, 'Hey Alec, thanks for fucking up the best thing I have going for me right now. We're done sleeping together forever'? Because I will do that."

"You're mad at him for coming over while I was here because it means you have to explain yourself to me now! You're not mad he came over! You're not sorry you fucked! If I weren't here, you'd be on that couch with him right now!"

"You're so wrong, Eric! What I have with you is so different from what I had with him! It was never real with him. I was playing house, waiting for something real to come along! We had fun. We did. But I promise you, it's over."

"Look, Lyren. All that is well and good. And maybe it is. Maybe you do go over there and say you're into me and things with him are completely done. But that doesn't mean your feelings are completely done. And I can't even say that I'd really like you to stop seeing him. He's going to be in your life. I can't get rid of him. He's not just some random fling from the past that can just disappear. He's your best friend's brother! He's always going to be around, Lyren."

I can't dispute this. My worst fear throughout my entire situation with Alec was falling for a guy that couldn't handle my past with Alec. I wasn't going to dump Olivia as a friend. I couldn't get rid of Alec.

"He doesn't have to be around that much. Just because I'm friends with Olivia doesn't mean her brother has to be around. Please just don't give up on us over this. I'll sort it out. I'll tell Alec I can't be his friend. You're worth it to me. You're worth losing a friend over. I'll stop seeing him. I won't go out when I know he's there. Please, Eric. Please."

"I can't think about all this right now. I need to sort things out. I don't know. I really like you, Lyren. I was really feeling this with you. I just don't know how you could be feeling the same about me and still have him on the side. He's one of your best friends, and I don't know that I want to ask you to end that. I think it's selfish. But I don't think I can deal with having him around, knowing you guys have had so much history."

"It's nothing," I whisper, fighting back tears. This can't be happening.

"Look, I'm not saying we're done for good. I need some time to figure things out and figure out what I'm really OK with and what I can handle. And I think you need to sort things out for yourself. And be honest with yourself. Because until you are truly over Alec, you can't really be in a relationship. I'm sorry."

I just look at him. I can't think of anything to say.

"I'm so sorry," I manage.

"You don't have to be sorry, Lyren. You didn't do anything wrong. You're right. We never talked about monogamy or anything like that, and you guys have a past. I should have been more curious about it earlier on. But I just don't know that we can have something real with all that still so there. This is obviously moving too fast already. We started to let ourselves get comfortable, and I didn't consider that you're not really ready for that. I don't care if you say you are. Your actions speak otherwise. I'll call you in a while." He hugs me, and I never want to let him go.

I want to scream and cry and beg him to stay. Tell him I'll do anything it takes to prove him wrong. Tell him that I'm crazy about him and falling for him. But I don't.

I let him walk away. I stand there, frozen. I don't even know if I can cry. I feel dead and empty. A first impulse is fury at Alec. But Alec didn't know any better. I barely told him anything about Eric, and it's not like Eric is the first guy I've seen since Alec and I started sleeping together. None of the other guys mattered, so how would he know that Eric did? Besides, it's not his fault I slept with him again. No more than it is mine, anyway.

Is Eric right? Is there something between me and Alec that I'm completely ignoring? It's over. I meant that. Alec is fucking up my relationship. If Eric and I are over, then he'd only fuck up the next one. I need space from Alec. I can't be his friend the way things were. I always knew this was coming. And Eric is right; Alec and I have been such good friends. It seems foolish to throw that away. But I have to. I know that I have to. I text him to see if he's home.

"Hi Alec," I say and walk into his place.

When I woke up here last Sunday, I felt sort of refreshed knowing things with us were going to be OK. Like we'd rekindled our friendship. But that meant sex. Alec and I can't exist as friends without sex. There is too much history. Too much attraction. Too much of something.

"Lyren, I'm so sorry about earlier."

I nod. "I know you didn't know or anything. It's not your fault, and it probably needed to happen. I was lying to myself about some things, and it wasn't fair to Eric."

"So, what happened?"

"Well, he obviously knows you and I have been fooling around, and no matter how much I tried to assure him that it's nothing, he didn't believe me."

"I'm so sorry, Ly. Is he . . . is it . . . over?"

I can almost hear the hope in Alec's voice.

"No, I don't think so. Not yet. I'm not going to give up that easily. This guy, Alec. This guy is the real deal. There is something there. There really is. He's amazing. He's everything I could have ever dreamed up. And I'm fucking it up over you."

"I don't know what to say to that. What do you want me to say? Why are you here?"

"I'm here because I want to end this officially. Regardless of what happens with Eric. I kept telling myself that we were just friends, so we didn't need to break up or talk about anything or deal with anything. Those are the rules, right? The rules of friends with benefits. You don't have to talk or fight or be cuddly. You avoid affection and relationship behavior. It's actually really fucked up."

He awkwardly looks away.

"We had something, Alec. I don't care what you say. I know it was casual and that we never wanted to be officially dating and all that. But we kept coming back to each other. Every time I wanted to kill you this past year proves that there was something. I would sit there thinking what a disgusting scum bag you were for having some 20-year-old fucking you. I'd get pissed because you were taking her to all these places and doing and saying all these sweet things. The thing is, I was so fucking jealous. I became the default. The last-resort option to fill your bed.

"You were more to me than that, Alec. You always were. I knew we'd never date. I knew I didn't want us to date, but I deserved more than what I settled for because there were those moments. Those moments are why I kept coming back. Why I slept with you last weekend. And those moments are how I know that it meant something to you, too. You were sweet to me. You cared about me. And you can't be screwing someone you care about and you're attracted to, and say it's nothing and assume it's just going to go away when the time is right. This was going to end in flames, and so far, we've handled it quite well. But this is over. And I don't just mean the sex. This is over the way a relationship is over. I promise not to make things awkward with Olivia, and I'll always be cautious of how this affects her, but it's over. No more Sunday Fundays, no more pubs, no more wake-up sex, or drunk sex, or text messages, or lame movie days. We have to end this if we ever want to be in real relationships with people who are right for us. Maybe that's not what you are looking for in anyone right now, but I am. I am ready for that. I deserve that."

He is quiet for a while and doesn't look at me. I can't believe I just said what I said. I never wanted to end things, even if it was inevitable. I never wanted to lose Alec. I'm right, but I don't feel relieved. I feel terror at the thought of not having Alec in my life. We've only been good friends for barely over a year, and this feels like a real breakup.

"You're dumping me as a friend?" He pouts as he says it in a way that is playful and adorable, and that's why I like him.

I pout back and nod my head.

"God, I guess you're right. Lyren, I never wanted to make you a default. Please know that hurting you was the last thing I ever wanted to do. I really do care about you. So much. I'd have cared about you the same way if we'd never started doing each other, but you're so goddamn beautiful. How the hell could I stay friends with a girl like you and not at least try to get her into bed?"

I laugh, and he puts his arm around me.

"Look, I think I always knew deep down that this wasn't going to work. It never works. And I've been afraid cause of my sister. I've tried pushing you away. And just seeing you as a friend and all that. You're right. We really cared about each other, and you mean so much to me. I think you're ridiculously sexy, but we don't have the makings of a relationship. Maybe if the timing had been different, or who knows. You can be crazy about someone and know they aren't right for you, so I get it. And we do need to break up. I'm so sorry if I've gotten in the way of a good thing for you. OK, enough of this. I'm getting sad. Fuck you."

No one wants an ex around, and I think a hot sex friend might be worse.

"I'm kind of sad, too."

"Alright, it's time for you to get out of here. We're done. We're over. Go. Get your man back. And wish me luck in finding someone. Preferably someone who is just like you, only not good friends with my little sister. Maybe with bigger tits."

I slap him playfully. "Good luck with that. You'll never find another me." I smile.

"I know."

I don't want to hug him one last time. It's too sad.

I walk down his street to my car, not sure what I feel. Eric wanted me to sort things out with Alec, and I did that the only way I know how. He's right. Everyone was right. I have feelings for Alec. And I don't know how the hell we're really going to stay away from each other. But we've never made things official before. Alec needs someone who will boost his ego. He and I aren't even close to right in the long haul. I need to get Eric back. I have this burst of emotion that's a combination of extreme sadness over no more Sunday Fundays with Alec coupled with an absolute need to get my dream man back. It's overwhelming. Do I cry? Do I hide under the covers?

This isn't in the movies. I can't run to the airport to stop Eric from getting on a plane and leaving me. I can't orchestrate a flash mob. I'm gonna have to figure this out like a real person. And he wants time to sort things out, so I need to give him that. He deserves that. I just hope to god that he sorts things out and realizes I'm worth forgiving.

Chapter Twenty-four

"So what are you gonna do?" Olivia asks over frozen yogurt.

"I haven't figured it out yet. It's only been a week."

"Don't wait too long. He'll think you don't want to be with him, and technically you're the one who needs to beg for him back."

"I know. I just don't know what to do."

I have been a wreck all week. Staring at my phone, willing it to light up with his name. Debating texting him, but wanting to respect his space. Feeling like I messed up the first real potential relationship I've had in years. Chastising myself for being so weak around Alec.

"Think about it. Whenever Chris and I get in a fight, I'm mad that he never does anything big enough to get my attention and really prove that he wants to be with me. I mean, I'm still a sucker and always go back to him. But I'm always mad that he doesn't do something."

"Yeah, but we're girls and we want our lives to be like a romantic comedy where the guy comes in after he fucked up and holds a radio above his head or storms a press release to win back the girl's affection. Eric is a guy. He doesn't watch romantic comedies."

"Well, I mean, porn is the male equivalent. You could just show up at his house in a trench coat with lingerie underneath it eating a lollipop."

I laugh. "I could . . . but that doesn't send the message: 'I'm not a slut, and I do want to be with you exclusively,'" I imitate.

"True. I'm not saying to blast opera while you hold flowers through a limo sunroof. But do something that shows you care about him. Do something that shows you've been listening to him when he talks and that you really do want him back, and that you want him exclusively. Admit you were wrong."

"I know I was wrong. I just don't know what to do. It's funny. We get disappointed that guys don't think to do these great sweet things when they fuck up, but here I am trying to think of how to get the guy back, and what I really want to do is send a fucking text message."

"Be brave!"

"I'll figure something out." I look out the window a second, trying to think of what I can do that is bigger than words to show Eric I'm really in this with him and only him. In the long run, I'm going to end up just calling him. "So how is Alec doing, anyway?"

"He's OK. He misses you a lot, you know."

It's the first time we've talked about Alec since I first told her the way I ended things. I miss him too, of course.

"Really?"

"I know you wanted to, like, cut him out of your life and all, and I think that's good and what you should do. But I figure it doesn't mean you can't know what he's been up to."

"You're absolutely right. What'd he say?"

"He won't admit it. He just asks about you and gets sort of sad. I think he thinks maybe a part of him is realizing that he should be with someone for real. He really did care about you, you know."

"I know," I say, and mean it.

"I'm not saying it would have ever worked. Granted, I do think he needs a strong girl like you to kick his ass into shape. But you guys started all wrong, and you knew too much about him and all that. But I think he's realizing that you were real and that he ran away from you."

"I don't know, Liv. He's great. And I really hope he finds someone who makes him happy. I wanted his attention and affection so desperately, and it just wasn't right for me at all."

"I know. I just thought you should know. I know you don't like to talk about it with me since I'm his sister. And I appreciate how you tried not to talk shit about him to me. But you really cared for him, and he really cared for you. I think the clean break was what you really needed. And honestly, I'm not gonna miss your disgusting PDA."

"Fair enough," I laugh. "Sorry about that."

"It's OK. Anyway, I thought you should know. He took the job in New York."

"Wow." It's my only response. So this break is cleaner than I thought. This is a good thing. For both of us. I need him away, and this will make that easy. He needs a new start and new people. This is fitting for him.

"Yeah. They are paying for his relocation and everything. New York will be a big change for him. I think he realized he has very little reason to stay here."

"He'll be back. He needs your family too much."

"Maybe."

"Well, good for him. This is what he needs. See? I want stability and sense; he needs constant adventure. It never could have worked."

"Well, who knows? He probably took it because of you. Maybe you made him realize he needed to move on to something new, too. But I think it's a good thing." She doesn't elaborate, and I don't want her to. The last thing I need is to sit here wondering what could have been with Alec if we hadn't both messed things up the way we did.

TWO WEEKS LATER

I still haven't figured out what to say to Eric. I miss him. I really do. But I'm afraid of getting re-involved with him and doing something to mess it all up. Eric is the greatest guy I have known, and yet he isn't nice in the way that always turns me off. He's stable. He's manly. He's passionate. What if I'm truly just bad for him? He has his life together. Mine is a mess.

I finish frosting my last set of cupcakes I'll be delivering later. Caramel Apple for some teacher's party. I feel on fire with productivity. Like I'm ready to explode with ideas and energy all the time. Sort of like a personal renaissance.

I take my apron off and check the mail. A couple of bills, a pay stub. And a letter from someone I don't know. I scream upon opening it and run and grab my phone.

"MOM!" I shout into the receiver.

"Oh my god, what? Are you okay? What is happening?"

"I got a personal invite to partake in Chicago's first annual Cupcake-Off!! Only small businesses are allowed, and it says they read about me in the paper. There are only ten places from the city! They secret-sampled mine! I didn't even know that could happen!" My heart is exploding. I can't even get the words out fast enough. I'm trying to comprehend it as I re-read the invitation.

"That's awesome, Lyren! Congratulations! What do you have to do? What can you win?"

"There are rounds. I guess sort of like *Cupcake Wars* on The

Food Network. The winner gets ten thousand dollars! I don't know; I barely read it. I had to call you! I can't believe it! I could open a storefront and quit my job! Oh my god! It's in one month! They have themes and give you ingredients and stuff! You get all kinds of press attention, too! MOMMY!"

I'm jumping up and down, screaming. Someone actually judged *my* cupcakes and personally invited me to a contest. Of all the small bakeries and cupcake companies in Chicago! There is so much potential here. I have to win. My head is swelling.

"Well, I have to go, but I cannot wait to watch you! Where is it going to take place?"

"It's at McCormick Place. GAH! I have to call Sarah and tell her how much I appreciate her letting me make the cupcakes for her shower! That's where it all started!"

"No. No, baby. It all started when you decided to start your own little company. It all started when you got serious about this. You have really made your dad and I proud, Lyren. You are an unbelievably talented young lady."

I laugh. I'm in too good of a mood to bother making fun of my mom for being cheesy.

I go through my phone book, calling everyone that means something to me. Sarah, Emma, Olivia, Gail. I think of Alec and stop myself. *Friend break up.* That means no more calling to catch up or tell exciting news. I briefly wonder how he is doing with moving plans. Knowing him, I'm sure he'll be fully acclimated, making friends and having sex with beautiful New York women in two weeks. The thought makes me laugh.

I dial another number into my phone. I've taken so much of my life into my own hands. No more selling myself short. Not with my career, not with my relationships. He may not be ready to trust me, but I'm not letting it go without a fight.

"Hello?"

"Eric . . . it's me."

"Hey Lyren. How are you?" His tone is surprisingly pleasant, and it gives me a bit more confidence.

"I'm absolutely fantastic actually and was wondering if you wouldn't mind grabbing a cup of coffee with me. I have to drop off some cupcakes sort of near your house in an hour. My treat?"

"OK. That sounds nice. I'd like to see you."

My heart skips. "I'd really like to see you, too. And I have a few things I really need to say."

Acknowledgments

What an incredible dream to breathe life back into a project that lay dormant for over a decade. I still cannot believe I get to hold a finished physical product of nearly 100,000 words I somehow weaved into a semi-cohesive story.

I need to begin by thanking whatever cosmos came together to reignite this idea at the right time. Diving into this novel and finally making it a reality grounded me during a period of anxiety, heartache, and restlessness. I had previously looked into self-publishing, got overwhelmed quickly, and gave up again. I'm not sure that I believe in fate per se, but timing is everything, and the timing on this was perfect. So thank you to the Instagram algorithm that brought me to Brittany Evans and Chelsea Lauren at Represent Publishing.

Chelsea, your edits and suggested revisions helped me see this book in reality and took it from being some silly thing I did in my twenties and made it something I'm proud to have created. Thank you for taking it seriously, providing constructive feedback, and listening to my absurd stories in the interim. Brittany, thank you for taking my vague concept of a cover design and coming up with visuals so much cooler and more powerful than I imagined.

To the friends who inspired me then and now, better and worse, I appreciate the crying shoulders, the advice both genuine and fully delusional, and maybe most importantly, the antics, some of which may or may not have gotten immortalized in writing. In absolutely no order: Julia, Cece, Jaime, Meg H., Megan F., Molly, Felicia, Michelle, Jenn M., Jen F., Jake, Anthony, Rafal, John W., John C., Lou, Richie, Torrey, Zach, Abby, Ryan B., Ryan also B., Ellen, Colleen, Kelly W., Kelly C., Maya, Chuck, Rachael, Amy, Nate, Brendan, Chad, Ocean, Tim, Brad, Kelly O., Justin H., Justin L., Erin, Alexa, Kylie, Liz, Bart, Jenna. Note: If you share a name with a character in the book, I probably met you after I started writing it. Any resemblance to actual people is coincidental. Mostly.

To the teachers who encouraged my creativity and writing, you have no idea how much you did. You gave me an outlet. A vision. The most valuable personal resource I have ever had, which has carried me through my life. Special thanks to: Mrs. Ryan, Mr. Schmittgens, Mr. Juillard, Ms. Delaney, Ms. Boose/Gries, Ms. Pelle, Dr. Kleiman, Dr. Frager, Dr. Schaengold, and most significantly, Dr. Romano. This novel does none of you justice, but more will come.

My Pepper Sprout, with whom I have a serious pandemic codependency, I have no idea what I'd have done these five years without your snorts and your snuggles. Thank you for being the emotional support bestie you never knew you were signing up to be.

To my parents, who are in many ways significantly cooler than Lyren's, thank you for challenging me, supporting me, and giving me space to grow on my own. Mom, for sharing your love of reading and allowing me to take on books way beyond my appropriate age group. And for not dismissing my outlandish imagination and my ability to tune the world out and live in my daydreams. I'm sure it wasn't always fun wondering where my brain was despite my body being in front of you, but from that tangled web of castles in the air, novels are born. Dad, for finally accepting I was never going to be a computer scientist and being proud of me anyway, and also for grounding me in responsibility and practicality when I needed it.

Re-reading and revising a novel written during a period of immense confusion and extreme highs and lows with the experiences I have had since makes me want to wrap my arms around younger me in both sympathy and celebration. Thank you to all who have helped validate that a fulfilling life may not always be a traditional one and that chasing electricity isn't always crazy. In fact, I plan to keep doing it forevermore.

Thank you!

Thank you for reading *This Fine Line*! I would greatly appreciate it if you could leave a review on Amazon and/or Goodreads to share your thoughts with others. Each review helps another reader find this story.

   Scan the QR code to check out my website, or follow me on Instagram and TikTok @zaylnzofer to stay in touch!